MISTAKEN IDENTITY

MISTAKEN IDENTITY

A Lucinda Pierce Novel

Diane Fanning

This first world edition published 2010
in Great Britain and in the USA by
SEVERN HOUSE PUBLISHERS LTD of
9–15 High Street, Sutton, Surrey, England, SM1 1DF.
Trade paperback edition published
in Great Britain and the USA 2010 by
SEVERN HOUSE PUBLISHERS LTD

British Library Cataloguing in Publication Data

Fanning, Diane.
   Mistaken Identity. – (A Lucinda Pierce mystery)
   1. Pierce, Lucinda (Fictitious character) – Fiction.
   2. Women detectives – Fiction. 3. Murder – Investigation –
   Fiction. 4. Detective and mystery stories.
   I. Title II. Series
   813.6-dc22

ISBN-13: 978-0-7278-6866-4   (cased)
ISBN-13: 978-1-84751-223-9   (trade paper)

All Severn House titles are printed on acid-free paper.

Severn House Publishers support The Forest Stewardship Council [FSC],
the leading international forest certification organisation. All our titles that are
printed on Greenpeace-approved FSC-certified paper carry the FSC logo.

Mixed Sources
Product group from well-managed
forests and other controlled sources
www.fsc.org Cert no. SA-COC-1565
© 1996 Forest Stewardship Council

Typeset by Palimpsest Book Production Ltd.,
Grangemouth, Stirlingshire, Scotland.
Printed and bound in Great Britain by
MPG Books Ltd., Bodmin, Cornwall.

A special thanks to Liz Nichols, Andrea Campbell and Don White for helping me find answers to my questions on genetics, forensics and firearms.

ONE

The crisp taps of Pamela Godfrey's heels on the concrete echoed through the garage. She clenched and unclenched her jaws, the clack of her teeth matching the rhythm of her shoes. She was not pleased with her day. He had no good reason to keep her waiting that long. He asked for that meeting. Then to cut her off because he had another appointment compounded his sin. The next time, she'd make him wait – if she showed at all. That lack of consideration on top of the mess she'd had to handle first thing in the morning. *It was all just too much.*

She pressed the lock release on her key chain. The responding beep made her flinch. She opened the door and stepped up into her Escalade. 'Dammit,' she said as she spotted a piece of paper stuck between the wiper blade and the windshield. She didn't care, let it fall where it may, she thought, as she reversed out of the parking slot quicker than she should. Shifting into drive, she hit the windshield wipers to dislodge the nuisance as she made the turns toward the exit.

It didn't work. The paper clung to the blade arcing back and forth across the glass. It wasn't an advertisement after all. It was a typewritten note. Curious, she stopped, slipped the transmission into park and stepped out of her SUV. Behind her, a horn honked. She turned and glared at the silver Lexus. The engine revved. The horn blared again. She couldn't see anyone through the tinted glass but flipped the bird in the driver's direction anyway. She stepped to the front of her car, grabbing the document. She was back at the side of her car with one leg raised, ready to step inside, when the horn blasted a third time.

She lowered her foot to the pavement, turned with hands on her hips and stared at the driver. As the door of the Lexus started to open, she realized that she really didn't want a confrontation with a stranger – she'd had enough grief for one day and it wasn't even noon yet. She hopped into the seat and left the other driver standing by his car and shouting obscenities as she pulled away.

The piece of paper crumpled between her hand and the steering wheel. Stopping at a red light, she opened it up and read: 'CALL 9-1-1 NOW!!! 6423 James Landing Drive.'

A polite tap of a horn brought her back to her surroundings. The light was now green. She jerked forward, driving half a block before turning into a parking lot where patrons pulled into numbered spaces and stuffed money into the corresponding slot in a big metal lock box. She stopped in the middle of the lane; glanced in her rear-view mirror to make sure no one was on her tail again. *I must have read the address wrong.* She reread the note. *Who left it here? Who knows about my connection to that house? What is the best way to handle this situation? Should I do what seems natural and place this call or simply toss the note into the first dumpster I see?* She considered driving to the address but worried that might confirm someone's suspicions. *Wouldn't it be better to call from miles away and react as if the address was not familiar to me?*

She wanted to return to her office, accomplish something positive and forget this morning ever happened. But she knew someone could have seen the person placing the note on her SUV and could even have recognized her car. If she ignored it, it wouldn't look good for her. She had to make the call.

Pulling out her iPhone, she slid the digital lock to the left, hit the green phone button, then the keyboard icon. She paused, rethinking her decision. She didn't believe anyone knew of her ties to that address. But if she was wrong, it was probably too late to save her professional image anyway. She turned back to her iPhone just before it faded to black. It brightened at her touch. She hit the three digits.

'Nine-one-one. What is the nature of your emergency?'

TWO

Confusing. Contradictory. Like two crime scenes in one. The old Doublemint commercial jingle skipped like a naughty child through her thoughts. Homicide Lieutenant Lucinda Pierce stood beside the female victim in the master bedroom of 6423 James Landing Drive.

A summer-weight blanket, the same shade of scarlet as the drapes over the windows, stretched from the foot of the bed over her body, up to her armpits. Over the top three inches was folded a crisp gold-colored sheet matching the shade painted on the walls. The sheet and blanket were as smooth and wrinkle-free as if someone made the bed with her in it.

Her bare arms lay on either side of her body, hands palm side down. The natural nails were moderately long and well-tended with a blunt cut and a French manicure. No jewelry adorned her fingers but the flesh was flattened in a band at the base of her left ring finger. Was a wedding band removed? Ante or post-mortem? No ring rested on the surface of the nightstand next to the body.

The female victim's shoulder-length hair formed a honey-brown corolla around her head, spreading wide over the pillow – obviously brushed as she rested there. A fresh application of make-up brightened her face. No doubt that was post-mortem as well. The foundation obscured much of the stippling around the wound in the center of her forehead but nothing could cover the angry red edges of the blood-blackened hole.

Except for that solitary defect, all else indicated a woman who died in her sleep – a quiet, peaceful departure. No sign of blood spatter on the headboard or the bed linens. Perhaps she, too, met her end in the bathroom.

The Tyvek booties on Lucinda's feet whispered as she crossed the carpet to the doorway of the en suite bath. One hairy leg hung over the edge of the deep, soaking tub. A dark patina of partially dried blood covered the porcelain, the walls, the ceiling, the floor.

Lucinda took two steps into the room, stopping just outside the perimeter of the red. On the polished marble surface of the vanity, two brilliant blue glass bowls sat beneath pewter faucets. Between them, a chainsaw rested, its bar spattered with blood and bits of flesh.

Lucinda caught a glimpse of her face in the mirror above the saw and jerked her head away. The last procedure granted her no satisfaction. It did not return the symmetry to her features she desired. The doctor had warned her it would take multiple operations, but Lucinda was not a patient woman. She did not expect miracles. She demanded them.

She looked again at the sprawled, nude male in the tub.

The murder was fresh; a tiny rivulet of fluids still traced a thin line from the body to the drain. The body no longer had a head or hands. Officers searched for the missing parts in the house and yard. She did not expect they would be found anywhere near the property.

The scene where this victim rested jarred with the other one like an orchestra engaged in a simultaneous performance of Brahms and Tchaikovsky. What did the contrast tell her? Two perpetrators? Or one killer with different feelings toward the two victims? But how could one overcome two? Were they both shot point-blank in the head quicker than either one could respond? Impossible to know without the other head.

Maybe, though, it had nothing to do with emotions toward the two. Maybe, his identity needed to be concealed. If so, why was hers irrelevant? To be found here together meant there had to be a connection. In that case, wouldn't it be easy to deduce his once hers was known?

'What kind of mess have you got for me today, Pierce?' a gravelly voice barked from the hallway.

An involuntary smile crossed Lucinda's face. 'Doc Sam, welcome to my world. I hope the timing of this one meets with your approval.'

He grunted as he crossed the threshold. 'Very considerate of you, Lieutenant, to arrange this one during regular business hours.' He crossed the room to the far side of the bed. 'Well, how nice. You laid her out pretty for the viewing and I'm not even family.' He leaned over the body in the bed, observing every detail before slipping his hand under the victim's fingers. The elbow didn't bend, the whole arm lifted. 'Looks like just past three hours since she died. You touch anything?'

'Of course not.' Lucinda bristled.

'Don't get your knickers in a wad. Had to ask.'

Lucinda's lips twitched. She bit back a retort.

'Any idea of the cause of death, detective?'

Lucinda snorted. She refused to take his bait. 'Of course not, Doctor, that is your purview.'

'Ha! Like you have any respect for those boundaries. Photos taken?'

'Yes. From every angle.'

Doc Sam grunted his approval and gently pulled down the sheet and blanket, sliding it from under the dead woman's stiffening arms. The victim was nude, her legs together, stretched in a straight line. They looked at the soles of her feet – as clean as if she just stepped out of a bath.

The doctor lifted the right hand, moving his face close to her fingertips. He set it down with care and examined the left one. 'Looks like someone might have cleaned her nails. Better bag them just in case they missed something.'

A silent, hovering tech stepped between Lucinda and the coroner, efficiently covered both hands and retreated to his current role as wallpaper.

'Help me turn her over,' Doc Sam said.

He and Lucinda slipped four hands under the body, making her body flip like a solid board. Three washcloths, soaked in blood and cerebral fluid, sat stacked in the center of the pillow. The exit of the bullet left a messier and larger wound on the back of her head.

'Find the bullet and you'll know where she died. Think you can do that, Pierce?'

Knowing he was baiting her again, she did not respond.

'Where's the other one?'

Lucinda led him to the bathroom.

'You certainly left a mess for me in here,' he said staring down at the body. 'Husband? Lover? Lousy plumber?'

'Can't locate the husband – never showed up at work today. No word on a lover – one way or the other – yet. And there are no abandoned service vehicles in the immediate vicinity of the house. Of course, that would be an interesting variation on the theme. We can, however, eliminate murder-suicide from the list of possibilities here.'

'Really, Lieutenant. I thought that was *my* purview.'

'Of course, Doctor. How presumptuous of me. Could you please explain how a suicide could dispose of his hands and head or how the woman could apply make-up and brush her hair after putting a bullet in the center of her forehead?'

Doc Sam grunted and kneeled down by the side of the tub. He found it difficult to manipulate the body with the stiffened leg forming a hook securing it in place. 'I see no signs of bullet wounds or stabbing . . .'

'But if he was shot in the forehead like . . .'

'I don't make guesses, Lieutenant,' he snapped.

'Yes, sir, Doctor Sam, sir.'

He rewarded her with a baleful glare, muttering 'Smart ass', as he turned back to the body. 'Find the head.' He placed his gloved hands on the side of the tub and pushed up. His right hand slipped on the slick surface. Lucinda leaned forward, extending a hand to assist. 'You think I'm too old to do my job, Pierce?'

'No, sir,' she said, jerking back upright as if her hand had been slapped.

A disembodied voice shouted, 'Lieutenant.'

Lucinda stepped out of the bathroom and walked to the bedroom doorway where a uniformed woman patrol officer stood. 'What is it, Colter?

'There's a boy downstairs claiming he lives here.'

The detective glanced over to the dresser to a framed snapshot of a man, a woman and a boy, all with drenched hair, grinning at a camera. 'The son?'

'He says so, yes, ma'am.'

'Where is he?'

'We took him out back by the pool to get him out of earshot of any grisly conversations. But he's full of questions.'

Lucinda sighed. 'How old?'

'Eleven, twelve, maybe thirteen. And he's none too happy that none of us would give him answers.'

'He'll be less happy when we do.'

THREE

Lucinda spotted him through the French doors before she stepped outside. He stood there looking lost in his own backyard. His face sported Harry Potter glasses with his hair styled in similar fashion. In dim light, he could pass for Daniel Radcliffe, the young actor who portrayed the title character in the movie. His solemn face and intense eyes betrayed his worried mind but he appeared to work hard at being the epitome of geek cool.

'I'm Detective Pierce,' Lucinda said as she approached him, flashing her badge as quick as she could in the hope he would not see the word homicide but his eyes were quicker than her hands.

'Homicide?' Is my mother dead?' he said. Then he blushed and thrust out his right hand. 'Sorry. I forgot my manners. I'm Frederick Sterling.'

'Frederick?'

'Yes. But my mom called me Freddy.' His lower lip trembled.

'What should I call you?' she said, placing a hand on the boy's shoulder.

'Freddy would be good,' he said as tears welled up in his eyes.

'Well, Freddy, let's go sit and talk.' She moved her hand from his shoulder to the center of his upper back and steered him to the two chairs under an umbrella on the far side of the pool. 'Freddy, where were you before arriving home?'

'At school,' he said as he took a seat.

'In the summer?'

'It's a computer programming enrichment course. Dad thought it would help with admissions at university this fall.'

University this fall? He barely looks old enough for middle school. 'You're in high school?'

'Yes. Chesterfield High. I'll be a senior when school starts.'

'A senior?' *Is this a sign I'm getting old? He looks like a baby.*

'I know,' he said, ducking his head to hide a fierce blush. 'I don't look old enough. Technically, I'm not.'

'How old are you, Freddy?'

'Thirteen.'

'I'm impressed,' Lucinda said.

'Well, yeah, it's no big deal. College will be the big test. If it's not easy, I'm not as smart as everybody thinks.'

Smart or not, this wasn't going to be easy. Lucinda sighed. She didn't really know where to start.

Before she could form the words, Freddy took charge of the conversation. 'Somebody killed my mom, right?'

'I'm afraid so, Freddy.'

His shoulders slumped, his head hung, his right foot banged into the leg of her chair once, twice, three times. Then he stopped mid-swing and looked up, embarrassed by the realization he'd been kicking her chair. 'Sorry,' he mumbled.

'No problem, Freddy. Do it again if you want.'

He looked into her face, his hands clenched into tight fists in his lap. 'I worried this would happen. I was afraid it would get this bad. I should have done something.'

Lucinda leaned forward, her elbows pressed into her knees 'What do you mean, Freddy?'

'I know who killed my mom. And I know why he did it.'

'Who did it, Freddy?'

Freddy turned his head away.

'Freddy, you can tell me. Who did this?'

He swung his gaze back to her face. 'What happened to you?'

She focused her eye on his furrowed brow and the darkness lurking behind his stare, deciding to allow him to control the reins of the conversation for a little while. 'I came between a man and the woman he wanted to kill. The shotgun blast grazed this side of my face.'

He pointed as he said, 'That eye isn't real.'

'No, it's not,' she admitted. Somehow a child asking about her face did not irritate or anger her as it usually did when an adult posed questions or made unwanted comments. *A child?* She thought. She didn't spend much time around children. She was really thinking of Charley, a girl who lost her mother to homicide, and now Freddy, a boy who lost both parents. Maybe it wasn't their age but the knowledge that they possessed kindred spiritual scars, the kind that reach far deeper and with far more cruelty than the ones on her face.

'You don't sound mad,' Freddy said.

'I was mad – very mad.' Lucinda smiled. 'I was angry at the world for a long time. I've just learned to deal with it, to accept it and move on.' They sat in silence for a moment then Lucinda spoke again. 'Freddy, who do you think did this?'

'I don't think,' Freddy said with quivering lips, 'I know.'

'Who, Freddy?'

'My dad.'

Lucinda leaned back in her chair, stunned by his answer. How could she explain to him that his father was dead, too? 'Freddy, your mother's body was not the only one we found. It appears that your father was murdered, too.' The lump in her throat caught her breath; she held it there, half-released, as she awaited his response.

'No. My father's not dead.'

What now? She didn't know if she should allow him his delusion or break through his denial. 'But, Freddy . . .'

'No. You don't understand. My dad is not dead. It's impossible. He is immortal.'

Lucinda wondered if it was time to call in a social worker or a psychologist.

'That's why he had to kill my mom. That's why. I should have known it when I heard them the other day.'

'Did they fight, Freddy?'

'No,' he said with a shake of his head. 'They never fought.'

'OK, so did they argue?'

'No. Never. Well, one time. I remember them arguing one time.'

'When was that, Freddy?'

'I don't remember,' he said. 'It was a while ago. My mom was upset with my dad. She thought he was pushing me too hard. They stopped talking when I walked into the room. They looked at each other and I could tell they were trying to figure out how much I overheard. So, I said, "Mom, don't hold me back." My mom started to cry. I just walked away. I didn't want to see that. I wish I didn't say that,' he sobbed and tears dropped from his eyes to his pants, making round darkened spots on the khaki. 'All she did was love me.'

'Is that when you knew your dad would kill your mom?' Lucinda said in a whisper, hoping it was the right thing to say but fearing she was in over her head. *Maybe a psychiatrist?*

'No. No.' Freddy shook his head. 'Not then. It must have been Tuesday.'

'Last Tuesday?'

'Yeah. I'm pretty sure it was last Tuesday.'

'What happened, Freddy?'

'Well, Mom and Dad were in the kitchen fixing a salad for supper that night. Dad started teasing Mom about her hair. He said it was turning gray. She gave him a hard time and said it wasn't fair that his hair was still black. She accused him of dyeing it behind her back. They were laughing. I don't think Mom knew how serious it was. But I know Dad did. I saw it in his eyes.'

Lucinda struggled to comprehend his reasoning for painting his father as a murderer. 'You think he killed your mother because her hair was turning gray.'

'Well, sort of. But more because his wasn't.'

'Freddy, I'm sorry but this isn't making any sense to me. Maybe you should be talking to someone else.'

'Like who? A minister? A shrink?' he shouted, jumping from his seat so quickly, he turned it over.

'Well, Freddy . . .'

'No. Don't patronize me. You think it's all in my head. You don't believe me.' He picked up the overturned chair and set it upright with a slam.

'Freddy, I . . .'

'Don't. I'll prove it to you. Just take me to that other body upstairs and let me see it.'

'No, Freddy, I cannot . . .'

'Yes, you can. It won't upset me. I know it's not my dad. It's just a stranger.'

The image of the leg hanging over the tub, the slumped body without a head floated through Lucinda's thoughts. She knew the vision would haunt her dreams for months, maybe years. It would be traumatic for anyone. 'Freddy, it's against procedure.'

'It's not my dad,' he yelled. 'Are you going to show me or do I have to go see for myself?'

Lucinda rose to her feet. Her jaw moved but words did not come out.

'Fine,' Freddy said and turned on his heel.

She grabbed his arm and spun him around. 'Stop.'

He glared up at her. 'Let go of mc, One-Eye.'

Lucinda stared back at him and exhaled forcefully. 'Cut it out, kid. It won't do any good to go up there and see the body. You won't be able to tell if it is your dad or not.'

'Why not?' he said, his angry countenance morphed into a fearful one.

'Just trust me, Freddy, you won't,' she said, releasing her grip on his arm. 'C'mon, let's sit back down.'

Freddy slumped into the chair as Lucinda sat down beside him. 'Dad messed up the face?' he asked.

'Well, not exactly.'

'His face was skinned?'

Lucinda grimaced. 'Skinned?'

'Yeah, it's kinda gross. I saw it on a TV show.'

Lucinda shook off her disgust. She wasn't enjoying this guessing game at all but she wasn't sure how to make it stop except by cutting him off and walking away. It might be what she wanted to do, but she would not walk away from her responsibility. 'No. Not skinned.'

'The head's gone, isn't it?'

The nonchalant way he said it made her head spin. *Did he really know?*

He nodded his head. 'I bet the hands are gone, too.'

She looked at him in horror. *He does know. But how? No. A thirteen-year-old boy is capable of taking a gun and shooting both his parents in the head. But beheading one parent? No. Impossible. Or is it?* She wanted to believe it was impossible and she didn't know what to say to this child sitting beside her.

'You don't need to answer. I can tell by the look on your face that I'm right and maybe you think I did it. I didn't,' he said, shaking his head. 'It was my dad. It was bad but he couldn't help it. He had to. He made his deal with the devil and he had no choice. Honest.'

Lucinda looked at the earnest face, heard the pleading in his voice, but didn't know what to think. *The Devil? That's often the refuge of the psychotic. Did he kill his parents and mutilate his father's body while disassociated from reality? That's the only way he could have done it, if he even could then.* She knew she had to find an adult relative for the boy before she asked another question.

'Freddy, do you have any other family besides your mom and dad?'

'There's my grandma but I'm not allowed to see her anymore.'

'Why not, Freddy?'

'I don't really know. My mom said she was a bad influence but that doesn't make sense. My mom is good and grandma raised her. I tried to tell Mom that but she said I shouldn't talk back. I tried to explain I was just being logical but she sent me to my room and said she didn't want to hear another word about it.'

'Would you like to see your grandma?'

He raised his head and nodded up and down; for the first time since she'd seen him, a tiny smile teased at the corners of his mouth.

'We'll see if we can find her, then.'

'I have her number on my cell,' he said, digging his phone out of his pocket and handing it to her.

'OK, any other family? Is there a grandpa?'

'No, all of my grandpas are dead, I think. I don't know about my dad's dad – he never talked about him or showed me pictures or anything. But I guess they didn't have photographs that long ago. But my grandma was married, maybe five times, I think. She showed me all their pictures. The only one I really remember was my mom's dad. He was in a uniform.'

His comment about not having photographs of his paternal grandfather bothered Lucinda but she set it aside for later rumination. 'OK,' she said as she rose to her feet. 'I'll call your grandma and, while I'm doing that, I'm going to turn you over to a couple of officers. You tell them what you need from the house and one of them will get it for you.'

'I can get it myself. I'm not a little kid,' Freddy objected.

'No, Freddy,' she said, lifting his chin with one hand to meet his gaze. 'You do not want to go in there, now. No matter how old you are, this is something you don't ever want to see.'

'But . . .'

'Trust me, Freddy. I honestly wished I had never seen it and they are not my parents.'

He jerked his chin out of her hand. 'I told you, my dad is not dead.'

'OK, Freddy. I've heard you. I understand what you are saying. And it is a possibility we will investigate. OK?'

He nodded his head. 'Promise?'

'Yes, Freddy. I promise.'

'He needs to be stopped.'

FOUR

Pamela Godfrey stuck her head out of the interrogation room, shouting down the hall. 'Hello. Hello. Hello.' She paused a moment for a response before striding down the corridor, teeth and heels clacking in unison.

The noise drew Ted's attention away from the computer. He jumped up and chased after her. 'Ma'am? Ma'am?'

Pamela stopped, placed her hands on her hips and spun around. 'Yes!' she said, the trailing sibilance of the last letter causing the image of a coiled snake to pop into Ted's mind.

'Ma'am, we really need you to wait for Lieutenant Pierce. She'll be here as soon as she clears the crime scene.'

Pamela's nostrils flared and her mouth turned down as if she smelled a bad odor. 'I am here, officer, because I agreed to come down and answer a few questions – not because I wanted to take up permanent residence in that ugly little room. Ask your questions and be done with it.'

'Lieutenant Pierce needs to talk to you. I'm sure she'll be back as quickly as she can.'

Incredulity washed across her face. She tilted her head to the side. 'Do you know who I am, off-i-cer?'

Normally Ted was not a stickler for titles but the sneer that wrapped around 'officer' as it left her mouth hit a nerve. 'Sergeant, Ms Godfrey, Sergeant.'

'So, you *do* know who I am. Good. Then I won't need to explain to you that my time is valuable and I can't afford to lollygag here any longer.' She spun on her heels and headed for the door.

'Ma'am, you can't leave,' Ted said as he followed her.

Pamela ignored his entreaty but she had to acknowledge the uniformed bulk that stepped in her path. She stopped an inch before contact, looked up at the man's eyes and snapped, 'Excuse me.'

The officer folded his arms across his chest, planted his feet and returned her glare.

Pamela turned back to Ted. 'Am I under arrest?'

'No, ma'am, but you are a material witness,' Ted said as he stepped forward, hemming her in a place of no retreat.

'Material witness? To what?' She laughed. 'A note?'

'Please, ma'am. I'll be glad to get you a cup of coffee, a soft drink, water? But please return to the room and wait a bit longer.'

'A glass of cab, perhaps?' She laughed again, then set her jaw tight. 'I really do regret making that call.'

'I'm sorry to hear that, but . . .'

'Forget your buts. The least you can do is explain to me what you found at that address. I assume it was more than a cat up a tree.'

'Yes, ma'am, it was.'

'And?'

'I'm not at liberty to discuss an ongoing investigation with you, Ms Godfrey.'

'Fine. Get my lawyer or let me leave.'

Ted looked her over. She certainly was a fine-looking woman – he had to admit he enjoyed watching her walking away. But she exceeded the allowable level of bitchiness by an excessive amount. He blew a disgusted breath of air out of his mouth. 'I'll tell you what. I'll give the lieutenant a call.'

Her hands gravitated to her hips. 'I'll wait. For one call.'

Looking at the sharp angles of her jutting elbows made Ted want to grab her arms, pull them back and snap on a pair of cuffs. The urgency of the impulse surprised him. He pulled out his cell and punched up Lucinda's number. He grimaced when his call went straight to voicemail. He left a message and disconnected.

'Time's up,' Pamela chirped. 'Lawyer or departure? Your call.'

'You're free to leave, Ms Godfrey.'

She smiled and turned to face the broad blue shoulders. She raised an eyebrow and tilted her head. 'Excuse me.'

The officer raised his chin and looked down at her through slitted eyes for a moment before stepping aside. He swiveled his head, watching her until she'd turned a corner and was out of sight. 'Lieutenant's not gonna be happy 'bout that.'

'Tell me about it.' Ted shook his head and walked down the hall to his office.

FIVE

While Lucinda spoke to Freddy's grandmother, another call came to her cell. She let it roll to voicemail. She walked over to the patrol car where Freddy sat looking very small. Opening the door, she said, 'Have you got everything you need?'

He gave a tight nod. 'I think so.'

'OK, I'll see you later. Here's my card. If you need me before I get there, just call my cell, OK?'

'Yes, ma'am.'

Lucinda straightened up and closed the door. She spoke to Officer Robin Colter across the roof of her car. 'I'm not sure how long it will be before I can get over to his grandmother's house. I would appreciate it if you could remain there until I do.'

'In the house?'

'Until we know why this happened to his parents, it might be best. But if the grandmother gives you a hard time, sit out in your car and keep a close eye on the house. Go back in if anything makes you feel uncomfortable, no matter what she says.'

'Got it.'

'Don't ask him anything about the crime or his family while you're driving over. He's made some odd comments and I think it would be better not to question him without an adult family member present.'

'No problem.'

'Go on,' Lucinda said.

Robin ducked her head, slid behind the wheel and backed out of the driveway. Lucinda watched as she pulled away, still not knowing what to think about the boy. His reactions seemed odd but then what did she know about thirteen-year-olds?

Lucinda checked her voice mail and returned Ted's call. Without giving him a chance to say a word, she started talking. 'Ted, how old is Pete?'

'My Pete?'

'Yeah. Pete Branson. Your kid. Who else?'

'He's eleven – gonna be twelve soon. But, Lucinda, I have to tell you . . .'

Lucinda cut him off. 'Is there a big difference between an eleven-year-old boy and a thirteen-year-old boy?'

'How should I know? Pete hasn't gotten there yet. Lucinda, I . . .'

'But you've been there. You were a thirteen-year-old boy. You must remember something.'

'Ha. I tried to block it all out. It was an awkward, clumsy, insecure year. What's this all about?'

'The son of the two victims. I just can't figure him out. None of his reactions seem normal.'

'There's nothing normal about thirteen.'

'Yeah, it wasn't a romp in paradise for me either.'

'Do you think the kid's the doer?' Ted asked.

'I have a hard time wrapping my mind around that possibility but I just don't know,' Lucinda said with a sigh. 'So why did you call?'

'Pamela Godfrey.'

'Who?'

'The woman who made the nine-one-one call for your crime scene. We brought her in . . .'

'You'll have to amuse her for a while. I've got to go over to the grandma's house and see the kid when I finish up here.'

'But, Lucinda . . .'

'Just ask her some questions about the note and her reaction to it. There may have been a reason it was left on her car – or maybe she's the one who wrote it. Press her a bit and see what pops out.'

'I can't, Lucinda.'

'What?'

'That's what I've been trying to tell you – she left.'

'She left? You let her go?'

'Yes, but . . .'

'Right now, she's a possible suspect and you just let her go? You didn't even question her first?'

'Lucinda, she asked for her attorney.'

'All the more reason to keep her there. What were you thinking, Ted?'

'Do you know who she is?'

'You said she was the nine-one-one caller, right?'

'Yeah, but beyond that?'

'No. Tell me.'

'Her father is Malcolm Godfrey – the Godfrey in Drummond-Godfrey.'

'The law firm?' Lucinda asked, hoping it wasn't true. Drummond-Godfrey was the largest – and most influential – law firm in the state; and, with offices in New York, Miami, Houston and Los Angeles, a dominant force across the country.

''Fraid so,' Ted acknowledged.

'Shit. Is she an attorney, too?'

'No, but her public relations company does a lot of work for the firm. Most of it typical corporate image stuff but Pamela's personal specialty is dealing with situations when crime and corporate culture overlap.'

'A PR flak? Damn, that's worse than a lawyer.'

'So, that's why I backed off when she squawked. I . . .'

'No need to explain, Ted. I get it. What I need you to do now is start digging to find out everything you can about that woman and her company.'

'Pamela Godfrey Management.'

'Gee, I wonder how long it took her ego to settle on that. Dig up everything you can. Look for any connection between her or her company and Jeanine or Parker Sterling – at least for now; I'm assuming that's Parker we found in the tub.'

'You got any reason to doubt his identity?'

'Other than his son? No. But the kid's story makes no sense. Look for any background you can find on the Sterlings, too. Even rumors about infidelity by either one of them might be useful. But I have a feeling that the answer might lie in a connection with Godfrey – find it for me.'

Lucinda disconnected from Ted and walked back to the house. After donning Tyvek booties and latex gloves, she went upstairs. 'Spellman?' she called from the bedroom doorway.

Forensics team leader Marguerite Spellman, covered in blue from the hood over her head to the toes of the matching foot coverings, rose from the floor on the far side of the bed like a spooky apparition. 'Yes, Lieutenant?'

'One of the most important things for me right now is establishing the identity of the male victim.'

'Of course, Lieutenant. We have bagged and tagged all the toothbrushes, hairbrushes, a man's electric razor, two used disposable razors and a pile of dirty male garments from the hamper to compare with the vic's DNA.'

'Good,' Lucinda said, pleased that Marguerite was living up to her reputation for thoroughness. 'Could you spare someone to come with me to get a buccal swab from the boy we think is his son?'

'Sure. Give me fifteen, twenty minutes to check in with all my team members, Lieutenant, and I can follow you over there.'

'Terrific. I'll be downstairs,' Lucinda said, starting to turn away until a thought brought her back to face Marguerite. 'Listen, you've been at this for a long time. Seen a lot of homicide scenes.'

'Sure have. It'll be seventeen years in September.'

'Give me your gut reaction to this one – could it be the work of a thirteen-year-old?'

After barking out a startled laugh, Marguerite said, 'You're kidding, right?'

'No.'

'Oh, man. Oh, my God, Lieutenant. A thirteen-year-old?' She turned and looked across the bedroom into the bloodied bathroom. 'I suppose anything is possible – but a thirteen-year-old kid? Whoa. I sure hope to God not.'

'Me, too,' Lucinda said. 'Me, too.'

SIX

Lucinda turned into an older neighborhood, on a street filled with fifties-era ranch homes and lined with tall trees. The address of Freddy's grandmother was a tidy brick home with roses, irises and gladioli adding a riot of color to a small yard inside a split-rail fence.

As Lucinda opened her door, Robin stepped out of a patrol car. 'She didn't want you in the house?' Lucinda asked.

'Oh, she did. But she plied me with tea and cookies while asking a steady stream of questions that I didn't want to answer. I told her I had to check in with the dispatcher and retreated out to the car.'

'Anything about her questions cause you any concern?'

'Lieutenant, I wouldn't presume . . .'

'Colter, cut the crap. You have an opinion, I want it.'

'Yes, sir – uh, ma'am. I, uh . . .'

'Colter, listen. You impressed me when you stood up to that school superintendent who was twice your size a year or so ago. You didn't let him intimidate you. Don't let me.'

Colter gave a tight nod. 'Yes, ma'am.' She cleared her throat, took a breath and said, 'Her questions seemed strange to me not because of what she wanted to know but because of the way she asked. She sounded curious but she didn't seem concerned. Do you know what I mean?'

'Yeah, I think I do. What's going on in the house?'

'Freddy brought his Wii from home and I helped him set it up on the television in the basement. When I came outside, he was still down there playing a video game and the grandmother was sitting in the living room.'

'Marguerite Spellman from forensics is on her way here.

I'm going in to find out if Grandma will let us have a buccal swab from Freddy. Bring Spellman in when she arrives. Pay close attention to Freddy and the grandma's behavior; I'll want your feedback after we leave.' Without waiting for confirmation, Lucinda turned and walked up to the front door. Victoria Whitehead opened it before Lucinda could ring the bell. Her hair was the consistency of dried straw, the make-up on her face a bit too thick to look anywhere near natural and the deep V-neck of her red dress revealed a bounteous but tired-looking bosom.

'Oh, my lands, officer! What happened to your face?' Victoria sputtered.

Lucinda flashed her badge. 'May I come in, ma'am?' *Maybe, just maybe, she'll forget she asked.*

'Of course, of course. That was rude. Sorry. Please have a seat. Would you like a cup of tea?'

'No, thank you,' Lucinda said as she studied her surroundings. The living room looked like Victoria, colorful but worn, wafting the fragrance of lilacs offset by an undertone of chicken soup. A long teal sofa nestled under the picture window, facing two overstuffed floral-patterned chairs. A glass-topped coffee table filled the space between them – an assortment of crystals rested on its surface. On the far wall, the mantel of the brick fireplace was adorned with family photographs, candles and more crystals.

'Please, please, have a seat,' Victoria insisted. 'Freddy is downstairs. Should I fetch him?'

'Not yet, ma'am. Would you please have a seat?' Lucinda said as she slipped into one of the chairs. 'I need to ask you something.'

Victoria settled in the middle of the sofa, spreading the full skirt around her as if it were an ante-bellum gown and she was Scarlett entertaining at Tara. 'Yes, ma'am. What would you like to know?'

'We'll get to that in a minute. But first, I need to get your permission to take a DNA sample from Freddy.'

'DNA?' she asked, her eyes widening, the fingers of her left hand flying to her throat.

'It's really simple, ma'am. We take what looks like a giant Q-tip and rub it on the inside of his cheek.'

'That's it?'

'Yes, ma'am.'

'Why do you need to do this?'

'We need to confirm the identity of Freddy's father.'

'Are you referring to the dead man in his house?' Victoria asked.

'Yes.'

'That's not his father,' Victoria said with a shake of her head.

Lucinda decided to pursue that line of questioning later. Right now, she simply wanted permission to get a sample before the tech came through the door. 'Fine, Ms Whitehead. That is important information. We simply need to confirm it with a DNA test.'

'I suppose that could be useful,' Victoria conceded. 'If you are sure it won't hurt Frederick, then that will be fine.'

Lucinda pulled the release form out of a pocket, unfolding and smoothing it on the coffee table. 'Won't hurt at all, ma'am. Thank you so much for your cooperation,' she said, handing the woman a pen.

As Victoria touched the paper with the nib of the pen, the doorbell rang. Lucinda bounced to her feet. 'I'll get that, ma'am. It's just the technician who's come to get Freddy's sample. You go ahead and sign that and we'll put her to work.'

Opening the door, Lucinda nodded and said, 'She's signing right now. Colter, would you please take Spellman down to the boy.'

As they walked by, Victoria came to her feet. 'Shouldn't I go with them?'

'No need,' Lucinda said, scooping up the document from the coffee table. 'I'd really like to speak to you alone for a moment.'

Victoria looked at Lucinda; cast her eyes toward the retreating backs of the other two women. 'I don't know.'

'Please have a seat, Ms Whitehead.'

Biting her lower lip, Victoria eased herself back on to the sofa, arranged her skirt, folded her hands in her lap and tilted her head to the side. 'Yes?'

'Your grandson?'

'Yes?'

'You call him Frederick?'

'That *is* his name,' Victoria said.

'I understand your daughter called him "Freddy"?'

Victoria rolled her eyes. 'I am afraid so. That wasn't the only thing I didn't approve of.'

'What else, Ms Whitehead?'

Victoria closed her eyes and shook her head. 'I don't want to go into that. It is personal – between me and my daughter.'

Lucinda bit back a retort, letting her response rest for a moment. 'Do you think the deceased male in your daughter's house is not her husband?'

'Oh, no, it's not a matter of what I think. I'm certain he is not. Her husband killed them both. I tried to warn my daughter.'

'Really? Why is that, Ms Whitehead? Was your daughter having an affair with the deceased man?'

'Absolutely not. No daughter of mine would ever – no, ma'am. I can't believe you even suggested that.'

'Forgive me if I gave you cause for offense, Ms Whitehead. I am simply trying to understand. You said that your daughter and a man were found deceased in the same bedroom suite, killed by your son-in-law, but there was nothing going on between your daughter and that man.'

'Well, I sincerely doubt that Jeanine even knew that poor man.'

'Help me, ma'am. I'm struggling to put this information together in a way that makes sense to me. You are saying your daughter and a man are killed in her bedroom and they don't know each other.'

'I'm pretty sure of that. Parker wouldn't want to make it easy to identify the man so he wouldn't kill someone connected to the family. He would want everyone to assume it was him.'

Lucinda waited to see if she would say anything more without prompting. I *know the head and hands are missing but she doesn't – or rather, she* shouldn't.

'You did make that assumption, didn't you?' Victoria asked.

'Ms Whitehead, what are you saying about your son-in-law?'

'He's still alive.'

Lucinda stared hard at Victoria, willing her to continue talking. Instead, without saying a word, Victoria turned her head away, casting her glance down to the floor.

'Ms Whitehead, why do you think your son-in-law is still alive?'

Victoria turned toward her, and then turned away. 'I'm sorry, Lieutenant. I find it very difficult to look at you. I know that's rude but – I'm sorry.'

Lucinda wanted to jump up, grab her by both the shoulders and shake her hard. Instead, she said, 'That is understandable. You don't have to look at me. But I do need you to answer my questions.'

Victoria rubbed the back of her neck, raised her chin and turned her face toward the window next to the fireplace, her focus on the yard beyond the glass. 'Certainly.'

'You think your son-in-law is alive?' Lucinda asked again.

Victoria turned her glance toward the hallway when she heard the sound of an opening door. Marguerite and Robin stopped in the archway of the living room. 'Got it, Lieutenant. You need anything else?' Marguerite asked.

'No, thank you, Spellman. I'll see you back at the scene. Colter, could you go downstairs with Freddy? I'm not quite through talking to his grandmother.'

As Robin turned away, Victoria said, 'I should be there when the boy's being questioned.'

'She's just keeping him company, Ms Whitehead.'

'Yeah.' Robin grinned. 'He promised to teach me how to play "Punch Out".'

'Well, OK,' Victoria said.

'Ms Whitehead, about your son-in-law?'

'Yes, yes. Of course, he's alive. Frederick told me he explained that to you already.'

'Yes, ma'am, he did. But I'd like to hear it from you. He didn't really give me a lot of detail.'

'I must admit the boy had a hard time understanding it, at first. He is bright but he is only thirteen. You still tend to accept the world at face value at that age. It is hard to accept that evil can come in very attractive packages.'

She's not making any more sense than the boy. Maybe the whole family is whacked. 'Could you start at the beginning?' Lucinda asked.

'Oh, dear, I'm not really sure where the beginning is. But I can start with when I first met Parker.'

'Fine. Go ahead, ma'am.'

'I didn't like him. And let me tell you,' she said with a wag of her finger, 'these are not the words of the mother-in-law from h-e-double hockey-sticks. I was ready to accept my daughter's choice of a life mate – more than ready, actually. And Parker was brilliant, competitive, and on the fast track to the top of the heap. After all, who am I to criticize? I've been married five times and now I'm living with a sixth man. I was ready. Yes, ma'am, I was ready.'

'You were ready, but . . .?'

'Oh, but – oh yes, oh yes. I was uncomfortable from the moment he stepped into the room,' she said, leaning forward. 'His aura was black. Solid, pitch, black.' She leaned back in the sofa, folding her arms softly across her chest as she nodded. 'Oh, my, yes. His aura was as black as the heart of Satan himself.'

Here comes the devil again. 'Did you share this with your daughter?'

'Well, of course. But at the time, I didn't know what I know now.' Her folded arms kept flying apart and coming back together as she spoke. 'If I had known, I would have taken her away, out of the country, into an asylum – whatever it took. I knew his aura was bad, but I had no idea. I didn't even know it was possible.'

'Didn't know what was possible?'

Victoria leaned back again and spoke in a tone that made it clear she thought Lucinda asked a stupid question. 'Didn't know he was immortal, of course.'

'Be patient with me, Ms Whitehead, and please explain why you think your son-in-law is immortal.'

'Because he sold his soul to the devil,' she said, laughing at Lucinda's ignorance.

'And when did this happen?'

'Now, that I'm not sure of yet. Jason's been doing the research. So far, we've tracked it back to 1845. But it could go further. It gets difficult following a trail that old.'

'Who is Jason?'

'My boyfriend. Jeanine didn't approve. He is a bit younger than me,' she said as a blush penetrated through the thick layer of cosmetics on her face.

'And what did he track back to 1845?'

'Parker Sterling, of course. Naturally, he's used other names. Many other names. Sometimes he simply disappeared and turned up in a distant location with a new life and a new identity. Other times, he faked his death by sinking a ship or seeming to get lost in an avalanche. But on other occasions, like this one, he faked his death by substituting the body of someone he murdered. And this time, he killed his wife – my daughter. This time, he went too far.'

'And you are convinced of this, Ms Whitehead?' Lucinda said, trying hard to keep her incredulity out of her voice and off of her face.

'Most certainly, Lieutenant. After all, my boyfriend is Parker Sterling's son, too.'

An image of this woman in a passionate embrace with a teenage boy flashed through her thoughts, making her stomach churn. 'Your boyfriend Jason is your grandson's age?'

Victoria gasped and then tittered. 'Oh, Lieutenant. Oh, Lieutenant, I should be appalled but I can't help but laugh.' She giggled. 'Oh, my, my. What a dreadful vision you must've formed in your head. Jason and Frederick don't have the same mother. They're both Parker's sons but only Frederick is my daughter's child. Oh, my, that would be absolutely outrageous, wouldn't it?'

Lucinda squirmed at her reaction. 'But with the same father, Jason and Freddy would be close to the same age?'

Victoria glanced at Lucinda and jerked her eyes away. 'I really wish you wouldn't call him Freddy.'

'Ma'am, please, how old is your boyfriend?' Lucinda asked, pressing down her impatience.

Victoria chuckled, her eyes twinkled. 'Why, he's old enough to be Frederick's father. Which means, Jason is young enough, I suppose, to be my son, but once you're out of your thirties, the age difference doesn't matter quite so much, does it?'

'So, Jason, is . . .?

'In his forties.'

'And your grandson is thirteen, right?'

'Yes, that's right.'

'And you think they have the same father?'

'Oh, yes, I'm sure of it. Different names but the same man.'

'Different names?'

'Yes. When Jason was born Parker went by the name Samuel Houston King.'

'Where is Jason right now?'

'He's in Texas. Visiting his mother.'

'How long has he been there?'

'His flight left, I believe –' she looked at her wrist watch – 'about three hours ago. He should be in San Antonio by now, I think.'

'Today? He left town today?'

'Yes. Frederick was so disappointed. He really likes Jason. They love playing together on the Wii. It's a nice way for the brothers to bond.'

Lucinda was certain she'd slipped into another dimension. *No wonder Freddy was acting so strangely.* 'I'll need to speak with Jason, Ms Whitehead. Could you give me his cell number – he did take it with him, didn't he?'

'Well, yes, but I don't know. I can't see why Jason needs to be involved. And his mother is sickly.'

'Why don't you get me his mother's home address, too? I have to speak with Jason. Like you said, he's done the research. He knows more than anyone about Parker Sterling, or Samuel King, or whoever he is.' Lucinda plastered what she hoped was a look of sincerity on her face.

'Oh, yes, of course. How silly of me. I'll go get my address book.'

At that moment, a loud 'whoop' echoed up from the basement, followed by footsteps pounding up the stairs. 'I beat her,' Freddy crowed as he bounded into the living room. 'I beat a police officer.'

Robin followed him, grinning and nodding. 'He sure did. The kid gave me a righteous stomping.'

'Yeah,' Freddy said. 'Righteous.'

'Congratulations, Freddy,' Lucinda said with a smile. She dreaded bringing him down to earth – away from games and back to reality. She crouched down, resting an elbow on each knee. 'Hey, Freddy . . .'

The joy drained from his face as rapidly as floodwaters from a ruptured dam. 'Yes, ma'am?'

'Did you think of anything else I need to know?'

'Not really, ma'am. But I don't think I explained things too well.'

'That's OK, Freddy. Your grandmother filled in the blanks. You still have my card?'

He pulled it out of his pocket and held it up as he smiled. 'Sure do.'

'Good, you keep it safe and call me anytime. And

congratulations again; Officer Colter needed someone to bring her down a peg.' Lucinda pushed down on her knees and rose to her full height.

Victoria returned with a piece of paper in her hand containing the address and phone number for Karen King, as well as Jason's cellphone number. 'Just remember, when you speak to Frederick's brother, his mother is sickly.'

Lucinda jerked her head over to Freddy. She saw no indication that his grandmother's mention of his brother surprised or bothered him in any way. It seemed as if the boy believed Jason was his brother.

'Please don't distress her,' Victoria said as she handed the address to Lucinda.

Lucinda and Robin walked out of the house and stopped by Robin's patrol car. 'So what's running through your head?' Lucinda asked.

'Something's off. Something's odd.'

'Yeah, odd's a good word.'

'Does Freddy really have a brother?' Robin asked.

'The grandmother says so – a half-brother anyway. His name is Jason.' Lucinda looked down at the address in her hand. 'Jason King, I believe.'

'Which parent do they share?'

'The father, she said.'

'How old is Freddy's brother?'

'In his forties, she said.'

'What?'

'Yeah, about thirty years' difference in their ages. I imagine it is biologically possible but it sure doesn't sound probable to me.'

'You believe her?' Robin asked.

'No, but Freddy does.'

SEVEN

Returning to the Sterling home, Lucinda donned booties and latex gloves before crossing the threshold. She went up the stairs to the bedroom. The bed was stripped of its linens. Rectangular holes scarred the surface of the mattress.

Marguerite emerged from the bathroom and smiled at Lucinda. 'Glad you're back. I've got something to show you.'

Lucinda pointed to the bed. 'Blood on the mattress?'

'Nah, but we did find some body fluids and took them for testing.'

'Good. If someone other than Jeanine and Parker Sterling were in that bed, we need to know.'

'My thinking exactly. I found two bullets in the bathroom. Wanna see?'

'Excellent,' Lucinda said, following Marguerite into the adjoining bath.

Marguerite pointed to a spot on the wall and both women leaned toward it, their noses just a hair's breadth from the surface. 'Thirty-eight?' Lucinda asked.

'That'd be my guess. The ballistics labs will let us know for sure.'

'Where's the other one?'

Marguerite led her into a luxurious, large shower. A broad rain shower head pointed down from the ceiling. Four water jets pointed at each other from opposite walls. 'Right here.'

Lucinda looked at the cracked slate tile. 'You got a flashlight?'

Marguerite pulled one from her tool belt and handed it to the detective. Lucinda studied the bullet. 'Looks like the same caliber.'

'Yeah. But not the same victim.'

'You sure of that?'

'I did a quick blood typing test around each bullet. Type A in the shower, type O on the wall.'

'Nice, Spellman. Very nice. If we could only find the head, we could get trajectory and have a shot at recreating the scene.'

'We haven't found it in the house.'

'I doubt if it's anywhere near here. But, I've got a cadaver dog coming over to check the grounds, just in case. Any sign of a gun in the house?'

'Not yet. No gun. No ammunition. But we're still going through the house,' Marguerite said. 'They all know to alert me if they find a gun, a head, hands or anything else of interest.'

'Thanks, Spellman.'

'Lieutenant, there's one thing that's bothering me.'

'What's that, Spellman?'

'There are two adults in this house. Two cars in the garage. But we've only been able to find one ring of keys. Doesn't make sense.'

'No, it doesn't. Any theories?'

'Got me, Lieutenant, it's just odd. We'll keep looking. They might still show up somewhere.'

'Let me know if they do.' Lucinda went downstairs and went from room to room observing the techs at work. Pleased with their thoroughness, she was, nonetheless, impatient for them to finish and get out of the house. She wanted to spend some time here alone.

That would have to come later. For now, her priority was the nine-one-one caller, Pamela Godfrey. She climbed into her car for the drive downtown. On the way there, she called Ted. 'Did you find a connection between Godfrey and the Sterlings?'

'I sure did. Parker Sterling is the founder and former CEO of Dodgebird.'

'Dodgebird?'

'A computer software company. They were bought out by Microsoft last year but in the negotiations, Sterling secured the vice-presidency of the Dodgebird division and he still manages the facility. Dodgebird's legal representation is handled by Drummond-Godfrey.'

'Aah . . . and?'

'A couple of years before the Microsoft acquisition, Sterling and Godfrey spent a lot of time together. Remember that child porn ring the FBI busted up?'

'Yeah. How can I forget a swarm of those vainglorious jerks?'

'Oh, did you and your Special Agent have a fight?'

'Don't start with me, Ted.'

'Well, I thought . . .'

'Ted, I just pulled up to a meter downtown, so drop it or I'll throw Ellen in your face.'

'OK. Never mind. Anyway, one of the folks arrested was the sales manager at Dodgebird. Pamela Godfrey personally handled the media flak and public relations damage control for that.'

'Anything else before I tackle Godfrey?'

'Just a little scuttlebutt that might prove useful. It seems Ms Godfrey has a reputation for mixing business with pleasure.'

'An affair with Sterling?' Lucinda asked.

'I haven't heard anything that specific – just a general rumor that she has a tendency to climb into bed with her clients.'

'Lovely,' Lucinda said. 'Thanks, Ted. I'll call back when I finish with Godfrey.'

Lucinda strode into the high-rise, checked the board for an office number, stepped into the elevator and pressed the button for the fourteenth floor. When the doors opened, she saw that there were just two offices on that level – straight ahead of her were the oversized double glass doors leading to the law offices of Drummond-Godfrey. Beyond the doors and past the receptionist, the panorama of the city filled the far glass wall. To her right, an apparently smaller space with a single door was marked 'Pamela Godfrey Management'.

She entered and approached the front desk. 'Pamela Godfrey, please.'

A cute and perky dark-haired young woman smiled and asked, 'Do you have an appointment?'

Lucinda hated that question. It always spoke of a sense of superiority and a spirit of exclusion. She pulled out her badge and held it close to the woman's face. 'This is all the appointment I need. Tell Ms Godfrey I'm here.'

The receptionist's face turned beet red and her jaw moved without making a sound. She picked up a receiver and spun around in her chair, turning her back to Lucinda. She whispered into the phone, pivoted back and hung up the receiver. 'I'm sorry, ma'am. It just isn't convenient for Ms Godfrey to speak with you at this time. Umm . . .'

'Yes?'

'I'm sorry. But she told me to tell you that y'all ate up enough of her time today already.'

'Fine,' Lucinda said and walked toward the hallway that led to the offices.

The flustered receptionist jumped up and blocked her path. 'I'm sorry. But I can't let you go back there.'

Lucinda looked down on her – at five feet eleven inches and wearing three-inch heels, she made the petite woman standing in front of her look like a small child. 'Really?' she said. She placed a hand on both of the woman's upper arms and gently moved her out of the way. She strode down the hall to the door bearing Pamela's name and threw it open.

Pamela bolted up out of her high-backed office chair. Anger curled her lips into a sneer. In the chairs opposite her desk, two dark-suited men bounced to their feet, with widened eyes.

'How dare you?' Pamela said.

Lucinda smiled at the visitors in the room, pulled out her badge and flashed it first in their direction and then at Pamela.

One of the men said, 'We were just leaving.'

'No, you were not,' Pamela snapped.

'Hey, Pamela, we can come back,' the other man said.

'Sit.' When they didn't respond immediately, she said, 'Now!' They slid back down but their bodies remained tensed, ready for flight. She turned to Lucinda. 'You'll need to make an appointment with the receptionist. Right now, as you see, I am occupied.'

'OK. If that's your attitude, fine,' Lucinda said pulling a pair of cuffs out of the waistband at the back of her skirt. 'We can go over to headquarters, if that's the way you want to play it.'

The two women stared at each other across Pamela's desk. Pamela looked away first. Seeing the receptionist standing in the doorway wringing her hands, she said, 'Jennifer, would you please escort the officer down to the conference room?' Turning back to Lucinda she plastered a sour smile on her face. 'Just give me a minute, please. I'll be right with you.'

Lucinda continued to stare for a few more seconds before turning and following Jennifer. She understood that power play. *We made Godfrey wait in an empty room. Now she's going to return the favor. That's OK. Once she thinks she's put me in my place, her cockiness will make it easier to catch her off guard and corner her in a contradiction.*

Lucinda barely heard the stuttered apologies of Godfrey's embarrassed employee. Her thoughts had already moved forward, forming a strategy. The challenge of the upcoming interview made Lucinda smile.

EIGHT

The vibrations of the phone in her pocket pulled Lucinda's thoughts away from Pamela Godfrey. Grabbing hold of the cell, she groaned when she saw the caller ID – Rambo Burns. She disconnected the call. She wished he'd leave her alone. He'd been calling her number and the office incessantly for the past ten days. She had no desire to talk with him – no desire for another round of reconstructive surgery. *Not now. Maybe not ever.* She ran her fingers over her lips, from the soft, full side to the thin, hard side. *He was supposed to eliminate scarring, not add to it.*

She felt the buzz of her cell again. Her first thought was to ignore it but she decided it was too soon for Burns to call her again and slipped a hand into her pocket. This time the ID read 'Spencer office'. Considering the timing, she felt certain that Spencer was calling for Burns. But she had doubts. *What if it's about Charley? What if something happened to Charley?*

She answered the call, 'Pierce.'

'Lucinda, it's Evan Spencer.'

'Yes. Is Charley OK?'

'Charley? Oh, yes, of course. I'm not calling about Charley. I'm calling for Rambo . . .'

'I'm hanging up now, Evan.'

'Please, Lucinda. Rambo just wants to talk to you.'

'Evan, I care about Charley. I'm always happy to talk to you about her – your daughter is very important to me. But I'm not going to talk to you about Dr Burns. And I have nothing to say to him at all.'

'Lucinda, please. He's not going to force you into anything. He just wants to talk.'

'Does Dr Burns take this much interest in all of his patients?

'You know Rambo and I are good friends. He has taken a special interest in you because of our relationship.'

Our relationship? Dammit, Evan! 'You mean because of my relationship with Charley?'

'Well, that, too,' Evan conceded.

Lucinda bit back the retort on the tip of her tongue. *Why does he assume I care about him because I care about Charley? Why does he read so much into my interest in his daughter? Why doesn't he just grieve the loss of his wife and stop grabbing for me as if I was born to be his crutch?* 'Dr Spencer . . .'

'Aw c'mon, Lucinda. When you start calling me Dr Spencer . . .'

'OK, Evan. But don't mention Dr Burns unless I bring him up first.'

'OK. But he just wants to talk.'

'Goodbye, Dr Spencer,' she said and hit the disconnect button before he could utter another word.

Lucinda had just enough time to refocus her mind on Pamela Godfrey before the door flew open and the woman strode into the room, clutching a cup of coffee in one hand. She stopped directly in front of Lucinda, slammed the mug down and placed her hands on hips with elbows jutting from her sides. She was an intimidating figure in an expensive suit and sporting an air of haughty indifference.

Lucinda rose to her full height and mirrored Pamela's stance – the four-inch advantage in height made it clear that Lucinda had the upper hand in this battle of wills. Pamela recognized and confirmed it. 'Perhaps we should both have a seat.'

They both stood for a moment longer, neither one willing to make the first move. Slowly, as if their movements were choreographed in unison, their knees bent and they lowered themselves to chairs on opposite sides of the conference table without losing eye contact for a second. 'I've told the officers all I know. I'm sure you'll find that in a report somewhere,' Pamela said.

Sliding a compact digital recorder out of her oversized shoulder bag and on to the surface between them, Lucinda said, 'I'd like to hear it in your own words and preserve it on audio, if you don't mind.'

'Actually, I do. It is a waste of my time to keep repeating the same story again and again.'

Lucinda placed her hands on the table and laced her fingers together. She cleared her throat. 'There are two people dead, Ms Godfrey. I would think, on balance, their deaths are more important than polishing the image of another corporate jackass.'

'Lieutenant, I resent that depiction of my clients.'

'Fine,' Lucinda said through clenched teeth. 'You are entitled to your feelings. And I am entitled to hear a recounting of the events of your morning. Please start with when you arrived at the parking garage.'

'This is really tiresome,' Pamela complained.

Lucinda smiled, causing Pamela to flinch. She felt a spark of triumph, realizing that Pamela had worked hard not to show any reaction to the detective's face but she couldn't help that involuntary twitch at the off-kilter grin.

After a minute of silence, Pamela began. 'I arrived at the garage shortly before ten a.m.'

Lucinda interrupted. 'Did you have a preset appointment?'

'In a manner of speaking. I received a call from a client as soon as I entered the office this morning. He was panicking about the public relations plan for his company and wanted to discuss possible repercussions. I told him I'd be there right away.'

'You had a lengthy discussion, then?'

'Not exactly. I had a lengthy wait. And then I was dismissed.' Pamela's clenched jaw throbbed.

'Really? Does that happen often with your clients?'

'No. Absolutely not. In fact, because of his rudeness, his company might not be a client of my firm much longer.'

'Do you think your sexual entanglement with your client might have caused his rude behavior?'

Pamela slapped her hands down on the table and pushed to her feet. 'How dare you!'

'Who lives at 6423 James Landing Drive, Ms Godfrey?'

'How should I know?'

'Thought you might have bedded the homeowner at some point.'

'This is outrageous!'

'No, Ms Godfrey,' Lucinda said as she rose to her feet. 'What is outrageous is your pretense that you don't know who lives there and you don't know what happened there. One of your clients is dead, Ms Godfrey. I would expect that you would show some sign of concern about that fact – on a financial level, if nothing else.'

'What?'

'You heard me, Ms Godfrey. We went to the address you gave us and found one of your clients dead.'

'Dead?' Pamela said, sliding down into the chair. Her mouth opened and closed a few times as she stared at the top of the table. Raising her head, she asked, 'Who?'

Lucinda arched an eyebrow. 'You expect me to believe that you don't know?'

Pamela bowed her head. 'No. Yes. I – I – I mean . . .'

Lucinda sat back down, slouched in the seat, resting an elbow on the arm of the chair and bringing a hand to her face. She curled three fingers and her thumb around her chin. Her index finger lay flat across her cheek as she observed the woman struggle for words.

Pamela raised her eyes again. 'Who, Lieutenant?'

Lucinda held her gaze for a full minute before she said, 'Parker Sterling.'

'What?'

'Dodgebird, remember?'

'Of course I remember. But Parker? Someone killed Parker?'

'And his wife.'

'His wife, too? Who – who killed them?'

'That's exactly what I wanted to ask you.'

'Me? I don't know. I have no idea of anyone who'd want Parker – or his wife – anyone who'd want them – them – dead.'

'Really? Were you having an affair with Parker Sterling?'

'That is an outrageous allegation!' Pamela said, rising to her feet again. 'Absolutely outrageous!'

'Oh, sorry. Were you having an affair with Jeanine Parker?'

'That's it. That's it. I have had enough. I was not having an affair with Sterling or his wife. Any more questions, you can talk to my attorney. I'm done.' Pamela threw out her arm, gesturing to the door.

Lucinda looked at Pamela's coffee cup on the table. She really wanted it. She wanted Pamela's DNA. She couldn't use it in court if she swiped it, even if she did have a match with something in the Sterling home. But still, she wanted it. She wanted the advantage that information would provide. She intentionally left her recorder on the table as she left the room.

When they reached the reception area, Pamela said, 'Good

day, Lieutenant,' turned and walked back into her office, shutting the door behind her with a decisive click.

Lucinda walked to the office exit and stopped. 'Oh, my,' she said and walked back to the reception desk. She leaned over the counter and whispered to Jennifer, who was in the middle of a phone call, 'Sorry, I left something back in the conference room. I'll just be a sec.'

The receptionist held up a finger, signaling her to wait a moment, but Lucinda turned away as if she hadn't seen it and hurried down the hall. She pulled a pen from her bag and slid it into the handle of the mug. She slipped the mug into a paper evidence bag with care, making sure not to spill any of the quarter inch of coffee in the bottom. She placed it in her shoulder satchel, securing it in a corner, praying it wouldn't overturn as she made her way out of the building.

As she picked up her recorder, Jennifer stepped into the doorway. She cleared her throat and said, 'Excuse me, ma'am.'

Lucinda wiggled the recorder in her hand. 'Got it,' she said, maneuvering past the young woman and heading for the door. She tensed, expecting someone to call out and stop her. She did not relax until she was out of the building and in her car. *Now all I have to do is con Audrey into processing this sample.*

NINE

Pamela Godfrey felt betrayed by her own philosophy of life and men: When it costs you little, give it freely and then demand payment that far exceeds the value of the gift. She developed it first with her father. She awarded him a few smiles, the outward display of good behavior and a willingness to pretend total dependence. As a result, he never said no to anything.

It was no small feat. Her father, a prominent attorney, was known for his shrewd negotiation skills, his powerful courtroom presence and his ruthless ambition to win. Many feared him. All respected him – except for his own daughter who viewed him as nothing more than a ready source of cash and expensive gifts.

The same tricks, with the added tool of sex given or with-held, gave her dominance over the young men she met in college. She also discovered older men – the professors, the successful alumni, and local businessmen had far more to offer than students. She used them, got what she wanted and tossed them aside. If they tried to hang on after she discarded them, hissed threats of scandal made each one back away. In the process, she became adept at the arts of seduction and subtle manipulation.

After graduation, she applied these skills to building her business. It took no effort to obtain start-up money and a prime section of the law business floor from her father. He even referred clients without her asking. She bound them to her with contracts sealed in bed. Yet not one of them ever seemed to suspect he was not the only one. Was she that clever? Or was the power of denial even stronger than any loyalty she could conjure?

Along the way, they showered her with gifts of expensive jewelry, exotic trips and company stock. Her net worth grew at an extraordinary rate. Whenever she wanted a little extra cash, she pulled a bauble not to her taste from the safe and sold it to a jeweler friend who gave her more than good business sense dictated in gratitude for a semi-annual tumble.

The ease with which she used them all left her with no respect for any man. She held most women in contempt, too. They struggled and strived for influence and money, neglecting to use this birthright advantage to exert control over the men with power who stood in their way.

But, now, Pamela's confidence suffered serious injury. She harbored a secret that made her vulnerable – a secret that tied her to the murders at James Landing. The hot blast of that gritty reality rocked her sense of impregnability.

The police lieutenant seemed immune to intimidation or manipulation. Her vulnerability was her damaged face and her prosthetic eye but Pamela had not yet figured out how to use that to her advantage. Pointed comments about her flaws might throw her momentarily off balance but it was not enough. She had to keep that woman from sussing out her secret, but how?

She entered her condo that evening cursing her weakness, abusing herself for falling in love. Images of that beloved body taunted her – filling her with longing and dread. She went straight to the cabinet where she hid her cherished photographs, letters and other mementoes and carried them to her home office.

After emptying her shredder bin into the trash, she fed through every scrap of paper. She lined a bathroom sink with a triple thickness of aluminum foil and burned the shreds a handful at a time. She smashed, twisted or mutilated anything that wouldn't burn and tossed it on the ashes. She folded up the foil and slid it into a Bloomingdale's shopping bag. Pulling a piece of tissue paper from a shelf, she artfully crumpled it and arranged it atop the wadded bundle.

She walked back to her car, the bag swinging on her fingertips. Then she drove off to find a dumpster miles away – one that was at a great enough distance that, if found, could never be connected to her and her love.

TEN

B ack at the headquarters, Lucinda stood in front of the double doors to the forensics lab clutching the evidence bag containing the improperly obtained coffee cup. She knew if she did nothing to annoy Audrey, she'd have a far better chance of getting the mug into the queue without any awkward questions. She reminded herself to weigh every word before speaking and to make sure she didn't address Audrey by her first name.

She took a deep breath, pushed open the door and spotted Audrey right away – she was impossible to miss. She wore one of her signature bright-colored suits. And today's screaming hue was hot pink – extremely hot. Paired with Audrey's flaming red hair, it looked explosive. The color was so intense it seemed to saturate its surroundings, adding a blush to the clear glassware in the lab.

Lucinda attempted to suppress any sign of surprise at Audrey's attire but knew she had failed when the Forensics Lab Director turned her way and spoke. 'Did you know that in the Victorian Age, proper women did not wear pink? It was considered too strong a color for the female and was solely the province of men? Because of that past prohibition, I feel a strong sense of empowerment when I wear it. You could use some of that in your wardrobe, Pierce, instead of all those drab house sparrow colors. And it certainly wouldn't hurt if you got some highlights or some other treatment to put a bit of pizzazz in your hair.'

Lucinda swallowed the retort that sprang to her lips. 'Doctor Ringo, you certainly bring a bright note to these utilitarian surroundings.'

Audrey rolled her eyes. 'OK, Pierce. Out with it. What do you want?'

'I have a mug that I need tested for a DNA profile. There's still a little coffee in the bottom but I was afraid I'd contaminate the sample if I poured it out.'

'Oh, my, you are capable of sentient thought. What an unexpected surprise,' Audrey said and peered closely at Lucinda's face. 'That last round of reconstruction didn't go too well, did it?'

'If you don't need anything else, Doctor Ringo, I'll get your signature on the property form and get out of your hair.'

'You know, I've never liked you, Pierce. But I like you even less on those rare occasions when you maintain a firm grip on your self-control.'

Lucinda wanted to snap back, but she knew the consequences – Audrey would look at the form carefully, she'd note the location of the sample retrieval and she'd ask awkward questions.

As she scrawled her signature across the document, Audrey asked, 'What exactly are you looking for here?'

Lucinda could have directed her to the paperwork – the answer was there. Instead she said, 'I want this sample compared to any DNA found at the Sterling double homicide that does not belong to either victim.'

'I certainly hope this is the last of the DNA requests for this case. Spellman brought in a mountain of samples. You are really taxing our resources with this one case.'

'Well, I'll let you get to work,' Lucinda said, turning and making a fast exit. She retreated to her office, hoping for a few moments of solitude to gather her thoughts and plan the next steps in the investigation.

Downstairs, at the switchboard, the operator picked up an incoming call. 'Justice Center.'

'Is Lieutenant Lucinda Pierce in?' Doctor Rambo Burns asked.

'May I tell her who's calling?'

'No. That won't work. Listen, this is her doctor but if you tell her it's me, she'll tell you to tell me she's not in. And it's important for her to talk to me but she's a really stubborn woman.'

'Tell me about it,' the operator said with a chuckle. 'Hold on. She won't like it but I'll see what I can do.'

The intercom buzzed at Lucinda's desk. 'Line two, Lieutenant.'

'Who is it?' Lucinda asked but all she got was the click of a disconnecting line. 'Damn.' She pressed the button for the front desk operator. It rang and rang until Lucinda got impatient and pressed in the button for line two. 'Pierce.'

'Lucinda, this is Rambo.' When she did not respond, he added, 'Doctor Rambo Burns.'

'Like you think I know a whole lot of Rambos. Geez, doc. Later. Why do you need to talk to me anyway? I am not having another surgical procedure.'

'Because Charley wants you to talk to me.'

'Oh, good, Doctor. When bedside manner doesn't work, just grab hold of a little girl and beat me over the head with her. Charley has nothing to do with my decision.'

'I know that.'

'So why did you bring her up?'

'We had a barbecue over at the house this weekend and Evan came with his two girls. Charley took me aside wanting assurances that I was taking care of you. I tried to avoid telling her anything but that kid sticks to the point like a good hunting dog. You know what I mean?'

Lucinda grinned, in spite of herself. 'That sounds like my Charley.'

'Well, I told her there wasn't much I could do if you didn't want treatment but that wasn't good enough for her. She said, "What kind of doctor are you? When she acts all tough about stuff, it's because she's scared. And that means she needs you. So go do your job and take care of her." So, I promised I'd call. I really wish you'd just come in and talk with me.'

'Waste of time. I'm not going to get another procedure.'

'Fine. If that's your decision, I'll accept it. But before I do, you need to understand what's been done, the limitations of your current condition and the possibilities for the future. Then you can make an informed decision.'

'It's really a waste of time.'

'C'mon, Lucinda. Just show me the kind of professional courtesy or respect you'd show to one of your law enforcement peers or a supervisor.'

'Wrong assumption, Doc. Ask around. I'm not known for my charm among my colleagues and I'm well known for my pissy attitude toward my superiors.'

'Fine. Show me the same respect you'd show Charley.'

'You're playing dirty, Doctor Burns. Don't use that girl to get what you want.'

'I could've had her call you and give you a hard time – that would be playing dirty. All I'm asking for is conversation.'

'Fine. Because that's all you're going to get. I'll call the office tomorrow and set up a time.'

'Thank you, Lieutenant.'

'Don't thank me yet. I'm sure to be in a crappy mood when I get there,' she said, dropping the receiver into the cradle.

Ted stuck his head in Lucinda's cubicle and said, 'Hey, you wanna grab a drink – or two – maybe even dinner?'

'What about your wife, Ted? How long has it been since you visited her? Maybe you ought to go have dinner with her in the hospital dining room instead of coming in here and pissing me off.'

'Lucinda, why do you care about her? She wanted to shoot you, for crying out loud.'

Lucinda pointed a rigid index finger in his direction. 'Ted, don't you start. I am not in the mood. And you will *not* win this one.'

Ted raised his hands in mock surrender and backed out of the room.

Lucinda watched him but was not amused. She knew she was not fit company for anyone just now – maybe not even for her cat, Chester.

ELEVEN

Lucinda ended the day by trying to reach Jason King on his cell and at his mother's home phone. Each call went to voicemail but she chose not to leave a message. She arrived in the office just past six the next morning and started her day the same way. With the time difference, it was five a.m. in Texas but still she got no answer.

Where do I go from here? Lucinda wondered. She'd hoped to clear up some of the mystery by talking to Jason – it seemed like a logical next step. Blocked from doing that, she knew she couldn't sit still waiting for it to happen.

It was a challenge to plan the steps of a successful investigation when the identity of the victim was uncertain. *But is it really? Can't I discount Freddy's odd story as the product of an overactive imagination? No. His grandmother pushed the same tall tale. Is she the origin of it? Did she craft it out of animosity toward her son-in-law? Or does she actually believe it?*

Did Jason King plant that piece of outrageous fiction in her head? Is she that gullible? And how did he latch on to Victoria Whitehead? And why?

Lucinda knew she needed to talk to Victoria again but before she did, she wanted to know more about her. Freddy wouldn't be a good source – boys don't typically know much about their grandmothers' lives. Her daughter Jeanine was dead. That left her with Jason. A complete circle into a brick wall.

Lucinda knew a lot of her questions would be cleared up when she had the DNA test results but that required time. Besides, she knew that with the answers she would get an equally long list of new questions. She needed to go walk through the Sterling house – revisiting the crime scene always refocused her thinking and sparked new ideas. She stood and then remembered her promise to Dr Burns to call his office this morning and set an appointment. Before she could honor that commitment, the intercom squawked. 'Line three, Lieutenant. It's a lawyer named Richard Barksdale.'

'What does he want with me?'

'He said he represented Ellen Branson.'

'Thanks,' she said, snatching the receiver. 'Pierce here. What can I do for you?'

'Lieutenant, thanks for taking my call. I wanted to talk to you because Ellen Branson has a competency hearing next week.'

'Mr Barksdale, as much as I would like to do anything I could for Ellen, I don't think I can be much help to you. Everything I know about Ellen prior to that morning would be hearsay – I got it all from her estranged husband.'

'But you could testify about the notes she left on your car.'

'Yes, I could. And if you think it would help, I'll be glad to do it. But to me, that makes it sound premeditated, as if she were capable of thinking clearly. I can testify to her actions that morning but when I get to the point that she made me kneel on the ground and held a gun to my head, it won't make the judge very happy. Ted would know more about her state of mind – her disordered, paranoid thoughts – that led to the incident.'

'Unfortunately, Mr Branson has not been very cooperative. He usually doesn't accept or return my calls and he was all ready to begin divorce proceedings until his attorney told him it would be better if he waited until after next week's hearing.'

'Damn him.'

'Do you have any influence with Mr Branson?'

'If I did, counselor, he'd be falling all over you to help Ellen.'

'Can I count on you being there? It's only a hearing so hearsay is not as cut and dried as it is at trial.'

'I'll be there. Just give me the time and the place.' Lucinda jotted the information down in her calendar and left her desk without calling the doctor's office.

Lucinda entered the Sterling family home with the quiet reverence she otherwise reserved for entering a church after the service had begun. In her mind, it was hallowed ground – sacred to the memory of the two victims who waited on her to find justice. She tossed out any doubts she had about the male's identity and thought of her two victims as Jeanine and Parker while she walked through the house.

Downstairs, the only dishevelment in the home was the direct result of the search and confiscation of possible evidence. Smears of fingerprint powder marred the surfaces of door frames and knobs as well as table tops and edges. The living room was otherwise immaculate. Board heart of pine planks stretched across the floor to the stone hearth of the fireplace. The antique furniture looked lovely – and costly – but not comfortable for anything but a short chat.

The hardwood floors continued into the dining area. A long walnut table and ornate chairs with cushioned seats filled the center of the room. Hanging above it was an elaborate, crystal-laden chandelier. Straight ahead were French doors leading out to a spacious deck. A matching china closet and buffet lined up on one side of the room. On the opposite wall, a generous archway led into the kitchen. Both the living and dining rooms had a sterile, model home feel.

The kitchen was another story. It was a huge space enlivened by a sunny breakfast nook capable of seating at least six. An almost empty glass with a quarter inch of curdling chocolate milk stood sentinel by a plate littered with toast crumbs and a buttered knife. The remaining place mats were clean and bare. It appeared as if Freddy ate there the last morning of his parents' lives. She'd have to ask him about that.

A recycled glass countertop and walnut cabinets curled around the kitchen. The backsplash was an artful arrangement of recycled glass tiles. The copper-clad bottoms of skillets and saucepans winked at her from the wrought-iron pot rack hanging over the stainless stovetop on a spacious island. Cheerful red and yellow towels hung from a hook at one end.

Bright tropical fish magnets attached recipes, notes, cards and photos to the front of the oversized refrigerator. At the far end of the counter sat a built-in secretary desk, its top folded down and smeared with black powder, its contents looted and disorderly. Above it was a glass-fronted cabinet filled with assorted whimsical salt and pepper shakers. Lucinda smiled when she saw a pair of penguins that reminded her of the ones that sat in a place of honor in her mother's kitchen.

The ambiance in the kitchen embodied the essence of home – all of the memories and comfort of the idealized vision that beckons bruised hearts. Lucinda knew this was the essence of Jeanine. That awareness transformed Jeanine from a victim to a real person – so real that Lucinda could almost hear her voice.

Beyond the kitchen was a family room – another space exuding the personality of Jeanine. Built-in shelves were packed with books, mementoes and family photos – from the old black and whites of the past to contemporary color shots of Parker, Jeanine and Freddy at the beach, in the mountains and posing in front of an array of recognizable international landmarks. In every picture, the focal point was the never-ending, vibrant smile on Jeanine's face.

Lucinda studied every one of them, searching for any signs of the darkness that Victoria Whitehead had claimed was lurking behind Parker's eyes; seeking any clues to explain the horror that had visited them in their bedroom. All she saw was a happy family – and nothing more.

She moved on to the office. The techs had plundered this room more than any other outside of the master bedroom suite. At two computer workstations, all that remained were wires. The file drawers were empty, stray notes scattered across the floor, the chairs pulled away from the desks. Lucinda moved on, taking the stairs to the second floor. She stood by the stripped bed next to the spot where Jeanine's body lay. She sighed as she thought of how much Freddy would miss this woman with her radiant smile.

In the bathroom, she stared at the holes where bullets were once lodged, trying to make sense of the chain of events that led to the gory sight in the bathtub. She tried to visualize the room without gouges in the walls, bloodstains on the floor and the smell of death in the air.

Lucinda left the immediate crime scene and explored the rest of the second floor. The two guest bedrooms, slightly unkempt from the search, merited only a glance. She spent more time in Freddy's room. It was a second master with an en suite bathroom and a large walk-in closet. He had two workspaces; one for his computer – now in the forensics lab – and another for a microscope, chemistry set, bug collecting kit and other paraphernalia of a budding young lab rat.

There was a faint odor in the room that Lucinda could not place. At first, she thought it must be coming from the chemistry set but when she approached the desk, the smell grew fainter. Moving toward the boy's bed, it intensified. It wasn't the odd smell that wafts from a hamper full of an adolescent male's dirty clothes – it was a familiar scent.

When she pulled the bedspread back, the odor blossomed making it easier to identify – garlic. *But why would his bed smell like garlic?* She lifted the pillows and found the source – six cloves of garlic lay on the sheet next to a silver cross and a primitive voodoo doll bristling with pins. She stared at this hidden treasure in stunned silence trying to understand the why of it. Then she whipped out her cellphone and snapped a picture and slid all items inside an evidence bag.

Lucinda had even more questions now but, so far, no answers.

TWELVE

The last thing Freddy wanted to do was think but it seemed as if that was all he could do, no matter how hard he tried to avoid it. The only things that were any use in stopping the runaway train of his internal commentary were video games. He played until his thumbs felt tender and raw.

That discomfort was bearable but the more his thumbs hurt, the worse his performance. The resulting frustration destroyed his ability to concentrate and, thus, block out unwanted thoughts.

He tried to read but the words swam before his eyes and he couldn't grasp their meaning or sequence. His brain teaser book eluded him, too. Numbers and patterns shifted before he could focus in on them and draw conclusions. Then, he remembered that his mom always said, 'When something's bothering you, Freddy, it helps to talk to somebody about it.'

That memory nearly made him cry out in pain. Instead, he swallowed hard, took his mother's advice and sought out his grandmother. She was all smiles and tried to make him laugh. When he pressed for serious conversation, she said, 'Grief is a personal matter, Frederick. We do not inflict it upon others. It is not seemly. We grieve in private.'

She inhaled sharply then got all jokey again, making Freddy feel as if she didn't care that his mother was dead. He knew

that wasn't true, though. He'd heard the stifled sobs and snif-
fles coming from the other side of her closed bedroom door.

He didn't know how he could contain the pain of losing
his mother. He wanted to run into the street and scream his
anguish to the world – to beat on neighbors' doors and drag
them outside to weep and wail at his side. Instead he stuffed
it down, causing his stomach to ache and making his chest
tighten until he felt it would explode.

Maybe if he was haunted by bereavement alone, it would
be easier to bear but beneath his sorrow ran a riptide of fear.
Back at his house, he wanted to tell the officers to get the
talismans from under his pillow. He needed them for protec-
tion against his father and the evil forces at his beck and call.
He'd been too ashamed of his fear to ask. He had nothing
but his mind and his hands to stave off whatever darkness
lumbered his way.

At times of total clarity, his terror lifted and logic took
charge. Skepticism rose to the surface bringing with it doubt
of the protective powers of garlic, a silver cross and a voodoo
doll. Still, he clung to them in the maelstrom of emotions that
pulled him away and pushed him toward his father.

What if my grandmother is wrong? he wondered. He'd seen
Jason's genealogy charts. He'd followed all of his research.
He knew all the tales of death and disappearance stretching
back hundreds of years. *But what if it is all built on a faulty
premise? What if that lieutenant is right? What if my dad is
dead, too?*

He couldn't accept it. It was just too much. He'd felt
estranged from his father since Grandmother told him about
his history but no matter how hard he shoved his father away,
Dad kept trying to get close to him again. One evening, after
he'd been particularly cold and distant to his father, he'd overheard his mother say, 'Parker, just give it some time. Freddy's
going through a stage, that's all.'

Although Freddy tried to deny it, throughout this turmoil,
he still loved his dad and it pained him not to collapse in the
strength and warmth of his arms. His heart wanted to believe
his father was a good man – he really wanted that to be true.
But if he was, that meant his dad must be dead.

Freddy believed he was failing the first real intellectual test
of his life but was incapable of turning it around. His reason

told him one thing, his grandmother another. He had to believe her. He had to believe his father was evil – that was all that kept his dad alive.

THIRTEEN

L ucinda was descending the stairs in the foyer when the doorbell rang. She hadn't removed the crime scene tape when she arrived at the house – she just ducked under it. Now, someone else had done the same.

She approached the entryway and looked out the small window in the door. A curly-headed blonde woman looking very much like Gloria from *All in the Family* stood outside, wringing her hands as her eyes darted in all directions.

When Lucinda opened the door, the blonde turned her head to face her. Her jaw dropped, her lower lip quivered and she let loose an ear-piercing scream. She stuck her hands in her mouth, spun around and started to run, pulling the yellow tape loose from the column as she fled.

Lucinda stepped out on to the porch. 'Ma'am. Wait. Please, ma'am. I'm a detective. I'd like to talk to you,' she shouted.

The woman glanced back over one shoulder with widened eyes and ran even faster. Lucinda watched her cut through the neighbor's lawn, racing to the next house. *I've never had a child run from my face in fear, so why is this adult acting like such a ninny?* Lucinda heard the loud slam from two houses away. She sighed, locked the front door, refastened the crime tape and walked up the street toward the foolish woman's home.

Lucinda rang the doorbell and waited. She heard no sounds from inside the house. She pressed the bell again, clearly hearing the two-note chime echo inside, but still no response. She formed a fist, pounded on the door and heard movement.

Lucinda paused, listening, then blasted the door with three sharp raps.

'Stop it!' the woman inside shrieked. 'Stop it and go away. Go away or I'll call the police.'

'I *am* the police,' Lucinda bellowed. 'I am putting my badge and identification up to the window. Look at it and open this door.' Lucinda counted to thirty in her head. 'Ma'am, did you see that?'

For a moment, Lucinda heard nothing. Then the door creaked as it eased open a crack, privacy chain in place and a wild eye peering through the gap. 'I saw it,' the woman said with a whimper.

'Please open the door and talk to me,' Lucinda asked.

'What do you want with me?' the woman whined.

'I just want to talk to you. You can call the police station and verify that I am who I say I am, if you want. But I really need you to talk to me.'

'And if I don't?'

Lucinda sighed. 'Ma'am, if you don't, I'll have to call for back-up. Then, if you won't open the door for them, they'll knock the door down. After that, you get to experience being handcuffed, shoved into the back of a patrol car and stuffed in a cell until I can get there and talk to you. Your choice, ma'am. I'd rather talk to you here, but either way works for me.'

The door shut, the chain rattled and the door opened halfway, the opening blocked by the woman's outstretched arm. 'My choice? Humph. Like you're leaving me with any choice at all. What do you want?'

'How about you let me in?'

The woman flung the door all the way open. 'Please come in,' she said, acid etching each word.

Lucinda stepped inside, noting that the layout of this home appeared identical to that of the Sterlings' house but the decor was totally different. Everything here was ruffles and bows and lots of pink floral patterns. The living room and dining room definitely had that lived-in look: stacks of newspapers on tabletops, books folded open straining their spines, toys scattered on the floor and smiling kids' faces in the photos on the mantelpiece. It was a bit chaotic, but Lucinda had to admit she felt a lot more comfortable in this living room than in the one down the street.

The woman moved a child's blue windbreaker, a T-shirt and a baseball glove from the worn, flowery sofa and invited her to have a seat. She herself sat in a chair caddy-corner from Lucinda. Her blonde curls looked relaxed but the rest of her was rigid – ramrod posture, arms in a tight fold and lips grimaced in distaste.

Lucinda watched her in silence, waiting for the woman to speak first. Every time the woman tried to return Lucinda's stare, her head jerked violently away as if a mad Pavlovian had administered an electric shock. Finally, she turned her head to face Lucinda without actually turning her eyes in her direction. 'I thought the police department was trying to improve their image with the public.'

'Could you tell me your name, please?' Lucinda asked.

'I mean, really, if they are doing this big public relations effort to make cops our friends, then why do they send you out to scare people?'

'Your name?'

'Aren't you going to answer me?' the woman said, her voice rising an octave and becoming shrill. 'Aren't you going to respond like a normal human being?'

'Ma'am, as you've already pointed out, I am not a normal human being. And I am here to ask questions not answer them. First, what is your name?'

The woman huffed then said, 'Cynthia Littlejohn. Do I need a lawyer?'

'Ms Littlejohn, why would you need a lawyer? What have you done wrong – aside from violating a crime scene, which I am more than willing to overlook if you'd just answer my questions?'

'Violated a crime scene?'

'Yes, ma'am. When you ignored the tape blocking entrance to the Sterlings' porch, you violated a crime scene.'

'I was simply a concerned neighbor. I saw all of the ruckus over there and I wanted to check and make sure Jeanine was all right.'

'You really thought that someone would be in the house with crime scene tape strung across the steps?'

'Well, someone was. You were.'

'But you didn't expect someone would answer the door, did you?

'Well, I . . .'

'You weren't there out of neighborly concern, were you? You were there out of insatiable curiosity.' Lucinda paused in the realization that this was the wrong tactic with the woman. She changed her tone of voice and softened her expression. 'If I hadn't opened the door, I bet you would have gone round the house looking in windows, wouldn'tcha?' Lucinda grinned and, leaning forward, she whispered, 'If it was my neighbor's house, I would have.'

The corners of Cynthia's lips twitched. 'It is my neighborhood. I do have a right to know what's going on here.'

'Of course you do,' Lucinda said, stringing her along. 'Have you watched the news, read the paper?'

'It was on TV and in the paper?'

'Certainly was.'

'Oh, my. Hank is out of town on business – I don't pay attention to news unless he turns it on or tells me about a story in the paper. Boy, I missed out this time. Was my house on the news?'

'I don't know. I haven't had time to watch much myself, but what did you think happened?'

'Well, with all the corporate types getting in trouble these days, you can hardly blink an eyelash when a CEO's house is searched by police, can you?'

'You have children, Ms Littlejohn?'

'Yes, I do. A boy and two girls. They're all away at camp this week. A pity. I know they'd love to meet a real detective,' she said and then looked at Lucinda's face. 'Oh, never mind. Maybe not you. You'd probably give them nightmares. No offense.'

'Of course not,' Lucinda lied, stifling the urge to pistol whip the airhead. 'Did any of your children play with Freddy Sterling?'

'My boy did – well, he used to. That Freddy's gotten to be just a little too much of a brainiac for normal kids to hang with. Erin – that's my boy's name – kept coming home from playing with Freddy and wanting help to look up words in the dictionary and asking all sorts of questions. I said to him, I said, "Erin, what are you doing with Freddy, playing or going to school?" He said, "Mom, it's different with Freddy. He's real smart. He doesn't play like other kids." And I asked him, "Is that your idea of fun? Being outsmarted by a geek?" He said he never looked at it that way before. He moped around the house for a couple of days and then took up with the regular friends he'd been ignoring while he spent time with Freddy – which suited me just fine.'

Oh, I bet it did. 'What did you know about the family?'

'They seemed normal enough – a little smarter than most

of us, I suppose, but they didn't flaunt it. They acted like just folks whenever we had a block party or something like that. That little Freddy seemed like he had to prove he was smarter than everybody all the time. But that grandmother of his – now she's a real nutcase.'

'In what way, Ms Littlejohn?'

'Oh, you can call me Cynthia,' she said and waited for acknowledgement.

'Yes, Cynthia, of course. Now, Freddy's grandmother?'

'Well, I heard she's been married a dozen times. And now I hear she's got this young boyfriend. And she's always talking about crystals and how they can bring harmony and cure illness and all sorts of stuff. Now, if she just read palms or tea leaves or something, she'd be entertaining. But it's like she's on a mission with those stupid crystals.'

Maybe this woman did have a little bit of sense, after all.

'Cynthia, did you notice anything unusual yesterday morning?'

'Like what?'

'Anything you heard or saw, or anyone that looked out of place?'

'No.' She shook her head. 'Can't say that I did.'

'Tell me what you did see yesterday morning,' Lucinda urged.

'Let's see. I saw Freddy getting picked up in front of the house by this woman whose son goes to that summer class with Freddy . . .'

'Do you know her name?'

'No, but I recognize her car – it's a green Lexus, a fairly new one.'

'Then what did you see, Cynthia?'

'Nothing really. I didn't see Parker leave. I didn't see Jeanine leave. But I don't always see that. So, what did they do? Skip town with a barrel full of someone else's money?'

'No, Cynthia. I don't think either of them went anywhere.'

'What do you mean? They're still in there? Are you holding them under house arrest?'

'No. They are not still there. Two bodies were removed from the home and taken to the morgue.'

'The morgue? Two bodies? Which two? Not Freddy, oh please, not Freddy. He is a bit obnoxious. But he's just a boy. I'm sorry for what I said. I didn't mean . . .' Tears welled up in Cynthia's eyes.

'Freddy's fine. He's with his grandmother. Did you see anyone approach their home yesterday morning or the night before? Did you notice anyone? Or any vehicle at the house?'

'No. No. Can't say that I did,' Cynthia said, furrowing her brow. 'But I did hear something.'

'What was that? When was that?'

'I don't know what time it was exactly. Mid morning sometime. I stepped out into the backyard and thought I heard a chainsaw. I'm pretty sure it was a chainsaw. We hear them a lot around here after bad storms – cleaning up branches and stuff. But this time, it sounded like it was coming from inside of a house. But why would that be? And I listened for a while but it stopped before I could figure out where it came from.'

'Please, think, Cynthia. When did you hear that? What were you doing before you came outside?'

'Oh, my, so this might be important. Why would this be important? Oh, my, don't tell me they were killed with a chainsaw?'

'Cynthia, please. Concentrate. What time?'

'Oh dear,' she said biting her lower lip. 'Oh, I know. I just finished watching that show. It must've been just after ten in the morning.'

'Ten? Are you sure?'

'Yeah,' she said with a vigorous nod.

'Before that, you were watching television?'

'Yes.'

'You didn't hear anything that sounded like gunshots?'

'Gunshots? Oh, my, no. Gunshots? They were shot? So why was there a chainsaw? Oh, my, they didn't cut them up, did they?'

'Cynthia, tell me – aside from Jeanine, Parker and Freddy – who was the last person you saw visiting the home?'

'It had to be that crazy grandmother. But that wasn't yesterday. It was three days ago. And she didn't go inside the house. Jeanine came out and talked to her on the porch and then went into the house. The grandmother rang the doorbell again but Jeanine didn't answer.'

'What did the grandmother do?'

'She just stood there for a while. Then she pulled this big silver cross out of her purse and waved it all around the front door and left. Like I told ya, that woman is crazy.'

FOURTEEN

Lucinda stepped on the elevator in the justice center thinking about Victoria Whitehead. She had a lot of questions for her but even more about her. Ted might have found some of those answers by now. She didn't want to speak to him at all – she was too angry about his neglect of his estranged and hospitalized wife, Ellen – but she promised herself she'd be civil and professional.

Walking into his workspace, she said, 'What have you and your research moles dug up for me today?'

'I don't know where to start, Lucinda. I have volumes.'

'How about starting with Victoria Whitehead?'

Ted tapped on his keyboard and said, 'Born Victoria Dulaney in Baltimore on June twenty-eighth 1943. Married to Francis Pippin in 1964. First child born May third 1965. Widowed 1966 . . .'

'Wait. Did you say first child? Does that mean there is more than one?'

'Yes. She had three children, two girls and a boy.'

'Who else besides Jeanine?'

'The first child is Susan Victoria Pippin.'

'How did her first husband die?' Lucinda asked.

'You have a suspicious mind, Lucinda,' Ted said with a grin. 'Her first husband was a casualty of the Vietnam War – can't blame Victoria for that one.'

'You can't blame me for trying. OK, then what?'

'Married again before the year was out to Brian Jacoby – he was with Francis in the war. They were divorced in 1967, less than a year after the marriage – no children from that relationship.'

'And then?'

'Then, she married a Navy guy – an officer – Lieutenant Commander Frederick Winters in 1969. Six months after the nuptials, her second child was born – Jeanine Victoria Winters on December sixteenth 1969. Her third child, Frederick Victor Winters, was born on August thirty-first 1973.

He died when he was six years old in the same automobile accident that killed his father – head-on collision caused by a drunk driver who crossed over into their lane on July fourth 1979.'

'That had to be tough – maybe that's why she's so whacky.'

'Not too whacky – she found another guy to marry her in 1982. A civilian this time – Gary Finnerman – they made it to 1987 before they divorced. Then Victoria was single for nearly a decade. She married Charles Whitehead in 1996. She became a widow for the third time in 1999. Natural causes listed for that death and considering Whitehead was eighty-two at the time, probably legitimate. Looked like she was going to inherit a sizeable estate from husband number five until his children – four of them, who were all older than Victoria – challenged the new will. There must have been something questionable about it because Victoria backed down and agreed to a settlement which barely covered the bills she accumulated in her spending frenzy after Whitehead's death. That's when she moved here and into a home that her daughter and son-in-law bought for her.'

'Do you have that in a document you could print out for me?' Lucinda asked.

'I will in just a few minutes. I was about to format it into a chronological chart when you came in.'

'Have you located any of her living ex-husbands or her oldest daughter?'

'Haven't started looking yet.'

'When you find them, call the exes and see if you can fill in a bit more background information. But don't call the daughter – I'll do that.'

'So what are you seeing here, Lucinda? Do you think Victoria might be involved in her daughter's death?'

'I don't know. I do know they were having problems at least three days before the murders. It could have been because of her crazy story about Parker Sterling but I don't know. I just know there's friction and that bears examination.'

'Anyone else looking squirrely?'

'I'm bothered by Jason King and Pamela Godfrey – anything on them?'

'Haven't located anything on King yet and nothing I've found on Godfrey deviates from what I've given you already.

Her list of rumored affairs gets longer and longer – but I'm not sure which of them actually happened. I did find an interesting suspected paramour, though. His name is Rodney Conners. He was the CEO of "It Is", a rival software company that went bankrupt. He blamed Dodgebird in general and Parker Sterling in particular for his company's demise. He vowed more than once to get his revenge.'

'You know anything else about him?'

'Not yet, just picked up that morsel this morning.'

The intercom on Ted's desk interrupted their conversation. 'Sergeant Branson?'

'Yup,' Ted said.

'Is Lieutenant Pierce in there with you?'

'Sure is.'

'Tell her line four – it's Maggie Sutton.'

Lucinda didn't want to take that call. She knew she probably should take that call. The indecision left her mute.

'C'mon, Lucinda,' Ted said. 'It's your sister. You have to take that call.'

'Oh, that's just terrific coming from you. Why won't you answer the phone calls from your wife's lawyer?'

'Holy shit, Lucinda. My wife tried to kill you. I thought after that you would understand.'

'I understand one thing – you are an asshole.'

The female voice on the intercom jumped into the fray. 'Lieutenant?'

'Yeah, yeah. I'll take it in my office. And don't let Branson run like a girl the next time Ellen's attorney calls.'

'Uh, yes, ma'am,' the voice stammered.

Lucinda stomped out the door and down the hall.

Ted turned to the intercom. 'You still there?'

'Yeah.'

'Ignore that woman.'

'As if . . .' she said and shut down the connection.

In her office, Lucinda picked up the receiver. 'Yes?'

'Oh, that's nice, Lucinda. You haven't spoken to me for more than a year and you can't say "Hello. How are you?" or anything civilized. Just a "Yes?", like this is the fortieth call I've made to you today?'

'Cut the crap, Maggie. What do you want?'

'You are such a pleasant person. No wonder your husband walked out on you and no one else wanted you.'

'OK, Maggie, either you tell me why you called right now or I'm hanging up.'

'You are so infuriating. Uncle Hank died.'

'And?'

'I thought you'd want to come for the funeral.'

'Why?'

'Aunt Connie is asking for you.'

'Oh, that's rich. As if I would come on her account. Good grief, the woman threw me out of the house the day before my seventeenth birthday. You remember that, don't you?'

'She had her reasons, Lucinda, you know that.'

'Stupid reasons. Stupid woman. I'm sorry Uncle Hank is dead but since he's gone and I can't visit with him, I'm sure not driving up there to offer phony comfort to a woman who hates me.'

'She doesn't hate you, Lucinda. She's family.'

'Oh, so now, you're going to tell me that *you* don't hate me either?'

'You are my sister, Lucinda.'

'And that means what? That you hate me but you are not allowed to acknowledge it? Give me a break, Maggie.'

'She needs you, Lucinda. You are obligated to attend this funeral. It's family.'

'Oh, don't make me laugh – even without my experience with our family unit, my job has taught me there is no limit to the horror one family member can visit upon another.'

'Lucinda, this is a one-time event – it's a funeral. It is tomorrow at Whitten's. I will expect you to be here.'

A cynical laugh passed Lucinda's lips before she said, 'I never have lived up to your expectations, Maggie. Can't see any reason why I should start now.' A wave of anger and sorrow washed over Lucinda leaving ugly memories in its wake. She sought the only escape from them she knew – she plunged back into her work.

FIFTEEN

Lucinda rang Victoria Whitehead's doorbell and was surprised when Freddy answered the door. She'd been hoping to find Victoria there alone. 'I thought you'd be at class today, Freddy.'

'I didn't go. It's not seemly.'

'What?' Lucinda asked, certain she hadn't heard him use that phrase.

'That's what my grandmother said. She said it wouldn't be seemly until after my mom's funeral.'

'I'm sorry, Freddy. That should happen very soon. I'm not sure about your dad's, though, that's going to take a little longer.'

'How many times do I have to tell you: my dad is not dead. You need to arrest him. Do your job.'

Lucinda studied the boy. He seemed to believe what he was saying. She saw no signs of deception – just exasperation. 'Sorry, Freddy. Is your grandmother here?'

'Yes,' he said but didn't move.

'I would like to talk with her.'

Freddy didn't speak, move or give any indication he even heard her. He stood and studied her as if she were an anomalous lab specimen.

'May I come in, Freddy?'

Freddy turned away and walked off without uttering a word. Lucinda took one step inside the door. Although muffled by distance, she could still understand the conversation.

'Grandmother, that police lieutenant is here again.'

'Lieutenant Pierce?'

'Whatever.'

'Did you invite her in?'

'It's not my house.'

'Where are your manners, Frederick? Please go to your room.'

Freddy came through the archway, glared at Lucinda and went up the stairs. Victoria walked into the foyer, casting a glance up at Freddy's retreating back as she tsked and shook her head. 'Teenagers. Freddy is so intelligent. I expect more from him. Please come in. I'm terribly sorry for Freddy's lack of hospitality. Could you close the door behind you?'

Lucinda did as instructed and followed her into the living room. At Victoria's invitation, Lucinda took a seat while the older woman positioned herself in her skirt-flung pose on the sofa.

'What can I do for you today, Lieutenant?' Victoria asked.

'I can't seem to reach Mr King or his mother. I'm hoping you could tell me when would be the best time to call them.'

'I can't say that I would know. I never bother Jason when he's visiting his mother – she requires all of his attention. Her illness, you know.'

'Yes, ma'am. But if you do hear from him, will you let him know I am trying to reach him?'

'Certainly, Lieutenant, but I doubt that he will call.'

Lucinda nodded. 'Ms Whitehead, we've talked about your daughter Jeanine, but you've never mentioned your other children.'

Victoria sniffed and straightened her posture. 'It is a painful subject, Lieutenant – one that I prefer not to discuss – and it has no relevance to the current situation.'

'I can truly understand your pain over your young son's death, ma'am, but what about your other daughter, Susan?'

'Trust me, Lieutenant, that is painful, too – and irrelevant as well. Can we return our discussion to matters directly affecting the death of my darling daughter Jeanine?'

Lucinda leaned forward, resting her elbows on her knees. 'I need to know all I can about Jeanine, Ms Whitehead, to pull together a meaningful victimology. Her siblings are an important piece of this puzzle. Is your daughter Susan still alive?'

'I suppose so.'

'You suppose so, Ms Whitehead? You don't know?'

Victoria flung the back of one hand to her forehead in a theatrical gesture of suffering. 'Oh, just pound the bamboo slivers up my fingernails, Lieutenant.'

'Ms Whitehead, please. I am not trying to cause you unnecessary pain. I simply need information. When was the last time you spoke to Susan?'

'Alas, it has to have been at least twenty years, more than two decades, a fortnight of years . . .'

Alas? Give me strength! 'Ms Whitehead, please give me some straight answers about Susan. When did you last see her?'

Pursing her lips in obvious displeasure at Lucinda's lack of appreciation for her performance, Victoria primped her dress, patted her hair and cleared her throat. 'The summer before her senior year in college.'

'Where was she? What happened?'

'She was in her bedroom. Nothing happened. She was there and then she was gone.'

'Why did she leave?'

'I have no idea.'

'Did you file a missing person's report?'

'An officer came to the house. I was giving him the information when Jeanine came home. And that was that.'

'What do you mean?' Lucinda asked.

'She told the officer that she knew where her sister was. Susan was just avoiding me, she said.'

'Did Jeanine tell you where she went?'

'Back to college. After that, I have no idea. I don't even know if she graduated as she was supposed to do the next spring. Jeanine told me she did but I never got a graduation announcement and my card was returned unopened. Not much gratitude there from a child I fed, clothed and cared for.'

'Ms Whitehead, for your daughter to leave abruptly and never contact you again, there must have been a precipitating incident.'

'If there was, she never spoke to me about it and if she told her sister, Jeanine never shared it with me. Her sudden departure and lack of communication was bewildering.'

'Did your daughter Susan ever marry or change her surname for any other reason?'

'I don't know. I know nothing about her life. Nothing – from the moment she walked out more than two decades ago until this day. Nothing . . .'

Sensing Victoria was gearing up for another scene in the melodrama of her life, Lucinda rose to her feet. 'Thank you so much, Ms Whitehead. I'm sure I'll be back to talk to you again soon.'

'It will be my pleasure, Lieutenant,' she said with a gracious smile.

Lucinda let herself out and walked down the sidewalk to her car, grateful for her escape but disappointed in the amount of information she obtained. She'd just reached the side of her car when her cellphone signaled an incoming call. She looked at the caller's identity before connecting to the call. 'Not you, too, Ricky.'

'Yes, Lucinda, me, too. But I am not calling because of her; I am calling in spite of her.'

'Ricky, I see no reason to subject myself to the environment at Uncle Hank's funeral.'

'Well, I do. If you don't come, Maggie will bad-mouth you all day long. And because you didn't have the guts to show up, they will believe everything she says about you.'

'I don't care what they think.'

'I know you don't, but I live here and I care. I get sick of hearing the ugly talk. I stand up for you every time, Lucinda. But if you don't show up for something as important as a funeral, no one will ever listen to me again.'

'Geez, Ricky . . .'

'Listen, Lucinda, I promise I will stick by your side like glue the whole time you're here. No one will dare be hateful to you with your little brother by your side.'

'No one but Maggie.'

'I won't lie to you, Lucinda, I can't control Maggie. But you need to be here. She only called you so that she could tell everyone she tried but you just didn't care to come. That's what she wants, Lucinda. Don't let her win.'

'I don't know.'

'Yes, you do, Lucinda. I know you cared about Uncle Hank. And I know you were crushed when he kowtowed to Aunt Connie instead of sticking up for you. But you've forgiven him for that, haven't you? Please promise me you'll come – for Uncle Hank's sake. Come and protect his memory from those vicious, sordid stories.'

'OK, Ricky, OK. I'll be there unless something comes up in my current investigation.'

'Don't let that happen, Lucinda.'

'I can't control that, Ricky.'

'Oh, yes, you can. That's one thing I've always admired about you, big sister – you've always been in control.'

Lucinda snorted. 'Yeah, I play that part well.'

'Promise me you'll be here – no matter what.'

'Ricky, I'll do my best. Listen, I've got to go. I've got to get a lot done if I'm going to drive up there tomorrow.'

Dread dripped down on Lucinda's thoughts like acid rain. She had not been back to the farm since before the shotgun blast shredded half of her face. She didn't want to deal with the reactions. She was certain everyone knew – the local paper up there had covered the story, but actually seeing her in person would still be a shock. *Damn my sister. Damn that shotgun. Why can't people just leave me the hell alone?*

SIXTEEN

Lucinda drove back to the justice center musing over Jeanine's dysfunctional family. It blended in her head with her own. By the time she parked her car, she'd shifted to thoughts of Ted and how his relationship with his wife had fallen apart, and wondering about the impact on his kids.

Grudgingly, she reached the conclusion that although Ted had been a real jerk for the last year or so, she'd not been a good friend to him. In fact, she knew she'd been downright bitchy – ripping him to shreds for sins that were very much like her own.

She would go to the funeral tomorrow. She needed to start contributing to the emotional health of her family instead of being part of the problem. She needed to do the same for Ted – she'd been badgering him for far too long and it hadn't done a damn bit of good.

Getting out of the elevator, she almost hoped he wouldn't be there. If he was, she knew she'd have to act on her new-found understanding and she dreaded that his reaction wouldn't be what she hoped. But there he was, hunched over his keyboard performing heaven knew what digital magic.

'Hey, Ted, you got a minute?' she asked.

In a flash he was on his feet with his arms folded protectively across his chest. 'Yeah, what is it, Lucinda?'

'Look at you. Is that any way to greet an old friend?'

'Lucinda . . .' he said, taking a step backward and pulling his arms tighter.

'OK. I deserve that reaction. I've been a bitch and I know it – except you're not allowed to say that.'

Ted shifted his eyes back and forth, still wary. His shoulders relaxed as the tension in his posture eased up a notch. 'What are you up to, Lucinda?'

'Well, for starters, I wanted to let you know I'm going up to Charlottesville for my Uncle Hank's funeral tomorrow.'

'You are?' Ted said, dropping his arms in surprise.

'Yep. Somebody has to take the lead on calling an end to this tired, dysfunctional family drama. And no matter how long I wait, it'll never be Maggie.'

'Well, good.'

'There's something else I need to say, Ted. I really want you to shut up and listen and not interrupt me.'

Ted's arms flew back to their protective position. 'What?'

'I'm serious, Ted. If you start getting defensive and arguing with me, I'm apt to get pissed despite my best intentions.'

His jaw throbbed as he muttered 'OK' through tight lips.

'I know that part of my problem with my family is that I feel guilty for leaving my little sister and brother behind, even though I had no choice in the matter. And I believe that guilt is what is behind your reaction to Ellen and her problems.'

'Lucinda . . .'

'No, Ted, shut up. All I am asking you to do is think about that. Do you feel any unwarranted guilt over the death of your baby? Do you feel any guilt over not being able to keep Ellen from falling down so low? Do you feel any guilt for wrapping yourself in phony feelings about me to keep Ellen and her problems at a distance?'

'Lucinda, there is nothing phony . . .'

'Shut up, Ted. Don't defend yourself. Just listen and then think about it. That's all I ask. You can decide that I'm full of crap. That's fine. Just think about it. And think about the effect all of this discord is having on your kids. You can't move on with your life, Ted, until you've resolved the issues of your past. OK? Promise me you'll think about this.'

'I can talk now?'

'Yes, Ted. Don't be a jerk.'

'OK. I'll give it some thought. I doubt if it will make a difference.'

'Ted, that's life. I don't know that going to visit my family with a positive attitude is going to make any difference but I'm doing it. All I'm asking is that you open yourself up to other possibilities.'

'And after that, Lucinda. What then? What will it mean for us?'

'Ted, we had a relationship in high school. Right now, put that in the past and deal with the present. Both of our lives are too screwed up at this point in time to add that complication to them. Deal with today, Ted, and let tomorrow come. OK?'

'Yep.'

She wasn't certain if anything she said made any difference but she had to let that go – she was not responsible for Ted's reaction. 'Now, I'm driving up tomorrow morning and driving back as soon as I can – I'll get back sometime tomorrow night. Remember how you were talking about creating a virtual incident room?'

'Yeah, I've been tossing it around. I think it's doable and I think I can make it user-friendly and easy to understand even for a technological dinosaur now that I have a bigger flat screen that can display it all at once.'

'I'd like you to try creating one for the Sterling homicides. I'll give you my notes, my reports – everything I've got so far. I'm waiting for the forensics results – DNA, fingerprints, ballistics – and I'm also waiting for more information from your research team. I'd like a place where this information can be gathered and organized.'

'You got it. I'll try to have a working model for you by the time you get back.'

'Thanks, Ted. You've got my cell – feel free to call if you have any questions. I'll turn my phone off during the service so you don't need to worry about calling at an inopportune time. I'm going to go finish up my reports and get them to you tonight. We OK?'

'If I say what I'm thinking, you'll just tell me to shut up. So I might as well keep my mouth shut and save you the trouble,' Ted said with a grin.

Lucinda smiled back at him and felt the pull of scar tissue

on the damaged side of her face. She stuffed down her frustration over her limitations and took it out on the keyboard as she typed.

SEVENTEEN

As she walked through her apartment door, Lucinda's gray tabby Chester reminded her once again that dogs didn't have a monopoly on making you feel missed and loved. She cooed at him as she replenished his dry food bowl and filled his saucer with a scoop of the canned tuna feast he loved.

She threw together a turkey and Havarti cheese sandwich for herself but left it on the counter as she walked to the window and stared out at the lazy James River flowing far below. She focused on its movement to find the serenity she needed to banish her anxiety about tomorrow's trip and concentrate her mind on the case at hand.

Refreshed, she grabbed her sandwich, a legal pad and a pencil and curled up on the sofa to think through possible suspects and scenarios. Soon, Chester joined her, curling up in a ball between her leg and the sofa. She rested a hand on his back, feeling the comforting vibration of his contented purr.

She lifted her hand long enough to jot down: '1. Jason King'. *Is that his real name? And is he avoiding my call or am I calling at the wrong times?* She wrote down, 'Leave a message next time on both phones.'

There was no indication that anything was taken from the home, making the robbery-gone-bad scenario a non-starter. There was always the possibility of a love triangle. She wrote: '2. Jeanine's boyfriend?' and '3. Parker's girlfriend?' *That doesn't cover all the possibilities, does it?* She scratched out 'girlfriend' and 'boyfriend' and replaced them both with 'lover'.

Lucinda wondered who gained financially from the deaths. She knew the obvious answer was Freddy but, as snotty as he could be, she still could not see him wielding a chainsaw. In fact, as scrawny as he was, she doubted that he could lift the damn thing. There was always the chance that he had help, though. She added: '4. Freddy and unknown accomplice'.

She followed that on the list with '5. Victoria Whitehead'. Unless there was someone else specified, she'd be Freddy's guardian and, in all likelihood, have control of his inheritance until he reached legal age. Under Victoria's name she added, 'Check with Sterling attorney about will'.

Revenge was another motive to consider. Judging by the crime scene, it looked as if any vengeance was directed at Parker. But why would the avenger want to conceal Parker's identity? At number six, she jotted down Sterling Parker's business rival, Rodney Conners, followed by '7. Unknown avenger'.

She knew she had to add Parker Sterling to her suspect list – not because she found Freddy's story compelling but because it explained some of what she had found at the crime scene. If Parker did want to fake his death, he would have an interest in hiding the identity of the victim. On the other hand, although DNA might not be able to identify an unknown person, it would certainly sabotage that subterfuge. But Parker was an intelligent man, he would know that. Perhaps, for some reason, he only hoped to buy some time by making identification more difficult.

Then there was Jeanine's body – carefully cleaned up and placed in her bed. Whoever killed her either had to care about her or feel remorse for killing her. *Was her death unintentional?* A bullet through her forehead screamed execution. *Was it a professional hit? A murder for hire? And why?*

And what about the other victim? Did he die the same way? Who was killed first? And why? It always came back to 'why'. Lucinda knew the answer to this question wasn't essential for the arrest and conviction of a perpetrator. Nonetheless, it dominated her thoughts – she wanted a motive, she needed a motive. Even if it could never be proven at trial, 'why' pulled the puzzle pieces together, put the players in their proper places, made it all fit into a logical pattern. It might remain senseless on some level – the criminal mind often eludes rational thought – but still there was some sense of order, even if it was the product of a sick, disorganized mind.

Right now, though, she had no answer to that question. She would, however, have plenty of time to ruminate on it tomorrow on the road – three hours up, three hours back. She needed sleep tonight to make it through the drive and the family ordeal.

She got up and grabbed a glass of Australian Shiraz, popped a DVD from the third season of *24* in the player and settled back in her recliner. She could count on Jack Bauer's intense, over-the-top adventures to take her away.

In the morning, Lucinda hit the road and she attempted to focus on the questions of the double homicide. She wanted to gnaw on them, force her way into the marrow of the crime where the answers awaited. But the closer she got to Albemarle County, the more difficult it became to steer away from her dread of the coming encounters and concentrate on the case.

She arrived at the funeral home in Charlottesville two hours before the service. She knew she could go out to her Uncle Hank's farm and find the family gathered there. In fact, that's probably what she should do but she had no stomach to face either her sister Maggie or her Aunt Connie before it was necessary. She'd love to wrap her arms around her brother right now, but that would have to wait.

She pulled into a parking space in the lot that afforded a clear line of sight to the front entrance and settled back in her seat. She allowed her thoughts to wander back to the day that she moved to the farm.

She'd visited Uncle Hank and Aunt Connie's farm many times before but it was a lot different traveling out there for a picnic and horseshoes than it was moving out there to stay. On that day, it appeared lonely, forlorn and alien. She could still hear the gunshots ringing in her ears. Superimposed over everything were the slow-motion images of her mother falling after her dad fired the first shot, the vision of her father lying dead after the second shot. The smell of discharged weapons and the odor of death still permeated her nostrils, blocking out every other scent. Even out in the country, the air no longer smelled fresh.

Riding up their long driveway, Lucinda felt handcuffed by the recent past, imprisoned by the sins of her father. She sensed coolness in Aunt Connie's welcome as if she felt unduly burdened by the arrival of her orphaned nieces and nephew. Uncle Hank, however, greeted them with an unqualified acceptance. They were his sister's children and he loved them because he loved her.

Hank took a special interest in Lucinda, knowing that she had suffered the most trauma – she had seen her mother die, had found her father dead. He taught her to milk the cows, ride the horses, gather the eggs and drive the tractor. He filled the void left in Lucinda's life by an often-absent, ever-angry father.

Lucinda spent hours by his side, sweating in the summer heat as they toiled in the fields, shivering in the snow as they tended the stock. It was a year of healing for the young mother-less girl but it came at a price. Connie resented the time her husband spent with Lucinda. She looked at her niece and instead of seeing a wounded child in need of love and atten-tion, she saw a rival for Hank's affection.

She despised Lucinda for her flawless complexion, her long legs and her endless energy. Her resentment soon turned to loathing. And her loathing fed her suspicions. Lucinda often heard her aunt and uncle arguing behind their closed bedroom door. But she never knew she was the source of their conflict until one morning at breakfast.

Connie, holding a skillet in one hand and a spatula in the other, shoveled out mounds of scrambled eggs into every plate but one. Lucinda looked at the emptiness in front of her and over at her Uncle Hank. He furrowed his brow and shook his head. Connie returned with a plateful of sausage links and served them up to Uncle Hank, Maggie, Ricky and herself. But placed none on Lucinda's plate. Connie returned again with biscuits, doling them out to everyone but her oldest niece.

Connie slid into her seat, sprinkled salt and pepper over her eggs and began to eat. Except for Ricky, who'd begun eating as soon as the eggs hit his plate, the rest of the family stared with confusion at Connie. She looked up, scanned the faces on the table and said, 'Eat up, eat up before your break-fast turns cold. Nothin' worse than cold eggs.'

'Connie,' Hank said, 'you forgot to fill up Lucinda's plate.'

'Forgot?' she said as she sunk her teeth into a biscuit. 'I didn't forget,' she added, spewing biscuit crumbs.

'You didn't serve her anything, Connie.'

'I don't serve tramps, Hank. Be glad I served you.'

'Connie . . .'

'There's some leftovers on the stove. She can go in the kitchen and get what's left if she wants. I'm not serving the slut.'

'C'mon, Connie, how many times do I . . .'

'It doesn't matter how many times, Hank. I know what I know.'

A red-faced Hank pushed back his chair, rose to his feet and grabbed his John Deere cap from the rack. 'C'mon, Lucinda. I reckon we oughta run into town for supplies.'

As they walked out the door, Connie taunted them. 'Supplies? Is that what you call it now? Oh, yeah, Hank, go get your "supplies" hauled, you bastard.'

Lucinda was mortified and confused. She thought she understood her aunt's implications but they made no sense. She slid into the passenger's seat of the old Ford pick-up. 'Uncle Hank?'

'Forget about it, Lucinda. Your Aunt Connie's going through the change. It gives her weird thoughts, sometimes. Don't pay 'em no mind.'

'But Uncle Hank . . .'

'I'm not sure what we need in town – except for a good breakfast. We'll get that and think of something we need to pick up at the feed and seed store while we eat.'

They didn't speak through the twenty-mile drive. At breakfast, Hank talked about his hopes for that summer's bounty from the crops the two of them planted in the spring. Lucinda made a couple of stabs at turning the conversation back to the morning's conflict but Hank rebuffed every attempt.

Hank and Lucinda returned to the farm and tended to their chores until lunch time. When they entered the farmhouse for the midday meal, Lucinda gasped. A battered, stained, baby blue suitcase sat by the door – the same piece of luggage she'd used to move her clothes from her mother's house to here a year earlier. Next to it was a paper grocery sack with a folded over top. Without looking inside, she knew everything she owned was in those two bags.

'You're going to have to go back into town, Hank,' Connie ordered.

'Can we get a bite to eat, first?'

'You don't have time, Hank. Lucinda's bus leaves in less than an hour. But here,' she said, thrusting a wax paper-wrapped square at him, 'I fixed up a bologna sandwich for the road.'

'Her bus to where?' Hank asked.

'She's going to her grandmother's house in Greensboro.'

'My mother's house?' Hank asked.

'Yeah. The old biddy said she didn't care that the girl was a tramp and a home-wrecker. She even had the gall to blame me. I hung up on her. But she's taking the little bitch off our hands.'

'Connie, there's been nothing improper going on between me and my niece. She's family, Connie. What the hell is wrong with you?'

'Nothing's wrong with me that getting that slut out of my house won't cure. You'd better get moving. She misses that bus, I'm going to a lawyer. And you know, since this was my Daddy's farm, you'll get tossed out on your ear if I file for divorce.'

Lucinda looked at her uncle who seemed to shrink before her eyes. She stepped toward her brother and sister. Maggie spun away from her and flounced out of the room. Ricky looked at her with tears on his face and bewilderment in his eyes. She crouched down and wrapped him in her arms, kissing his eyes, his cheeks, his forehead. 'I love you, little brother.'

He clung to her as she tried to pull away. 'No, no, don't go.'

'I have to go, sweetie,' Lucinda said, as she uncurled his fingers from her shirt and stepped away. She bent down, grabbed the duct-taped handle of her suitcase in one hand, the paper sack in the other, and walked out the door. She breathed in the aroma of the farm – the air was filled with the scent of green, growing things, the earthy smells of fresh-turned soil and manure, and the musky tang of livestock. She listened to the distant cackle of the hens, the lowing of the cows, the snickering of the horses. Then, she stepped into the truck, slamming the door and leaving it all behind.

Standing in the doorway on his way out of the house, Hank turned and snapped, 'You've gone too far this time, Connie.'

'Oh, no, Hank, you ain't seen what too far looks like yet – just push me a little bit more and you'll learn mighty fast.'

Hank glared at her, then snatched the sandwich from her hand. 'You coulda made two,' he said and stomped out the door.

Hank started up the truck and unwrapped the wax paper. He handed a half of the sandwich to Lucinda, saying, 'I'm sorry, girl.'

'Don't worry about it, Uncle Hank. We all have to do what we have to do.'

Lucinda saw the sour face of her Aunt Connie come into view as the woman labored up the front steps of the funeral chapel. A small pleasure rippled through her at the sight of Connie dragging an oxygen cylinder behind her. Then she was ashamed. Connie was an old woman now and deserved her sympathy, not her scorn. She opened her car door, vowing to be compassionate and respectful as she girded herself with the armor she needed to guard against the pain.

EIGHTEEN

As Lucinda stepped into the foyer of the funeral home, she was greeted by a somber man in a dark suit. When he spoke to her, he didn't flinch, turn away or appear alarmed. Lucinda was grateful for the training that taught him the only two acceptable emotions on the job – sorrow and empathy.

He escorted her to the sanctuary where Hank lay in his coffin. Lucinda stood on the edge of the room looking over the people gathered there to pay their respects. The farm families were easy to identify. The men acted as if their ties were nooses as they shifted their feet in seldom-worn dress shoes. The farm women were devoid of cosmetics except for an occasional slash of petal-soft pink across some of their lips. They appeared as if they'd be far more comfortable with a basket of eggs resting in the crook of their arms or a jam-smeared apron wrapped around their middles.

Lucinda was content to observe from a distance until Connie spotted her and spoke her name. The clusters of people turned as one to look her over. All bore signs of shock at seeing the pretty young woman they once knew standing before them with a half-scarred face.

In some of their eyes, she also saw repulsion – not at her looks but at her character. She knew these were the people who listened to and believed the filthy lies that Connie spread about her and Hank. Lucinda wanted to tell them all to go to hell, but instead she moved toward her aunt, propelled by something other than her own free will.

She placed her hands gently on Connie's upper arms and, leaning down, placed a soft kiss on a withered cheek. Connie dug her fingers into Lucinda's arms and pulled her closer. She hissed into her ear, 'You shoulda worn widow's weeds. It woulda covered up your ugly face and shown everyone the truth about your relationship with my husband.'

Lucinda swallowed hard, pulled back and said, 'I'm sorry for your loss, Aunt Connie.'

Connie plastered on a plastic smile in perfect imitation of southern civility and loudly thanked Lucinda for coming. Lucinda kept her eye on the floor as she headed for a far wall, hoping to disappear on the sidelines. Before she reached it, a pair of suited arms stretched out to her. She looked up. 'Ricky!'

After a smothering embrace, they stood back and looked at each other, smiling. 'Thank you, Lucinda. Thank you for coming.'

At six feet five inches, he was one of the few men who towered over her, but to Lucinda he was still her baby brother. She reached up and brushed at the unruly hair that had fallen into his eyes, the same way she had done when he was a boy. His broad shoulders filled his jacket. He looked comfortable in his suit but she'd bet he'd rather be wearing a T-shirt and a pair of jeans. His smile reflected in his eyes, even though traces of tears clung to his long, dark lashes. 'How are you, you big lug?'

'Pretty good now that my big sister's here.'

Lucinda smiled, overjoyed at the sight of him after all these years. They were interrupted by a shout from Connie. 'Ricky, Ricky, come here. I need you, please.'

Ricky shrugged. 'Sorry. Got to see what she wants.'

Lucinda suspected she needed nothing. She simply wanted to tear Ricky away from her. She sighed as she watched him walk towards the old woman.

Over her shoulder, she heard another familiar voice. 'Not everyone is overjoyed to see you, Lucinda,' her sister Maggie said.

'Didn't expect they would be, Mags.'

'Don't call me that. No one calls me that any more. It's Maggie or Margaret. Or Mrs Sutton, if you prefer.'

Music swelled in the room. Lucinda hadn't noticed it playing in the background but now it filled the space, beckoning everyone to their seats. Ricky took Aunt Connie's arm and led her to the front row. He sat down beside her and she clutched his hand. Lucinda slipped into a seat at the end of the back row.

Lucinda listened as the minister spoke of Hank's reward in heaven and friends spoke of a good man lost. One joked about Hank terrifying the angels as he drove a plow up the streets paved with gold and planted it with corn. She could see how much they missed her uncle. She wanted to step to the front and talk about his kindness, patience and compassion, but she did not dare. The service ended with a prayer and the mourners drifted out to the parking lot to join the procession to the cemetery.

Lucinda headed toward her car but Maggie stopped her. 'Where do you think you're going?'

'To get my car, Maggie.'

'You don't need your car.'

'What are you telling me, Maggie?'

'Aunt Connie wants you in the family limousine. Actually, I don't think she really wants you in there but she thinks it would look funny if you're not.'

'I can drive myself over. I don't need to go in the limo,' Lucinda said, putting her hands up in protest.

'Oh, yes, you do. Don't be embarrassing this family again,' Maggie snapped.

Ricky stepped by her side, 'C'mon, Lucinda. You can sit next to me.'

Lucinda's knees stiffened but she forced them to function as she walked over to the long black car. She climbed inside and slid into the empty bench seat. Ricky followed and sat by her side.

'No, Ricky, please. I need you. Sit next to me and hold my hand,' Connie begged.

'In a minute, Aunt Connie,' Ricky said. 'Let me catch up with my prodigal sister, first.'

Connie's mouth folded into an unattractive pout but she

didn't argue the point. Ricky turned back to his sister. 'Well, Lucinda, what's new in the detective world?'

Maggie spun around in her seat next to the driver. 'Ricky, how could you? That's too morbid. The last thing we need to hear about right now are the dead bodies she messes with or the ones she shot dead.'

'Cut it out, Maggie.'

'Don't you tell me what to do!' Maggie snapped.

Ricky opened his mouth to respond but Lucinda gave a quick shake of her head and he kept still. For five minutes, the only sound in the limo was the snap, snap, snap of Maggie chewing gum. The relentless noise made Lucinda want to scream. Maggie had to realize how annoying it was; Lucinda wanted to tell her to keep her damned mouth shut while she chewed, but she gritted her teeth and bided her time.

A tune jingled from Lucinda's purse, announcing an incoming call. She grabbed the phone like a lifeline. 'Pierce.'

'Hi, Lucy. This is Charley.'

'Don't tell me Dr Burns made you call me.'

'Rambo? Why? Are you giving him a hard time, Lucy?'

Lucinda changed the subject. 'Why did you call, Charley?'

'I need help with fingerprints.'

'Fingerprints?'

'Yeah. I know. I gotta do a science fair project when school begins and I thought I could get started now and it would be fun to collect fingerprints around my house and compare them to me and Ruby and my dad. But I don't have the stuff and I'm not sure how to do it. I was kinda hoping you could help me.'

'I can do that. I'll get the powder, a brush, lift-off tape and fingerprint cards and ink . . .'

'And show me how to use it?'

'Yes, I will.'

'While you're here, could you touch something when I'm not looking, so I can see if I can find your print?'

'Sure.'

'Can you come over now?'

'I'm out of town, Charley.'

'Where are you?'

'I'm in Charlottesville.'

'How come?'

'I'm attending my Uncle Hank's funeral.'

'Oh, I'm sorry, Lucy. Pretend I just gave you a big hug. I'm sorry I bothered you.'

'I'm not sorry.'

'Will you call me when you get back and let me know when you can come over?'

'I'll do it. See you soon.' Lucinda ended the call with a smile on her face. It vanished at the sound of her sister's voice.

'You disgust me!' Maggie shouted. 'How can you sit here on the way to lay Uncle Hank to rest and talk business?'

'I wasn't . . .'

'Mags, cut it out,' Ricky objected.

'Shut up, Ricky, and don't you ever call me that again. We all heard her talking about fingerprints. I can't believe it. First she seduced poor Uncle Hank and betrayed Aunt Connie with her sluttish ways and you come to her defense – on today of all days.'

Connie's pout relaxed into a Mona Lisa smile.

'Maggie, do you really believe that vicious lie is true?' Lucinda asked.

'Vicious lie? Don't make me laugh. Aunt Connie told me what you're like. I know the truth. You can deny it all you want but I'd think you'd at least have the decency to leave your nasty work behind to pay Uncle Hank a moment of respect.'

'Maggie, that call was not business.'

'You lying bitch!' Maggie shrieked.

Ricky jumped in again. 'Mags, please. Even if it was business, what business is it of yours? This is not the appropriate place for this conversation.'

'You're a pathetic excuse for a man, Ricky, if you'd come to that tramp's defense.'

Lucinda squeezed Ricky's hand and shook her head again. He suppressed the retort on his lips. Lucinda placed her hand over her mouth and looked out the window. When Maggie got no return fire, she snapped, 'You both make me sick,' and swung around in her seat to face forward.

They traveled the rest of the way to the gravesite in silence. While words were spoken over Hank's casket, Lucinda stood on the fringes of the gathering, hoping not to be noticed or acknowledged in any way. For the most part, she was left in peace.

Back in the limo, she kept her gaze out the window and spoke to no one, listening to Ricky talk to Connie about his favorite memories of Hank. It was a conversation she would've loved to join, but knew she didn't dare.

In front of the funeral home, Lucinda embraced Ricky. 'Goodbye, little brother. You ought to come down and see me sometime.'

'I'd like to, Lucinda, but I can't just walk away from my milk cows and hope for the best. I'll see if I can get someone to fill in for a couple of days after harvest. I'll give you a call. I guess you're not coming back to the house.'

'Do you have to ask?'

Ricky smiled. 'Guess not. Have a safe drive back.'

'Thank you, Ricky. It was worth all the hassle to get to see you again.'

Lucinda took her longest strides as she headed to her car without looking back. She heard her Aunt Connie say, 'Ricky, does she still know the way to the farm?'

She heard the low murmur of her brother's voice followed by a grating shriek: 'What do you mean, she's not coming back to the house?'

Lucinda pulled out of the parking lot and turned left. The highway back home was to the right but she didn't dare drive past Aunt Connie. She circled around the block and hit Interstate 64, pulled out her cellphone and called for updates on the Sterling case. Even a double homicide was a cheerful prospect after a couple of hours with her family.

NINETEEN

As soon as Lucinda got her car up to speed, she pulled out her cell and stuck the Bluetooth in her ear. She made her first call to Ted.

He answered on the first ring. 'Branson.'

'Did you find anything out about Jason King?'

'Lucinda?'

'Yeah, did you?'

'Well, gee, Lucinda, hello. How are you doing?'

'Can it, Ted. Answer my question.'

'Oh, I guess this means the funeral didn't go so well.'

'It was a real blast, Ted. We stood around the hole in the ground, held hands and sang "Kum-Ba-Yah". What about King?'

'Don't know much. If the addresses we have are correct, he does not have a driver's license here or in Texas. But there are a helluva lot of Jason Kings in both states. We're still running them all down.'

'Anything else?'

'Robin Colter led a team on a canvas of Victoria Whitehead's neighborhood. A lot of people said they knew King but when pressed for any details they all ended up saying that they didn't really know him at all. I talked to a couple of law enforcement agencies in Texas but they're all still digging through all the Jason Kings they have on file. I got one detective to go by and pay King's mother a visit but no one appeared to be at home. He stuck one of his cards in the door with your name and cell number written on the back. Margueite Spellman has a tech combing through all the recovered evidence from the Sterling home looking for the missing key ring. So far, no luck.'

'What about the lab? Heard anything from there?'

'I called to get an update on their progress but Doctor Ringo's out today.'

'So, Audrey's not in. Where is she? When will she be back? Did you talk to anyone else?'

'You know how tight Ringo runs that office. The secretary was not at all forthcoming with information.'

'Did you press her?'

'Of course. But she's more scared of Ringo than she is of me.'

'Jeez. Do you have anything for me?'

'Freddy Sterling called three or four times.'

'What did he want?'

'You. All he'd say when I asked was that he needed to talk to Lieutenant Pierce and he said you can't return his call because he didn't want his grandmother to know he was talking to you.'

'OK, fine. Later,' she said as she disconnected the phone. She keyed in Jason King's cellphone number and went to voicemail after four rings. She left a message for him to return her call. She had the same result with the phone at his mother's home. The next call she made was to the forensics lab. 'This is Lieutenant Pierce. Where is Audrey?'

'Dr Ringo is not in today.'

'Fine. I need a report on lab results and I need it now.'

'You'll need to talk to Doctor Ringo, Lieutenant. I am not trained nor authorized to convey that information.'

Lucinda knew that line had to have been scripted by Audrey. 'Who am I talking to?'

'Laurie Johns.'

'Listen, Ms Johns, I don't want to cause you any problems but waiting for Audrey to get into the lab is not an option for me. Do you understand?'

'Yes, ma'am.'

'Now connect me to whoever is running the DNA analysis for the Sterling double homicide.'

'That would be Beth Ann Coynes, ma'am.'

'Well, put her on the line.'

'I can't, ma'am. She's . . .'

'What do you mean, you can't?'

'She's in court, ma'am. She's testifying in another case, ma'am.'

Lucinda felt a momentary twinge of guilt hearing the quaver in the secretary's voice, but she shrugged it off, knowing that working for Audrey meant Laurie was bullied on a daily basis. 'OK, fine. Would you please have her call my cell when she gets back in?' After giving the secretary the number and disconnecting the line, Lucinda wanted to scream in frustration. Instead, she floored the gas pedal, daring a state trooper to stop her. She didn't ease up until the speedometer hit seventy-five. An hour later, the phone rang and Lucinda slowed down to the speed limit as she answered the call.

'Hello, Lieutenant, this is Beth Ann Coynes. Dr Ringo is on medical leave. I talked to her at the hospital and she told me to give you whatever you needed.'

'What's wrong with Audrey? '

'I don't know. All she would tell me is that you made her sick. I know that's not true – not literally,' she said with a laugh. 'But when it comes to her personal life, it's as hard to get information from her as it is to squeeze honey from a lemon.'

'I hear ya. What have you got on the Sterling murders?'

'I'm pulling that together now. I just spent most of the day at court being badgered by a defense attorney. But I'm organizing all of our preliminary results and should have something for you shortly.'

'I'll be back in town in about an hour. Will you still be there?'

'Yeah. Probably be here half the night. Come on in to the lab. I'll be waiting for you. But don't feel you need to rush, I'll be here quite a while.'

Lucinda sped back up and barreled back to town. Although she didn't need to hurry for Beth Ann's sake, she felt an intense urge to make up for lost time. In the parking lot of the justice center, she opened the car door with one hand while pulling the keys out of the ignition with the other. Rather than wait for the elevator, she took the stairs, two at a time. As she burst through the double doors of the lab, a head popped out of a room down the hall.

'Lieutenant Pierce?'

'Yes. Are you Beth Ann Coynes?'

'Sure am, come on down and let me show you what I've got.'

By the time Lucinda got there, Beth Ann was already back to work, bent over tubes and Petri dishes on the bench. The lab tech's long, dark blonde hair was clasped in a silver barrette at the nape of her neck. When Beth Ann turned toward her, her petite face and ready grin made her look no more than fifteen years old.

As if reading her mind, Beth Ann said, 'Don't worry, Lieutenant. I do know what I'm doing. Despite appearances to the contrary, I've actually been doing forensic DNA analysis for nearly ten years.' She picked up a clipboard packed with paper and flipped through the sheets. 'OK. The first big question is the identity of the male victim, correct?'

'Yes. You have something there?'

'Well, here's the deal: the male victim is not the biological father of Freddy Sterling.'

'What? You mean the victim isn't Parker Sterling?'

'Didn't say that. In fact, I think he probably is. The DNA of the male matches that found on a toothbrush, a hairbrush and all the other objects the techs picked up in the bedroom. In fact, it is the only male DNA found in the bed.'

'So, he had to be living there.'

'Yes. And, the samples taken from Parker Sterling's office also matched that of the male victim.'

'So the victim was Parker Sterling but he was not Freddy's father?'

'Exactly. That sure is what it looks like. We also found something else of interest in the bed.'

'Besides the female victim's DNA?'

'We found DNA from two females on the sheets.'

'Really?'

'And you know that mug you brought in? It was a perfect match.'

'You're kidding?'

'Wouldn't dare! Your reputation precedes you,' she said with a grin.

'Anything else?'

'Not yet. I talked to the fingerprint guy before he left for the day. He'd been through all the ones lifted in the bathroom. All he found were the prints of the female victim and one of an unknown male – in all likelihood, the male victim – but without his hands . . .'

'What about the chainsaw?'

'Wiped totally clean – not a print on her.'

'Thanks, Beth Ann. That gives me a lot to think about.'

'Sorry, Lieutenant, but I'm afraid I may have given you more questions than answers.'

'Yeah. But at least now I have the right questions.'

TWENTY

As Lucinda drove to her apartment, two phrases pounded in her head: *Pamela in the Sterling bed, Parker not Freddy's father* – the repetition too relentless to allow her to concentrate on either one. If she did manage a momentary banishment of one, the void filled in an instant with a melange of thoughts about the day at the funeral and the past it resurrected.

Chester diverted her attention from all of that the moment

she opened her apartment door. First she heard strange, muffled chirps that sounded more like a bird than a cat. The gray tabby marched toward her in apparent pride, his tail stiff and straight, and he high-stepped like a majorette, his mouth full of something unrecognizable. He laid that something at her feet.

She remembered the little yellow mouse she gave him that morning. Now its pink ears were gone, its goggle eyes departed, its leather tail non-existent. Only shreds of its yellow, tufted skin remained and a trail of its stuffing ran through the kitchen and disappeared down the hall. Chester sat, looking up at her, expectant and quite pleased with himself.

She laughed as she scooped him up in her arms and snuggled his warm body against her face. 'What a fearless hunter! What a courageous protector! What a consummate warrior!'

Throughout the praise, the sound of Chester's purr increased in volume and the vibrations of it thrummed against her arms and chest. She rewarded him with a bowl of his favorite canned food and listened to his snarls of delight as he gobbled it all down. She settled into the sofa with her list of suspects and a smile still on her face. She added Pamela Godfrey to the top of her list and then wondered if it made any sense. She couldn't envision Pamela wielding a chainsaw. *Did you have an accomplice? Or perhaps one of your other lovers was a sole perpetrator?*

Although Lucinda knew neither scenario was impossible, they didn't seem to fit with the evidence at hand. Neither one explained the reverential treatment of Jeanine's body. *If it was a crime of jealousy by one of Pamela's sexual partners – why was Jeanine dead?*

Lucinda could not locate the logic that would provide answers to those questions. But still, she had the note on Pamela's car, her feigned ignorance of the address and the DNA in the bed. She knew it couldn't be coincidence and she was certain that Pamela had lied about her relationship with Parker Sterling.

At five thirty the next morning, Lucinda rang the doorbell at Pamela Godfrey's apartment. She pressed the button two more times without getting a response. She raised her fist and pounded three times in quick succession.

An eye popped into sight on the other side of the peep-hole. A chain rattled, a deadbolt clicked open, the door knob turned and a two-inch gap opened. 'Do you know what time it is?' Pamela demanded.

Lucinda lifted up her wrist and looked down. 'I've got five thirty-two. Could be off by a minute or two either way but that's close.'

'Come back at a more civilized hour,' Pamela snarled, slamming the door.

Lucinda's finger hit the bell and held it down until Pamela jerked the door back open. 'What the hell do you want?'

'I'd like to talk with you.'

'It's not a good time. Come back later.'

'Not an option, Ms Godfrey. If you'd like your neighbors to know the police are at your doorstep, that can be arranged.'

Pamela flung the door open. 'Can't stop the Gestapo, now, can we?'

'I'm surprised you know that term at your age, Ms Godfrey,' Lucinda said, stepping into a contemporary living room dominated by black and stainless steel. She thought the decor generated less warmth and comfort than a crime scene.

Pamela planted her feet in the middle of the room and crossed her arms over her blue silk dressing gown. 'The Gestapo may be history but you are living proof that their tactics are eternal. I will be filing a complaint.'

'That is your right, Ms Godfrey. May we sit down and talk?'

'I don't want to sit down and I don't want to talk. I imagine that your idea of "talk" is more my definition of "interrogation". I believe I should call my attorney before I say another word.'

'That is your right, Ms Godfrey. Please call him and tell him to meet us down at the justice center.'

'I am not going down there. You have no right to make me.'

'Fine, Ms Godfrey,' Lucinda said, pulling out a pair of handcuffs.

Pamela dropped her arms and stepped backwards shouting, 'You have no right to arrest me. I've done nothing. I have rights.'

A head covered with tousled gray and black hair poked around the corner, followed by an attractive barefoot man wrapped in a terry bathrobe and sporting the shadow of a beard. 'What's going on here?'

His voice was authoritative and tinged with menace. His face bore an expression of distaste when he looked at Lucinda. She knew that look – the gaze of someone who assumed that no one as disfigured as her could possibly be up to any good.

Lucinda turned her attention to Pamela. 'I thought you lived alone.'

'I do. But what business is it of yours?'

'Is he a client?' Lucinda asked, nodding her head in the man's direction.

The man stepped toward Lucinda, thrusting his chest into her space, his hands forming loose fists. 'Who the hell are you?'

Lucinda whipped the wallet containing her badge and identification out of the waistband of her skirt. 'Pierce. Homicide. I'm here to speak to Ms Godfrey.'

'Keep out of this, Todd,' Pamela snapped. 'This is none of your business.'

'None of my business? I have a reputation to protect.' He turned from Pamela to Lucinda. 'What is this all about? Is she a hooker?'

'How dare you!' Pamela shouted.

'Whether or not she is a hooker is irrelevant to me, sir,' Lucinda said. 'I am investigating a double homicide.'

His jawed dropped. 'Murder?'

Lucinda nodded.

Todd turned back to Pamela. 'Murder? You're mixed up in a murder?'

'A double murder,' Lucinda corrected.

'Two murders, Pamela. How could you expose me to a situation like this? What have you done?'

'I have done nothing, you idiot. This is police harassment. Get your clothes and get the hell out of my apartment.'

'Gladly,' he said as he disappeared down the hall.

Pamela glared at Lucinda and tapped her foot while the two women waited for him to gather his belongings. He emerged from the bedroom, a loose tie looped around his neck, his shirt tail hanging out unevenly from his hurried lopsided buttoning. He turned as he reached the door. 'Our lawyers will call your office later this morning to arrange for the cancellation of our contract.'

'Don't expect it to be easy or cheap,' Pamela snarled at the slamming door. She turned to Lucinda. 'You've cost me money now. You're going to pay for this.'

'Could we sit at your dining table and chat?' Lucinda suggested.

'Chat? Sit and chat? Have you lost your mind?'

'Have a seat, Pamela; and, if you please, we will need a piece of paper and a pen or pencil?'

'You want me to fetch something for you to take notes? You've got to be kidding.'

'You are going to need to write things down, Ms Godfrey. Not me.'

'You know, you're right. I should keep notes to give to my attorney to file harassment charges against you.'

She stomped down the hall, returning with a legal pad and a pen as Lucinda slid into a chair at the table. Pamela sat across from her and, with pen poised over the paper, she said, 'OK. Go.'

'Please write down the names and contact information for all your sexual partners in the last six months.'

'I will not.'

'Fine,' Lucinda said. 'We already have your client list. We'll call them one by one and inquire.'

Pamela's nostrils flared and her lips disappeared as she clenched her mouth tight. Lucinda suppressed her amusement at the woman's reaction. *If she were a spitting cobra, I'd be on my way to the emergency room now.* 'Your call, Ms Godfrey. Give me a list and we won't instigate a conversation about sexual matters unless necessary. Or, we'll call them all and ask upfront.'

Pamela bent over the pad, her pen nib digging deep furrows into the paper. She paused from time to time to think. Then she spun the list around to face Lucinda. 'There.'

Lucinda scanned down the dozen names but remained silent, hoping to provoke a response. Pamela didn't disappoint her.

'Having trouble reading that with just one eye?' Pamela taunted. 'Want me to read it to you?'

Lucinda pushed the pad back to Pamela. 'This is not a complete list.'

Pamela turned bright red from her hairline down past the V-neck of her dressing gown. 'How do you . . .?' she began and then pursed her lips and rotated the pad in front of her. This time, the pen tore holes through the paper in two spots. She shoved it back across the table.

Again, Lucinda studied the three new names without looking up at Pamela or making a comment. After a minute, Pamela broke the silence. 'Is that all, Lieutenant?'

Lucinda pushed the pad back. 'The list is still not complete.'

'Yes, it is.'

Lucinda pulled out her cell. 'Pierce here. Are you in the parking lot?' After a pause she added, 'Come on up.'

'Who was that? And what right do you have to invite someone into my home?'

'A forensics tech is coming up here to obtain buccal swabs from you.'

'What?'

'A DNA sample. It's simple, painless and quick. She'll swipe something that looks like an oversized Q-tip on the inside of your cheeks.'

'No, she won't,' Pamela said, rising to her feet.

'She is also bringing a search warrant authorizing her to take the sample. If you do not cooperate, you will be arrested and charged.'

'This is outrageous.'

'My thoughts exactly, Ms Godfrey, but for entirely different reasons,' Lucinda said as she rose to answer the ring of the doorbell.

Lucinda handed the document to Pamela, who scanned it, balled it up and tossed it in the general direction of the trash can. After that petty act of defiance, she followed instructions without saying a word until the tech departed. 'There. I co-operated. Now, I have a right to know why you wanted my DNA.'

'Tell me, is there anyone on this list who has expressed jealousy about your other lovers?'

'Please give me some credit. I take great pains to keep them from encountering each other. I deserve an answer to my question.'

'Is there anyone on that list who you think would do anything for you, Ms Godfrey?'

Pamela smirked. 'Most of them, Lieutenant.'

'Any who would kill for you?'

'Kill for me? What the hell are you talking about now? Kill for me? That is a stupid question. And you still haven't answered *my* question: why do you want my DNA?'

'Well, Ms Godfrey, we believe that your DNA will match the sample we found on sheets belonging to someone who is not on your list.'

Pamela blanched. She sucked in her cheeks in a vain attempt to still the quivering in her chin.

'Do you have an explanation for that, Ms Godfrey?'

'I . . . I . . . I need to talk to my attorney.'

'Fine, Ms Godfrey. You do that. We'll need to talk again real soon.'

TWENTY-ONE

Ted spotted Lucinda the moment she walked through the office door. 'I heard back from Texas,' he said.

'What did they have to say?'

'It's not good news. They ran down their list of Jason Kings in the state but none of them seem to be our guy.'

'Did they talk to his mother?'

'By phone. She claims she's not his mother. Said she didn't have any sons. And she doesn't know anyone named Jason King.'

'Did they get anything from her to verify or dispute Victoria Whitehead's story about him?'

'Actually, the detective seemed a bit disgusted – went so far as to call our request "a wild goose chase". When I pointed out that was a pretty stale metaphor, he said, "Your request didn't merit any creativity." When I attempted to ask for additional assistance, he cut me off and suggested I call back when I had a real person for him to locate.'

'Bastard.'

'Want me to go over his head to the Texas Rangers?'

'No, not yet. They'll listen to their local guy, not us, unless we find more. It's obvious Jason King is not his real name. We need to figure out what is. Could you put someone on it? Right now, I'd like you to focus your attention on finding some solid dirt on Pamela Godfrey. I need something I can use to apply more pressure.'

'You think pressure is going to work on the daughter of a high-powered attorney?'

'Dammit, Ted, I need something. You dug up some vague rumors – now find some solid piece of personal garbage. I don't need anything criminal – just a little tidbit of information that she wants no one to know. Just find something. I'm going to see if I can get a search warrant for her condo.'

Lucinda rode the elevator up to the sixth floor. She poked her head in District Attorney Michael Reed's doorway and said, 'Hey.'

'What do you need, Pierce?'

'A search warrant.'

'And why do you think that requires my personal involvement?'

'I want to search the condo of Pamela Godfrey, the daughter of Malcolm Godfrey.'

'Did you sit up at night thinking of ways to make my life more difficult?'

'C'mon, Reed. Equal justice for all, right?'

The District Attorney stared at her for a moment, then sighed. 'Why, Pierce? Why do you want me to lie down on Malcolm Godfrey's sacrificial table?'

'We found Pamela's DNA on the sheets on the bed at the Sterling double homicide.'

'And why is that important?'

'I can't believe you even asked that question.'

'OK, I give. You're right. Work with one of the ADAs on the paperwork – I don't care who. But I recommend you find one with no aspirations to go into private practice in the near future.'

'Could you jot a note so the lucky lawyer knows I'm not just jerking his chain?'

'Sure,' he said and reached for his memo pad and a pen. As he wrote, his phone rang. 'Reed.' After a brief pause, he said, 'Yes, she's in here with me. Send the call to my extension.' When the phone rang again, he handed the receiver to Lucinda.

'Lieutenant Pierce.'

'Lieutenant, this is Edwin Prager of Drummond-Godfrey.

My client, Pamela Godfrey, is in my office and we would like to speak with you. Could you join us here?'

'I'm at the justice center. How long will it take you to get here?'

'Lieutenant, my office is a lot more comfortable and the coffee here is far better.'

'I'm busy right now preparing a search warrant but I can give you a few minutes of my time. When will you be here?'

'Is the search warrant related to my client?'

'If you don't bring her over here, I'm going to have to send someone to pick her up.'

'An arrest is premature, Lieutenant. You do not have all the facts.'

'I never said "arrest". I do, however, have strong grounds to pick her up for further questioning.'

'We will be there within the half hour.'

'Make sure you are,' Lucinda said and hung up the receiver.

'That was Pamela Godfrey's attorney?'

'Yes, Edwin Prager of Drummond-Godfrey to be precise.'

'And you couldn't go to his office? It's less than a block from here.'

'I'm not a diplomat, Reed. I'm a cop.'

Reed shook his head. 'Fine. But let's wait on that search warrant until we hear what they have to say.'

'I call that wasting time. But you're the DA. It's your call. I just hope we're not giving her the opportunity to go home and destroy evidence.' Lucinda spun on her heels and returned to her office.

Arriving at her floor, Lucinda went straight to Ted. 'Anything on Pamela Godfrey yet?'

'Good grief, Lucinda, it's only been ten minutes since you asked.'

'Sorry. But she's on her way here with her attorney.'

'What's his name?'

'Edwin Prager.'

'If I find anything, I will get it to you immediately.'

Twenty minutes after Lucinda took the phone call in Reed's office, Pamela and her attorney arrived. The stunned and shaken woman of this morning's encounter was replaced by an über confident professional in Jimmy Choo shoes and a teal suit that would never fit in Lucinda's budget. The price tag for Prager's attire rivaled that of his client. Lucinda was not impressed.

She led them down the hall to the bare walls and fluorescent lighting of an interrogation room. They sat in uncomfortable chairs on opposite sides of a cheap, scarred table. 'You have something to tell me?' Lucinda asked, looking at Pamela.

The other woman turned to her attorney. 'My client,' he said, 'can explain the DNA match on the sheets. She was, as you suspected, having an affair with a resident of 6423 James Landing Drive. However, she had nothing to do with the homicides committed there.'

Lucinda turned back to Pamela. 'How long were you having an affair with Parker Sterling?'

'My client was not having an affair with Mr Sterling.'

For a split second, Lucinda was perplexed by what sounded like a contradiction. Then it clicked and the realization made sense of the care given to the female victim's body. 'Pamela, are you claiming you were having an affair with Jeanine Sterling?'

Pamela stared at her but did not say a word. A barely perceptible smile twitched across her lips and she swiveled her head to her attorney.

'Lieutenant Pierce, please address your questions to me. But, yes, my client Ms Godfrey was involved in an affair with Ms Sterling. I urge you, however, not to jump to conclusions. My client has an iron-clad alibi for the morning of the murders.'

'Iron-clad? Is this closing argument-speak or can you provide corroboration?'

Prager slid his briefcase on the table, opened it and removed a piece of paper. 'Ms Godfrey arrived in her office at nine thirty a.m. on the morning in question. Here is a statement from her secretary, who witnessed her arrival.' He slid it across the table and pulled out another document. 'Here is a list of other members of her staff who are certain they saw her that morning. Included are each of their extensions. Ms Godfrey received a phone call minutes after her arrival – you'll see that documented in her secretary's statement – and she left immediately afterward – also verified by multiple staff members.'

They were interrupted by a sharp knock on the door. Lucinda rose and opened it a crack. Ted slipped her a piece of paper. Before returning to the table, she read it: "Prager was divorced

six months ago because of an alleged affair with Pamela Godfrey.'
She made sure her smirk was hidden as she sat back down.

The attorney began, 'That leaves us with two hours before
the nine-one-one call, as you well know.'

'Excuse me, Mr Prager. I have an ethical question for you.
Is it appropriate for an attorney to be sexually intimate with
his client?'

Lucinda saw Pamela's head twitch ever so slightly as her
eyes widened. Prager's face turned to stone. Twice he appeared
ready to speak but changed his mind before he opened his
mouth. Finally, he continued. 'As I was saying, Lieutenant, it
took Ms Godfrey approximately ten minutes to drive to her
client's office, arriving just before ten a.m. She remained there
until just before eleven forty-five.' He pulled out another sheet
of paper. 'Here is the name of her client and the receptionist,
along with their phone numbers. We trust you will be discreet
when you contact them. Ms Godfrey is a professional woman
with a reputation to maintain.'

'Really?' Lucinda said, and then turned her concentration
to the documents, looking for holes. None were obvious. She
raised her head and stared at Prager. 'That still leaves an hour
unaccounted for. I hope you're not going to tell me she was
with you.'

'I will not dignify that question with a response.'

Lucinda had seen the crime scene; she knew the time frame
was impossible. Nonetheless, she turned to Pamela and said,
'Where were you between seven thirty and nine thirty that
morning, Ms Godfrey?'

'I was at home.'

'What was the reason that you arrived late to work that
morning?'

'I had something to deal with at home.'

'And what was that?'

'Lieutenant, you do realize that my client is not a magi-
cian. Travelling from her home – or from the Sterling house
– to her office in rush hour traffic would easily consume a
half hour. If she went straight to work, staff would have seen
blood on her clothing. That means she had to go home first,
taking another half an hour away, along with an additional
thirty minutes to drive from home to work. When you factor
in the time from the Sterling house to her condo and the time

required for her to change her outfit, that leaves us with a half hour or less remaining. Not even a professional assassin could kill two people and clean up in that short window of time.'

'Are these my copies?' Lucinda asked, lifting the papers from the table.

'Yes, Lieutenant, they are.'

'If you'll excuse me for a moment,' she said as she rose. A part of her wanted to pretend she never saw the paperwork in her hand but she did what she needed to do anyway. She went up to the sixth floor and presented it all to the District Attorney.

Reed read them over and said, 'Fine. Check it out. You find one lie or distortion of fact and the search warrant is yours; otherwise it's a no go. Do you need me down there?'

'No, sir,' she said.

'Pierce. It's time to play nice, now.'

'Yes, sir,' she said and returned to the interrogation room. She thanked both of them and shook their hands. Then, she scurried off to check out Pamela's alibi.

By the time the day was over, Lucinda had confirmed all but the mysterious gap of time between when Freddy left for school and Pamela arrived at work. Even if she operated at the assumption that Pamela was already at the Sterling home watching when Freddy left for school, the time frame seemed too tight – squeezed down close to impossible unless she had an accomplice. But a jealous lover doesn't usually have one. She dropped Pamela down to the bottom of her suspect list, for now. She wasn't ready to eliminate her yet. She knew any alibi could be obtained with money, threats, promise or pressure. But for the moment, she would shift her attention to the new star of her list – Jason King.

TWENTY-TWO

Lucinda went in to work early again, determined to do whatever she could to uncover Jason King's real identity. She knew of one place in her jurisdiction where she might find fingerprints or DNA. She filled out the paperwork for a search warrant for Victoria Whitehead's home.

Even though it was Saturday, she was confident she could find a prosecutor willing to get a judge to rule on it. She went up to the sixth floor and roamed around until she found one. She rolled her eyes when she spotted Matt Cummings at his desk. She could not understand why a grown man would sport that licked-up-front style that made him look like a kitten overgroomed by its mother.

As she approached him, Matt said, 'Ah, c'mon, Lieutenant, I'm here because I have work to do, not because I'm bored. Can't it wait until Monday?'

'If your mother and father were murdered in their home, would you want it to wait?'

'That's foul play, Lieutenant. But, go on, now that you've induced my guilt, tell me what you need.'

Lucinda thrust the documents at him and said, 'It's all here.'

'Give it a few brush strokes before I read it.'

'I want a search warrant for the home of the female victim's mother in the Sterling double homicide.'

'You think the mother did it?'

'No, Cummings. But I'm missing a head and a pair of hands from the male victim.'

'And you think his mother-in-law is hoarding his body parts?'

'Maybe. I don't know. But I want to be able to search for them there and I need to see if I can get any fingerprints or DNA samples for Jason King, the grandmother's boyfriend.'

'Why? You think he could be a suspect?'

'Maybe,' she said and launched into the questions about Freddy's paternity and the story told by Victoria Whitehead. Then she said, 'I'll also need to obtain buccal swabs for Whitehead as well as her and her grandson's fingerprints for the purposes of elimination.'

'You don't need DNA,' Matt contradicted. 'You can eliminate any of her DNA simply because it's female. What about the boy's DNA?'

'Already have that,' Lucinda said.

Matt grunted, leaned back in his chair and steepled his hands in front of his face. Lucinda squeezed her lips together to remind her not to blurt anything out until he gave some indication of his inclination to move forward. Just as she thought she could keep quiet no longer, Matt spoke. 'OK, let's go find the judge.'

With search warrant in hand, Lucinda gathered up a forensics team and led them over to the Whitehead home. Victoria answered the door with a smile that faded in a flash to an anxious frown when she saw the identity of her visitor. She recovered quickly, popping on a pleasant expression as she welcomed her inside. But when Lucinda pointed to the team standing at the foot of the steps, Victoria balked. 'What is this, Lieutenant? Am I being invaded by your retinue?'

'I have a search warrant,' Lucinda said, handing the document to her. 'You can stay here if you like, but you'll have to sit outside while we search.'

'What is this all about?'

'We need to search the premises for evidence related to the murder of your daughter and her husband. Read the warrant. It's all spelled out there. We also have two additional warrants to obtain fingerprint exemplars from you and your grandson.'

'You think I had something to do with the death of my daughter? You think Freddy was involved? This is an outrage. You are going to have to leave right now. I need to call my attorney.'

'Ma'am, you can call your attorney but we're not leaving. If you don't have a cellphone to call from outside of the home, an officer will loan you one. But you have to go outside now.'

Victoria snorted like a deer sensing danger and called for Freddy. When he appeared at the banister on the second floor, he said, 'What's happening, Grandmother?'

'We are being forced out of our home so these police officers can tear it apart for no reason whatsoever.'

Freddy's head jerked over in Lucinda's direction and then turned back to his grandmother. 'Yes, ma'am, let me get a book and I'll be right down.'

Lucinda watched without seeing any sight of Freddy for a few minutes and then started up the stairs. Freddy came out of his room with a book under his arm and his hand outstretched. 'Thank you, Lieutenant,' he said.

Perplexed at his reaction, she reached out and took his hand. The explanation of his greeting became clear when she felt a folded note scrape against her palm. She watched his back as he went out the door before unfolding the piece of paper. It read: 'Meet me in back of house. Don't tell Grandmother. Please!'

Lucinda instructed the search team and the forensics team

and then slipped out the back door. She scanned the backyard but didn't see Freddy. Then she heard him. 'Lieutenant,' he said in a whispered shout, 'over here.'

She followed the sound and saw the boy standing in the shadows of a tall blue spruce in the far corner of the property. She walked towards him, wondering how much she could trust him, how many of his words were the truth as he knew it or if it was all part of a game instigated by his grandmother. 'What's up, Freddy?'

'We had a seance,' he said, leading her to a hidden concrete garden bench tucked under the massive boughs.

Lucinda ducked down as she followed him but once seated she had plenty of headroom. 'Who had a seance?'

'Me and my grandmother and a couple of ladies and a man.'

'Did you know any of those people?'

'One of the ladies comes by and visits my grandmother a lot. I knew her even before I lived here. But I never paid much attention to her. She kind of gives me the creeps 'cause she stares at me so weird.'

'But you spent time with her during the seance?'

'Yeah, I didn't want to – I even had to hold her hand. Grandmother made me sit next to her when we formed a circle.'

'And besides holding her hand, what bothered you, Freddy?'

'Well, nothing bothered me then. I was kind of scared and kind of curious and kind of excited because they said I could talk to my mom.'

'Did you? Did you talk to your mom?'

'Yeah, well, that's what they said. But, I don't know. I mean, I believed it at the time but later I started thinking maybe they tricked me. And then, this morning, I was sure of it.'

'What gave you doubts, Freddy?'

'Well, I was talking to my mom and it gave me shivers – it was good but it was kind of icky, too. But I listened and I believed her and when it was over, I hugged my grandmother and even hugged the creepy lady, and thanked them for letting me talk to my mom. I was really excited – and scared, too. Then, in my room, I started thinking and it didn't seem right.'

'What didn't seem right, Freddy?' Lucinda asked as she studied his face for any indication of deception.

'What my mom said – or not my mom – it wasn't right. It sounded like my mom but she wouldn't tell me stuff like that.'

'How did your mom talk to you? What did she say?'

'Her voice – it sounded like her voice – came out of the creepy lady's mouth. She told me to believe everything my grandmother told me, but my mom told me before that my grandmother makes up stories. Mom said she loved my grandma, but she got some crazy ideas sometimes.'

'Yes?'

'And then this weird lady with my mom's voice said that Dad was evil and dangerous and I needed to keep away from him. She said Grandmother and Jason would protect me from him – but my mom never said "Grandmother" to me before she died. She always said "Grandma".

'And then she said I needed to do everything they told me to do and I shouldn't talk to the police or anybody about my mom or my dad except for them and she said if I ever get confused that I should come talk to her again. And I want to talk to her again but I don't think I talked to her then. I thought I did but I don't know. I mean, my mom wouldn't say those things. I don't understand. But I started wondering if they were making it all up to scare me or something. And then I heard my grandma talking on the phone and I think she was talking to her boyfriend Jason – you know, the one she says is my half-brother, which doesn't make any sense, and that's when I knew she was lying.' Tears streamed down Freddy's face. He brushed them away with the back of his hand.

Lucinda put an arm around his shoulders. 'Freddy, I know you are upset – and you have every reason to be upset. But tell me, what did she say to Jason?'

'She said, "We had a seance. The boy won't be any trouble at all."'

TWENTY-THREE

Lucinda went back inside the house, her thoughts focused on Freddy. When she reached the second floor, Marguerite Spellman stuck her head out of the master bedroom. 'Lieutenant, come in here. You need to look at this bed.'

A brief glimpse of a sheet-covered mattress was all Lucinda

saw before the forensics team leader flipped the light switch, plunging the room into a deep gloom. Marguerite's face glowed blue as she ran an alternative light source over the top of the bed. 'Nothing,' she said. 'Nothing at all. Not one single indication of any biological fluids. I'll take the sheets to the lab but I don't think I'll find anything.'

'So, she made the bed this morning. Where's the dirty laundry?'

'Checked that, it's not there. Sent someone in search of a washer and dryer but both were empty.'

'Damn. His DNA has to be on something.'

'I know. It should be here somewhere but there's only one toothbrush and one hairbrush in the bathroom – that doesn't look promising. The only male clothing in the closet is hanging in dry cleaning bags with the tags still on them. There are two empty dresser drawers which I suspect once held his T-shirts, underwear and socks. We swabbed the insides without much luck. We'll try to find his DNA, Lieutenant, but it doesn't look good.'

'OK. Well, maybe AFIS will give us a fingerprint match.'

Marguerite sighed. 'We have to find a fingerprint first.'

'What?'

'Every single surface in this room has been wiped clean. But we will not stop looking. We'll collect prints all over the house if necessary.'

'Damn, damn, damn,' Lucinda muttered as she walked out into the hall, down the stairs and out to the front porch. Victoria Whitehead sat in a wicker chair chatting with the officer watching over her as if they were best friends.

'Ms Whitehead, I have a few questions,' Lucinda said.

Victoria smiled apologetically at the officer and graced Lucinda with her most put-upon expression. 'Yes, Lieutenant. What is it now?'

'When did you change the sheets on your bed?'

'That is a very rude question.'

'Whatever. Just answer it.'

For a moment, Victoria looked as if she wouldn't and then she mumbled, 'This morning.'

'You haven't slept on them at all.'

'Oh no, not at all. They are brand new from the store. I just bought them the other day when I went shopping.'

'Where are the dirty sheets?'

'Cleaned, folded and put away, of course.'

'What did you use to launder them, Ms Whitehead?'

'The normal things – detergent, bleach, fabric softener.'

Lucinda stifled a groan. 'What about Jason's toothbrush or hairbrush or comb?'

'He took them with him, of course.'

'Do you have anything he used regularly? Any soiled clothing?'

'Oh, no, I washed all his clothes before I packed them. He takes nearly everything when he visits his mother. He never knows if a crisis might prevent him from returning when he planned.'

Lucinda considered confronting her with Karen's denial of having a son but decided against it. If she knew, she would either have a ready excuse or she might muck up the investigation with that knowledge. 'If you think of anything, please ask the officer to come and get me right away.'

'When will I have my house back, Lieutenant?'

'I honestly don't know, Ms Whitehead. After we get your fingerprints, I would be glad to drive you to a friend's house – or anywhere you like – if you'd be more comfortable elsewhere.'

Victoria sniffed. 'It's OK. For now. With the nice breeze, it's quite a pleasant day.'

Back in the house, Lucinda roamed from room to room on the first floor, looking for anything that might harbor a DNA sample or a good fingerprint. She stopped in the middle of the kitchen, spun around, and bounded up the stairs, calling out: 'Spellman! Spellman!'

'Yes, Lieutenant?'

'What is the one place men often touch, but women seldom do? The one place a woman might forget to eliminate a fingerprint?' Lucinda held her breath, watching realization wash away the confusion on the forensics tech's face.

'Why didn't I think of that?' Marguerite said.

Both women raced into the master bath. Marguerite carefully lifted the toilet seat and dusted powder on the front edge of the underside. They watched the ridges become visible. Four fists went into the air and a jubilant 'Yes!' echoed off the tiles.

'Is the crime scene at the Sterling house still sealed?' Marguerite asked.

'Yes.'

'I don't think we checked under the scat there. I'll get back to you if I find anything.'

It was early evening before the forensics team finished and turned the house over to Victoria Whitehead. Finally, Lucinda's long day was over. Hopefully, that fingerprint would provide her with Jason King's real identity. But she knew she still needed his DNA. She needed it to check out Victoria's story of a genetic link between King and the boy. She doubted that they were brothers but she wondered if King was Freddy's father.

Lucinda did not like Sunday afternoons. It was a day most folks spent with their families. The thought of that made her stomach queasy. It was also a time when she didn't feel right intruding on anyone else's life unless it was an emergency.

She spent her time trying to relax – playing with Chester, reading a book, watching a movie DVD. On this day, though, she was more restless than usual. She'd already spent over an hour working out in the gym, not stopping until her knees wobbled from the exertion.

She couldn't escape the relentless thoughts in her head. Freddy's words about the seance and the overheard phone call with Jason made her anxious for him and concerned about his safety. His grandmother's behavior troubled her, too – was she simply that tidy and devoted to cleanliness all of the time or had she intentionally set about destroying evidence?

It was all on an endless loop; she had to find a way to distract herself. She grabbed her laptop and stretched out on the sofa. Pulling up Google, she typed in Jason King. She was more than dismayed when 37,700,742 entries popped on the screen. She put quotation marks before and after the name. It helped some but she still had 248,000.

Scrolling through them she found a British TV series, a web designer, a journalist, a professor, a band, an architect and an expert on yeast infections – that certainly was something she never expected to find. She went through page after page without finding anything useful at all.

The answer seemed obvious. She needed to go to Texas. She should get the trip approved before she went. *But maybe*, she thought, *I should just head to the airport, fly out today and worry about the expense reimbursement later.*

She jumped up from the sofa and pulled a suitcase out of the hall closet and rolled it into her bedroom. Opening her dresser drawer, it hit her: *I can't go now. Ellen's competency hearing is tomorrow. And I promised I'd be there.* She slammed the drawer shut and stomped out of her apartment, hoping a walk by the river would clear her head.

TWENTY-FOUR

Lucinda slipped into the back row of the small courtroom – only four rows of pew-like benches for the audience behind the bar. The few observers scattered about like fallen petals. The defense and prosecution tables were surrounded by suited men.

Lucinda preferred the rooms in the old courthouse with their soaring ceilings, arching woodwork and tall windows that imbued the place of judgment with the sanctity and loftiness of a gothic church. The practicality and compactness of this space left no room for drama, as if what occurred between these walls was of little import.

A side door opened and Lucinda gasped. Ellen Branson shuffled into the room with a pair of guards at her elbows. She wore a tan, white and black shirtwaist dress that hung from the bony peaks of her shoulders. Ellen had lost a lot of weight since the day she pulled a gun on Lucinda in the parking garage.

That wasn't the most disturbing thing about her appearance, though. Her eyes were open but did not appear to see, her jaw hung slack, her hair lacked luster and she had no more color in her complexion than a corpse. She certainly did not look capable of aiding in her defense. It made Lucinda angry that the district attorney insisted on prosecuting this obviously pathetic woman.

Once Ellen was seated, a man in the row directly behind the defense table leaned forward and patted her on the shoulder. She turned and looked at him, emotionless. Her attorney, Richard Barksdale, flashed a smile at the man, reached out and shook his hand. *Is that Ted? It can't be.* Then the man turned enough in his seat that she could see his profile. *It is Ted. What a pleasant surprise.*

Lucinda paid little attention to the dueling psychiatrists on the stand with their shrink jargon. She wondered, though, if the one testifying for the prosecution had completely forgotten his oath as a physician to do no harm. She leaned forward in her seat when Ted Branson took the stand.

The attorney led Ted through the background of his romance and marriage to Ellen and the birth of their first two children. He smiled a lot, often looking over at Ellen with undisguised warmth. She, however, seemed oblivious to him and to her surroundings. When he reached the death of their third baby, Ted choked on his words, pausing to swallow and hold back the tears.

Barksdale walked Ted step by step through Ellen's deterioration from the days she spent silent, staring at walls, to the more volatile times when she shouted and cursed and her obsession with Lucinda consumed every day. 'And I was not the husband I should have been. I expected her to snap out of it. I grew impatient with her when she didn't. I escaped into fantasies about a high school girlfriend and how my life would have been different and better with her. In the process, I neglected Ellen and did not get her the help she so desperately needed. I am more than ashamed. I'm mortified by my self-centered behavior.'

That was the Ted Lucinda knew – the high school boy she once loved, the partner in crime she could trust. She realized that he was, at last, healing from the loss of his child and what he had perceived as rejection by his wife. In the back of her mind, though, the small cynic spoke, warning her that this could all be an act. She hoped that voice was wrong.

The prosecution called Lucinda to the stand. She described the morning in the garage when Ellen had her in handcuffs, on her knees, with a gun barrel against her head. She chose her words with care, hoping to minimize the terror she felt.

Barksdale asked, 'What is your opinion of Ellen Branson's state of mind at the time of this incident?'

The prosecutor objected. 'Lieutenant Pierce is not qualified as an expert in this field.'

Lucinda glared at him and wanted to tell him to shut up and sit down. The judge did it for her – although in far more diplomatic language. 'This is not a trial. It is simply a hearing to determine Ms Branson's competency to stand trial. Objection overruled.'

'You are the victim here, Lieutenant Pierce. So, please tell the court, what outcome would you like to see in this case?' Barksdale asked.

'That Ellen Branson gets the professional help she needs to regain her mental health and return home to her children.'

'What about the pending charges?'

'I hope they are dismissed.'

With those words, Lucinda noticed that the bored reporter in the second row snapped to attention and wrote furiously in her steno pad. Lucinda felt the woman's penetrating stare as she left the stand and returned to her seat.

After arguments from both sides, the judge ruled that Ellen was not competent to stand trial at this time. Lucinda hadn't realized how much tension had bunched up in her neck and shoulders until relief at the decision released the crunched muscles in her jaw and upper back. Lucinda remained seated as the judge left the bench and Ellen was led from the room, as lifeless and disconnected from her surroundings as when she entered.

Lucinda watched as the doors closed behind Ellen, then stood up and moved toward the front to speak to Ted. Out of the corner of her eye, she saw the reporter moving in to intercept her on her path. Lucinda turned abruptly and strode out of the courtroom. The quick clackety-clack of the reporter's heels on the marble floor echoed in the halls behind her, causing Lucinda to pick up her pace.

She pulled her cell out of a pocket as she walked, turning it on. She looked down as it beeped. She had one message. Without breaking her stride, she hit the playback button and held the phone to her ear.

'Lieutenant, this is Marguerite Spellman. We have a match for the fingerprint – both fingerprints.'

A fierce, tight fist formed in Lucinda's chest. She broke into a sprint, leaving a disappointed reporter far behind.

TWENTY-FIVE

Marguerite led Lucinda to the fingerprint analysis work-space, talking all the while. 'The print under the rim of the toilet seat in the Sterling master bath was identical to the one found at the Whitehead house. And your boy's been busy. We found three outstanding warrants for his arrest under three different names. Ten years ago, in California, Jason Kennedy was arrested for three counts of bigamy, released on bond and never showed up at court. But here's the good news: his denial of his name and identity caused the state to take a DNA sample to determine the paternity of one of the women's children. They are overnighting the profile to us. We should have it first thing tomorrow.'

'Good work, Spellman.'

'Thanks,' Marguerite said and continued, 'Jack Kraft is wanted in Florida on suspicion of scamming a handful of widows out of their life savings. In Rhode Island, they know him as Jimmy Kellogg. They arrested him when they discovered he was making duplicate imprints of credit cards of customers at the restaurant where he worked. He bailed out before the locals made a match of his prints to the warrants in California and Florida. When they went to rearrest him, he was gone.'

'But nothing connecting him to a violent crime?' Lucinda asked.

'No.'

'I wonder what else he's done without getting caught. Thanks, Spellman. Thanks for everything. Let me know what you get when you analyze that profile from California.'

'Captain?' Lucinda said, as she poked her head into Captain Holland's office. 'Got a minute?'

Holland grunted and Lucinda chose to interpret that as 'Yes'. Stepping into his office and sliding into a chair, she said, 'I need to go to Texas.'

'The Sterling homicides?'

'Yes.'

'Where in Texas?'

'I'm not sure if I can pronounce it.' Lucinda looked down at the piece of paper in her hand. 'New Bra-un-fels,' she said, stressing the second syllable.

'Let me see that,' Holland said, stretching out his hand. He looked down at the address and asked, 'German town?'

'Don't know.'

Holland grunted again and spun around to the laptop on the console behind his desk. He pulled up Google search and typed in the name. 'Yeah, it is. Must be New Brawn-fulls.'

'Are you sure about that?'

'Not totally. But I'm confident that I'm closer to the correct pronunciation than you are.'

'I can ask the locals when I get there. You will approve the travel, won't you?'

'Do you want local back-up?'

'I just need to talk to Karen King.'

'Talk, Pierce? Yeah, I bet that's all you want to do. You want local back-up?'

Lucinda stared at him, wondering why he had to ask.

'Of course not,' Holland said with a shake of his head. 'What was I thinking? Get out of here. I need to make some calls.'

'You're going to authorize the trip?'

'When I decide, I'll let you know. You can leave now, Pierce.'

Lucinda stood still for a moment, thinking about making a response. She decided against it and left Holland's office, heading for her own. On the way, she spotted Ted Branson. 'Hey, Ted, I was sure surprised to see you at the hearing this morning. Surprised and pleased.'

'Yeah, thanks. But we don't have time to go into that right now. I was just about to call you. The document analysis guys sent up copies of something interesting that was picked up in the search of Victoria Whitehead's home.'

'Show me.'

'It's a lot of pages. I'll need to spread them out for them to make any sense to you. Let's go to the conference room.'

Ted stretched out a line of paper that ran from one end of the table to the other, then went to the other side and laid down another.

'What are we looking at, Ted?'

'Family trees.'

'But William Blessing is at the top of each of these pages.'

'Yep. On this side of the table. With a different alias on each page and a connection to all these women, indicating that he fathered a child with each one of them, stretching over a forty-year period.'

'A bigamist?'

'Maybe with some of them – definitely not all of them. The second most current entry is "William Blessing aka Parker Sterling", married to Jeanine Whitehead Sterling with a son named Fredrick.'

'Damn!' Lucinda exclaimed.

'And the very first chronological entry down at the other end is interesting but not very revealing,' he said, walking to the other end of the table. 'Here William Blessing has no alias and the rectangular box has no name, simply "My mother". And under it, "Me".'

'That's got to be Jason King or whatever his name his. I got a report from Marguerite Spellman pointing to several other aliases.' She pulled a copy out of the folder and handed it to Ted. She walked down the line, scanning the other names, looking for one that was familiar. 'Look,' she said, '"William Blessing aka Samuel Houston King". Under that are Karen King and her daughter Trinity. We need to find out all we can about William Blessing and we need to cross-check all of the victims on the list of crimes from Spellman to see if there is any crossover with these documents.'

'I've got someone running down Blessing. I can handle the cross-check myself,' Ted said with a nod. 'But first, come over and look at the documents on the other side. They're even more baffling. They go back two centuries. It starts at this end with James Worthington in London in the middle of the eighteenth century. The down arrow indicates that he was married to one woman and had six children. Then the arrow to the right leads to another box that reads: "Charles Butler, Massachusetts". But the most interesting part is what is written above the arrow. "Disappeared and became". And that continues straight down the line for two hundred years. The words above the arrow either read that he disappeared or that he "faked death and became".

'Most of the children on these pages have no dates at all or just a birth date without the year they died, except for a couple of them where murder was indicated. Like right here,' he said,

moving up the line and pointing to another page. 'Beneath
Sarah Winslow Clark's name it says, "Murdered in 1847". The
same notation is below the names of each of her four children.
The right arrow next to Bartholomew Clark's name with "dis-
appeared and became" above it points to "Ezekiel Young in
Salt Lake City". He had seven wives and thirty-eight children.
I suspect a Mormon connection with plural marriages.

'He supposedly faked his death – heck, if I had seven wives
and thirty-eight children, I'd either fake my death or take my
life – one or the other.'

'If one of the wives didn't take you out first,' said Lucinda,
laughing. She walked down to the far end of the document
string and found William Blessing. Under his name again was
a box with 'My mother' and another with 'Me'. The arrow to
the right repeated the disappeared line and went to a box that
read, 'See full William Blessing file'.

Lucinda's cellphone beckoned. 'Pierce.'

'Come to my office, Pierce.'

'Captain Holland?'

'Yes.'

'You approving the travel?'

'Come to my office, Pierce,' he said and disconnected.

Lucinda put away her phone and went down the hall. When
she reached Holland's office, he said, 'Your flight is being
booked for tomorrow morning. You will not need to check in
with the local cops unless you want to do something more
than talk to Karen King.'

'Thank you, sir.'

'Pierce, I'm warning you. If Jason King answers the door
don't throw him to the ground and cuff him. Just pretend
you're peddling something door to door and get the New
Braunfels Police to bring him in. That clear?'

'Yes, sir,' Lucinda said with a sigh.

'I hear what you're saying but I need to make sure you
understand it and know I really mean it.'

That comment really ticked off Lucinda but she held her
peace, maintaining eye contact and responding with a quick
nod.

'OK. I'll accept that for now. Don't make a fool out of me,
Pierce. The documents will arrive on your computer shortly.
Get out of here. I have work to do.'

As Lucinda walked back down the hall, her phone rang again. 'Pierce.'

'Lucy!'

'Charley. What's up?'

'Me and Daddy and Ruby are going to the Outer Banks next week. So, I had to make sure you were taking care of yourself first.'

Lucinda grinned and laughed. 'Yeah, Charley, I'm taking care of myself.'

'No, you aren't, Lucy. I talked to Rambo. You didn't come in to see him like you said you would.'

Damn that Doctor Rambo. 'Sweetie, I'm really tied up with a case right now.'

'I know you're busy, Lucy, that's why I made a late appointment for you. Rambo said he'd stay and see you tonight at seven.'

'Charley . . .'

'Lucy, if you don't go I won't have any fun on the beach. I'll just be worrying about you and stuff the whole time. And I'll just make Daddy and Ruby miserable, too. Please, promise me you'll go. Promise?'

Lucinda knew she could see Burns and still have plenty of time to pack and make arrangements for her cat's care before her morning flight. She also knew that Charley wouldn't give her any peace unless she did. *Damn Burns for playing dirty and dragging in Charley.* She sighed. 'OK, sweetie. You have a deal. You have a good time on your trip and call me when you get back and tell me all about it.'

'You promise you'll go see Rambo today?'

'Yes, Charley, I promise.'

Charley was happy but Lucinda was filled with dread as they wrapped up the call. At her computer, Lucinda printed out her travel documents and headed over to the doctor's office.

'Even though it was pretty low of you to drag Charley into this, Dr Burns, I was on my way to your office because of her.'

'Don't get huffy, Lieutenant,' Rambo said. 'Charley is putting a lot of pressure on me.'

'She's a child,' Lucinda said.

'Yes, but a very persistent one, as you well know. I'll see you in a few minutes then?'

'No, something's come up in the investigation that requires my immediate attention. I'm sorry you stayed late on my behalf but I simply cannot make it.'

'I could stay a bit later.'

'I'm not sure how late it will be, Dr Burns. I'll have to call you back and reschedule.'

'Charley will be very disappointed.'

'There you go again with the dirty tricks,' Lucinda said with a grimace.

'I'm only asking you to listen to what I have envisioned for your care and consider one additional procedure at a time. You know as well as I do, if you don't, you'll have to answer to Charley.'

Lucinda didn't really care what Rambo Burns thought but Charley was another story. The thought of disappointing her put a lump in her throat and a burning in her eye. 'I'll think about it,' she said.

'Think about it? That's it?'

'I've got a homicide case as my priority right now. I've got to catch a man before he flies out tonight and then I've got a flight out to Texas in the morning to follow up a lead. When this is done, I'll get back to you.'

'Charley will be pleased to hear that.'

Lucinda sighed. 'Later, Doc.'

She disconnected and tossed the cellphone into the passenger seat of her car with a little too much force. It bounced down to the floor. 'Damn you, Burns,' Lucinda said. Part of her yearned to look like the woman she was before that shotgun blast. And another side of her wanted to tell everyone to go screw themselves. But she knew one thing unequivocally: even if Burns could repair all the scarring on her face, he could never return her missing eye and he could never heal her deepest scars – the ones with no physical manifestation. She knew she would never be the same woman she was before the day she leaped in front of that shotgun to push another woman to safety.

Arriving at the airport complex, she turned into the executive section and headed to the hangar where Ted told her she'd find Gary Finnerman. She approached a suited man with broad shoulders; a substantial guy with an impatient look on his face. 'Gary Finnerman?' she said, stretching her hand in his direction.

'Yes,' he answered, wrapping beefy fingers around hers. 'Lieutenant Pierce, what can I do for you? And what happened, line of duty injury?'

Lucinda ignored the second question and answered the first. 'I'm looking for background on your ex-wife Victoria.'

'Not a subject I like to think about but here goes. We were married for five years. Everything was fine for the first three, until she got all goofy on me. I filed for divorce but even though I instigated the separation, I was generous with the woman. Did I get any expressions of gratitude? Hell, no.

'I offered and dutifully paid her spousal support for ten years – twice the length of our marriage. But the first month the check didn't come, she was on my case – nagging about all the bills she had to pay and about how I owed it to her to help her maintain her lifestyle. I told her, "I owe you nothing. Go find another husband." And damned if she didn't. Picked an old guy that time – a bit too feeble-minded to notice her wacko tendencies, I think.'

'Mr Finnerman, you said she was "goofy" earlier and now you're saying she's "wacko". Could you explain what made you think that way?'

'You mean you didn't notice?' he said with a chuckle. When Lucinda didn't respond, he continued. 'It started out simply enough with her strange spending habits. She poured thousands of dollars in psychics, palm readers, tarot card fortune tellers, crystals, videos and books. Sure, I could afford it, but it was such a waste of my hard-earned money. I told her to cut it out and for a while I thought she had since I saw no other suspicious charges on the credit card bill. Then, I realized she was withdrawing large amounts of cash from our joint checking account. I confronted her and she admitted that she was using the money for the same old crap.

'But, you know, it was annoying, but tolerable, until it started impacting my business. At dinner parties for clients and cocktail parties with my associates, she'd go up to people like this,' he said, putting his face close to Lucinda's. 'She gets in their personal space and says all sorts of stupid shit, like "Your aura is damaged but I know just the crystals you need to set it right again" or "Your spouse's aura is as black as death, you need to leave your marriage or you will die."

'I told her over and over that she needed to leave that stuff at home when we went to social events connected to my business, but it was like talking to a child. She kept telling me that those people needed her help. But the final straw was the night we had a holiday party at our home. The guests were a combination of clients, associates and suppliers. I asked her nicely to put up her crystals for the night but she didn't – they filled every nook and cranny of the house.

'So, while she was getting dressed, I gathered them all up and shoved them to the back of a closet shelf. As usual, most of the guests had arrived by the time she made her grand entrance. Everything was fine for a few minutes. Then suddenly she shrieked, "Gary, Gary, where are my crystals?"

I went up to her and whispered, 'I just put them up for the party. They're all safe; we'll get them back out after everyone leaves.' She backed away from me with a look of horror on her face. She screamed out: 'Oh, my God, you are trying to kill me! I never noticed that darkness in your aura before but it's there now. I can see it. You put up my crystals because you knew they would protect me from your evil. And now, they are gone. Oh, my God, I'm going to die! All of you are my witnesses. When I'm gone, look to him – look to that evil man.'

'Fortunately, there was a doctor present, he retrieved his bag from his car and administered a sedative. But, that was it for me. I don't know why you're investigating that woman, but quite honestly, I wouldn't put anything past her.'

'How about homicide?' Lucinda asked.

'Murder? I never could have imagined that one. It's a bit hard to accept but, hell, by the time we divorced, I didn't know that woman any more. Listen, Lieutenant, anything else? I really need to get going.'

She asked for and got his alibi for the morning in question. It sounded solid – she'd check it out and, if she was right about this man, she'd eliminate him, too. *But Victoria Whitehead? That's another story. The more I know about her, the better I understand her; but the better I understand her, the less sense the whole situation makes.*

TWENTY-SIX

L eaving the San Antonio Airport, Lucinda took Loop 410 East to Interstate 35 and headed north. Half an hour later, she spotted the first exit for New Braunfels but kept going until she saw one pointing to downtown. No matter where she went, that area was the first thing she wanted to see. She believed that the main thoroughfare was very revelatory of any city or town – it held the key to its soul, disclosing its character, economics and dynamics. The better she understood a place, she thought, the better she was prepared for an interview in a strange town.

She drove a stretch of street dominated by newer commercial buildings. A couple of blocks later, older architecture prevailed – some buildings were constructed for commerce, others were once rambling homes turned into office space. Straight ahead, Lucinda spotted a large town square, an oval island of green grass, trees, a tall old fountain and a gazebo. Plenty of cars, lots of foot traffic – a vital downtown area like this one always made her smile.

She looped around the circle to the other side where she realized a bit too late that the right lane was not where she wanted to be. She waited in the neutral hash-marked area until other cars passed and she could slide behind them and follow the road as it dipped under a railway trestle. Beyond the overpass was a traffic light at a park entrance to her right. She detoured into the city oasis and was stunned – this was not the Texas she expected to see. A river flowed on her left that ran clearer than any she'd ever seen. On the far side of the river a cluster of upscale, balconied apartments graced its banks.

A little further on, a tiny train depot with its mini-train was followed by the lake with paddle boats and hoards of ducks, geese, anhinga and egrets. She knew she should head straight to Karen King's house but she couldn't resist a little exploration. She pulled into a parking space and walked into the grass. The broad, gnarled trees amazed her. Their massive branches, covered with small, glossy, dark green leaves, stretched out so far, they needed concrete columns and metal poles to hold them up.

She reached the side of the stream-like river and gasped. It rushed up out of the ground with waters skimming across the stones on the bottom. She wanted to walk through it instead of beside it but restrained herself. She kneeled down and stuck her fingers into the quick-moving flow and startled. Although the air temperature easily soared above ninety degrees, her fingers were numbed by the chill in the river.

She followed it until it reached the primitive gazebo by the lake. She continued around, approaching a large wooden bridge that arched over another branch of flowing water. She paused in the middle, amazed at the clarity below, laughing when she saw a turtle, with blue and red markings on its head, swim underneath her feet.

On the other side, she followed the bank to a small flat bridge leading over to a dammed area where young children splashed with their parents in shallow water. She went up a hill and saw that she was back where she started. She looked out across the park; from that vantage point, and realized it covered far more area than she'd walked.

Back in the car, she drove up a steep hill on California Street, slamming on her brakes when she reached the top as a doe and a fawn gamboled across the road. She slowed down, spotting deer in nearly every yard. She took a left on Ohio, where the large animals grew even more abundant. When she reached the high school, she turned left and entered a street where trees formed canopies across the road. She saw many of the same glossy-leafed trees she noticed in the park but had never seen before, as well as an unfamiliar evergreen. The foliage on the latter reminded her of juniper bushes but they soared higher. With their lower branches trimmed, they looked like the trees in a Dr Seuss book. She spotted a few others she recognized – crape myrtles, ash and the ubiquitous hackberry. She pulled into the driveway of a brick two-story home and headed for the front door.

She rang the bell and the door opened before she finished lifting her finger. The woman in front of her had big blonde hair, blatantly false eyelashes and wore a silk hostess gown in blinding brilliant colors. 'Not buying anything today. Not donating either,' she said as she started to shut the door in Lucinda's face.

'I'm here to see Karen King,' Lucinda said, whipping out her badge and identification.

'I'm Karen King. What happened to you?' she said, leaning forward to peer at Lucinda's face. 'Who are you? And what do you want?'

She sure doesn't look bedridden, Lucinda thought and, ignoring the first question, she said, 'I'm Lieutenant Pierce, a homicide detective from Virginia. I've been trying to reach you but you haven't returned any of my calls. I'd like a moment of your time to talk to you about your son, Jason King.'

'So you're the one who's been calling me. I assumed it was a wrong number. I told the police officer who stopped by that I don't have a son and I know no one named Jason King. It's just a coincidence that we have the same last name. There are a lot of Kings in the world, you know. We aren't all related.'

'I'd like to talk to you anyway, Ms King, because there's a woman in Virginia who claims you are his mother and who also said that you were bedridden.'

Karen arched her eyebrows and raised her arms, the over-sized sleeves trailing like wings by her sides. 'As you can see, I am hardly bedridden. The only person I even know of in Virginia is my boyfriend's mother, whom I have never met, so I doubt we have anything to discuss.'

'Could I please come in, just for a minute?' Lucinda asked.

'What do you want?'

Lucinda pulled out a photograph of Jason King and held it up facing Karen. 'Does this man look at all familiar to you?'

Karen laughed. 'Of course he does. That's my boyfriend. Where did you get his picture?'

'This, Ms King, is Jason King.'

'No, no, no.' She grinned. 'That's Jeremy Kneipper. Who gave you this photo?'

'His girlfriend gave it to me.'

Karen's mouth drooped and her brow furrowed. 'You'd best come in,' she said as she opened the door wide.

As Lucinda sat in a chair in the living room, Karen asked, 'Is she a younger woman?'

'Younger than you?'

'Yes, yes, of course that's what I mean. Is this woman in Virginia younger than me?'

Lucinda tilted her head and studied the other woman.

'Probably not, Ms King. You're probably the same age. Then again, she might be a couple of years younger.'

'What's her name?'

Lucinda paused, considering whether or not it was wise to share this information. She quickly decided that what she might gain from the revelation exceeded any risk. 'Victoria Whitehead.'

Karen flapped a hand at her and laughed. 'Oh, you silly thing. That's not his girlfriend. That's his mama. And, my stars, girl, she's a lot older than me.'

'Ms King, Ms Whitehead said the same about you. And she certainly does think she's his girlfriend.'

Karen's smile fled again and she stared, blinking her eyes. 'None of this makes any sense. I wish Jeremy were here. I bet he could straighten this all out.'

'So, he's not here?'

'No, he's out somewhere running errands.'

'I would like to wait until he returns home.'

'Well, I'm not really sure when that would be, Ms – uh, Lieutenant – Pierce. He's quite a bit younger than me and still has his wild times with the boys, if you know what I mean? What in heaven's name do you want to talk to him about?'

'His fingerprint was found at the scene of a double homicide in Virginia.'

'That's absurd,' she said, rising to her feet. 'Could you please excuse me for a moment.'

Lucinda listened to Karen's footsteps as they walked to the second floor. She heard a door open and close. Then, she heard nothing. She strained to hear any other noises. At one point, she thought she heard the sound of distant voices but she wasn't sure if they were inside or outside of the house or if it was just her imagination.

Karen returned to the room, with a forced smile plastered on her face. 'I was just checking my datebook and, as I feared, I'm fixing to go to a luncheon meeting in just a little bit, so it's not going to be possible for you to wait for Jeremy here. So, if you'll excuse me . . .'

'You know, Ms King, I sure would feel a lot better if you'd let me walk through your home and make sure he's not here – not that I'm doubting your word. But I have to report back and . . .'

'Of course, don't say another word. I watch those TV

programs. I know how that is. You just roam around down here. I've got to pop upstairs for just a moment. When you finish down here, I'll show you around the second floor.'

Lucinda walked through the kitchen, family room, bathroom and home office, peering in closets, behind draperies and under large pieces of furniture. She slid out a couple of drawers but knew she was overstepping her bounds when she did.

She hoped to find a clue to Jason/Jeremy's whereabouts or something more about him but uncovered nothing of use. She wanted a DNA sample, too, but knew she'd yet to find adequate grounds for the locals to issue a search warrant – even if they were willing to bend the rules a bit in the name of inter-agency cooperation.

Something was hinky about Karen, this house, this situation, but Lucinda couldn't put a finger on what it was. As she started up the steps to the second floor, a door to the left flew open and Karen popped out of the room and fast-walked to the top of the stairs.

'Finished down there, Lieutenant?' she asked. 'Come on up, I'll give you the guided tour of this floor.'

Lucinda wanted to go to the left to the room Karen just exited, but her hostess diverted her in the opposite direction. 'Let's go to this end of the hall and work our way back.' In the master suite, Karen pointed out the features as if she were a real-estate agent trying to sell the home. She flung open the door to a walk-in closet, proclaiming the glories of its spaciousness and design.

Most of the area seemed occupied by women's clothing and accessories but, over to the side, one section of a pole held menswear. 'Are those Jeremy's things?' Lucinda asked.

'Certainly are, Lieutenant; I make no secret of the fact that we are sexually intimate. I suppose that makes me a "cougar". But I'm proud of it; pleased that, at my age, I can attract and keep a younger man.'

Lucinda stifled a groan, knowing better than to comment on that statement. Special Agent Jake Lovett flashed through her mind. *If he and I did get involved, would that make me a cougar? Or would I have to be older?* 'Could I look through his clothing to see if there's anything that might help my investigation?'

'Absolutely not, Lieutenant. That would be a gross violation of his privacy. That is, of course, unless you have a search warrant.' She stepped forward into Lucinda's space and looked straight into her good eye. She arched her eyebrows and with a smug voice added, 'You don't have one, do you?'

Damn. 'No, of course not, Ms King. Why, in heaven's name, would I want a search warrant?' Projecting a look of startled innocence on her scarred face was difficult, but Lucinda managed a close approximation.

'Well, then, come take a look at the en suite bath and then we'll go explore the guest bedrooms.'

Despite herself, Lucinda was impressed. The bath was almost as large as the living room in her apartment and at least twice as tasteful and expensive. Karen prattled on about the recent upgrades – the jacuzzi tub, the multi-head shower, the travertine tiles. The moment Karen turned her back to leave, Lucinda's hand thrust out and grabbed a man's electric razor and dropped it in her pocket. She held her breath, wondering what she'd say if Karen noticed. She exhaled a breath when the woman displayed no indication of awareness at all.

In the first guest room, Karen droned on about the family heirloom furnishings and led her into the attached bath. Out of view of the hallway, Lucinda thought she heard another footstep out there. She stuck her head out of the doorway but, seeing nothing and hearing no further noise, she blamed the sound on the creaks of an older home.

Lucinda followed Karen past the steps to the lower floor and into the second guest room. Her fingers involuntarily flew to the holster under her jacket as she tensed to enter the space where the possibility of an ambush seemed most likely.

Nothing untoward occurred and Lucinda relaxed. Back at the top of the stairs, Karen led the way, taking two steps down before turning to point out the chandelier in the foyer below. After that, the sequence of events grew muddled in Lucinda's mind. She saw Karen step to the side and plaster herself against the wall and felt two palms land on her shoulder blades – but she wasn't sure which happened first. Then, she felt the shove that knocked her off balance.

Instinctively, her fingers grabbed for Karen's leg but slid off with nothing more than a breath of skin contact as she tumbled down. She grabbed the railing and a spindle bent back an index finger, sending a jolt of pain up her arm and into her chest.

Suddenly, she was aware that she was sprawled face down

on the oak floor with an aching head, a throbbing finger and a nauseous feeling. *Did I lose consciousness?* She wasn't sure, one way or the other. She heard the jingle of her cell but couldn't figure out where her phone was. She was afraid to move – worried about further damaging her battered body and anxious about the reaction that would greet any attempt on her part to stand. She strained her ears, listening for any indication of what might happen next.

TWENTY-SEVEN

A dazed Lucinda placed her palms on the floor, braced herself for another attack and pushed up to a kneeling position. Above her, Karen flapped her arms like a demented chicken and said, 'Are you OK? Are you all right? I tried to stop your fall, but . . .'

'Ms King, cut the crap. I know I was pushed.'

'Pushed? Whatever do you mean? I didn't push you. You lost your balance, poor thing. I was in front of you, remember?'

'And you conveniently stepped out of the way, just in time, didn't you? No, I don't think you did the actual pushing, Ms King. But I suspect I know who did.'

'Oh, my, Lieutenant, you banged your head real hard a couple of times on the way down. I think you're disoriented, a bit addled. Maybe you have a concussion.'

Lucinda rose to her feet and stared down at Karen, wanting to cuff her and haul her in for questioning. Knowing this was not an option – and angered that it wasn't – she stepped past her and out on to the front porch. Pulling out her cell, she called the local police.

A patrol car showed up in minutes. The officer listened to her story, before questioning Karen King. Returning to Lucinda, he said, 'I'm sorry, Lieutenant. Unless you can give me more, there's nothing I can do here. You say you were pushed but not by the woman in this house. The only uninjured witness says you tripped, fell, banged your head and are confused.'

Lucinda clenched her teeth. 'Officer, I am a fellow member of law enforcement and I have been assaulted.'

'Yes, ma'am. I understand what you're saying and I really want to believe your version of events, but, ma'am, you did bang your head – I can see a lump rising above your left eye.'

Lucinda's cell chirped, interrupting their conversation. She pulled out her phone and turned around to talk. 'Pierce.'

'Lucinda, it's Ted. I've been trying to reach you but you didn't return my call. I was getting concerned. Are you OK?'

'Yeah. I was pushed down a flight of stairs by my suspect who is still at large. But no major damage, except to my pride. I can't seem to get local law enforcement to take me seriously.'

'When are you booked to fly back?'

'Tomorrow afternoon. Why?'

'I think you need to get to the airport and get back today – you're chasing the wrong suspect.'

'What do you mean – the wrong suspect?'

'We've just arrested Pamela Godfrey.'

'Arrested? You arrested Godfrey? This is my homicide – my double homicide – how dare you arrest anyone without talking to me first!'

'Whoa, Lucinda. We didn't arrest her for murder.'

'For what then?'

'We nabbed her for breaking and entry inside the Sterling home.'

'You're kidding?'

'Nope. Wouldn't joke about that, Lucinda.'

'Damn. I'll be there as soon as I can.' Lucinda disconnected and turned back to the officer but he was gone. She saw his patrol car down the street, turning the corner. 'Double damn,' she muttered. *Something doesn't feel right about Karen King or Pamela Godfrey or even Jason King aka whatever. Could Jason King and Pamela Godfrey be in on this together?*

TWENTY-EIGHT

As soon as Lucinda's flight landed, she was on the phone to Ted. 'Please tell me you still have Godfrey.'

'Have a nice flight?'

'Ted, don't mess with me.'

'Yes, Lucinda. We still have Pamela Godfrey. She'll probably get bailed out in the morning. But she hasn't been transferred over to the jail yet. We still have her in a holding cell here.'

'Put her in an interrogation room. I'll be there in twenty minutes.'

'She asked for her attorney when we first brought her in. She wouldn't talk until he got here and he wouldn't let her talk after he arrived. You want me to call him first?'

'No, let me Mirandize her first. She might do the same thing but then again, we could get lucky. And see if you can dig up any connection between Godfrey and Jason King.'

As she drove, Lucinda thought about that possible partnership and how the pieces of the puzzle might fit together. On the surface, it seemed unlikely. Jason preferred to pair up with older women to take advantage of them. Choosing Pamela as a victim didn't fit. Pamela was a user, too, targeting men in power. Jason didn't have any. *What did he have to offer her?*

Of course, a romantic connection had to be considered but Lucinda doubted either one of them was capable of truly loving someone to the point of putting the other's needs above their own. It was possible, though, that both put up a false front of love and affection to manipulate the other without realizing that it was a two-way street. They'd both have to be pretty good at the game but, reflecting on their other liaisons, Lucinda believed they were.

It could also be a partnership of convenience. Both could be well aware that they were using and being used in turn and not minding it. Both could be willing to be manipulated to some degree because they believed they'd get exactly what they wanted in the end.

However they were connected – if they were connected – the crime scene made more sense with both of them present in the Sterling home than it did with either one of them there alone. *But do crime scenes always need to make sense?* Lucinda wondered as she pulled into a space at the justice center parking lot.

She stopped first at the forensics lab where Beth Ann Coynes was working late again. Audrey Ringo's office was dark. 'Audrey still out?'

'Yes, but Dr Ringo called this afternoon and said she'd be in next week.'

'Did she give you any reason for her absence?'

'When I asked, she just said, "When you're a woman, life sucks."'

'Audrey said "life sucks"?'

'Yeah,' Beth Ann said with a laugh. 'Kind of took me aback, too – like a Sunday School teacher cussing out a class of third graders.'

'Well, I've got another little present for you,' Lucinda said as she handed her a paper bag.

'A heavy present,' Beth Ann said as she unfolded the top and looked inside. 'An electric razor? You want DNA?'

'Yeah, like yesterday.'

'No problem. I should find a lot of skin cells in there. You want a profile comparison?'

'Yes. With Freddy Sterling.'

'Freddy? Isn't he a little young to shave?'

'Yeah,' Lucinda said, laughing, 'but I'm thinking of possible paternity here. I'd like to know if the owner of the razor is Freddy's father.'

'We know Jeanine is Freddy's biological mother so that comparison will be relatively easy. I'll get right on it.'

'Tonight?' Lucinda asked, not believing her good fortune.

'Oh, yeah. A double homicide in an affluent neighborhood takes precedence over everything else.'

'No, what I meant was, it's late. Don't you need to go home?'

'I'm stuck here waiting for a process to complete on a sample in another case. Might as well work on this while I wait.'

'Thanks, Beth Ann. I appreciate it,' Lucinda said before leaving and going up to the third floor. She met Ted in an interior hallway and they both went into the observation room to watch Pamela Godfrey through the glass. She sat with her legs crossed, the raised foot jiggling up and down. She shifted legs and the opposite foot went into motion.

'She's been more agitated this time than she was earlier today,' Ted said. 'I've seen her get up and pace more than once in the last fifteen minutes and the scowl on her face continues to deepen.'

'Good. Let's see what she has to say for herself.' Lucinda walked out one door and into the other. 'Hello, Ms Godfrey. I'm Lieutenant Pierce. Remember me?'

'Of course I do, Lieutenant. Your face is not one anyone would easily forget.'

'You have the right to remain silent . . .'

'Don't go through that again,' Pamela interrupted. 'I've already done the Miranda thing and listening to that is pretty depressing. This whole thing is really stupid.'

'Before I can ask you about that statement, Ms Godfrey, I need to read you your rights.' Lucinda read the Miranda statement from the top and then asked, 'What do you mean, "stupid"?'

'The whole thing is stupid. It can be easily explained.'

'Please, be my guest.'

'I'm sorry. But on the advice of my attorney, I cannot talk to you unless he is present.'

'OK, fine, Ms Godfrey, but I imagine he'll just stop you from talking at all.'

'Just the same, I am invoking my right to counsel. If you want to talk, get Mr Prager in here first.'

'Your call,' Lucinda said, walking out of that room and joining Ted in the other.

He was already on the phone. When he hung up, he said, 'Prager's on his way. Not real happy about it. But he's coming.'

'Did you find anything tying Godfrey and King together?'

'Not yet. A cross-check of their histories, as we know them, has not put them in the same place at the same time until King arrived here. I made a few quick calls and no one who knows King seems to be aware of Godfrey and vice versa.'

'Except for our victims.'

'Yes, there is that,' Ted agreed.

'And that doesn't get us much of anywhere,' Lucinda sighed. She went to her office to check her messages and plan for her next confrontation with Godfrey. She tossed three messages from Dr Rambo Burns in the trash and set one from her brother Ricky by her phone to return later.

She was in mid thought when Ted stuck his head in the door and said, 'Prager's here.'

Lucinda walked down the hall to the interrogation room where Edwin Prager sat by his client's side. All the muscles in his face were tight and drawn, making him look irritated and irritable. Pamela Godfrey's shoulders were rounded and her hands, on the table's surface, clenched together so tightly that her knuckles and fingertips were white. She gave her lawyer a sidelong glance that spoke of a brewing disagreement between the people on that side of the table.

'Mr Prager, I believe we've met.'

'I'd say it was my pleasure, Lieutenant, but I don't like to lie,' Prager snapped.

'Not outside of the courtroom, anyway,' Lucinda said with a laugh.

Prager was not amused. 'Can we get down to business here?'

'Certainly, Mr Attorney,' Lucinda said then turned to Pamela. 'Ms Godfrey, when we spoke earlier, you said that this whole thing was "stupid". What did you mean by that?'

'Don't answer that question,' Prager ordered.

Lucinda stared at Pamela, who focused her gaze on her own hands. Lucinda continued, 'Surely, you can answer this, Ms Godfrey. You were apprehended inside the Sterling home. Do you acknowledge being there?'

'Yes,' she said, without looking up.

'Ms Godfrey,' Prager chastised, 'do not answer any questions without getting my approval first.'

Lucinda continued. 'Why did you break into the Sterling home?'

'I didn't . . .'

'Ms Godfrey! Please!' Prager interrupted.

'But I didn't. I have a . . .'

'Not another word, Ms Godfrey,' Prager pleaded as he laid his hand on his client's arm. 'Ms Godfrey, look at me.'

Pamela breathed deeply, making her shoulders rise and fall. Then she turned her face toward her lawyer. 'This is stupid.'

'You have what, Ms Godfrey?' Lucinda asked. 'A key? Do you have a key to the Sterling home?'

'Yes.'

'Pamela, please stop answering questions. Lieutenant, may I please have a moment alone with my client? And could you turn on a light in the other room so I know you're not listening in to our conversation.'

'Not big on trust, are you?' Lucinda rose and nodded to Ted on the other side of the glass. The room beyond lit up and Ted exited. Lucinda joined him in the hallway. 'A little trouble in paradise, I believe.'

'I noticed. It seems she thinks she can explain everything away if her attorney would only let her talk. And he seems to think that if she doesn't shut up she'll never get out of here.'

'Wonder who's going to win that battle?' Lucinda mused.

'Usually, the odds are in favor of the lawyer but with Godfrey in the equation, I'd have to put my bucks on her.'

The door opened and Prager said, 'OK, Lieutenant. You can come back in.'

'Ms Godfrey,' Lucinda began, 'you say this matter is "stupid". Does that mean you have a simple, harmless explanation for your presence in the Sterling home?'

'Don't answer that, Ms Godfrey,' Prager warned.

'Damn it, Edwin. It's not you who will spend the night in that nasty cell wearing nasty jail clothes. It's me. If I don't answer her questions, it is certain I'll spend a nasty night in the nasty jail. Me. Not you.'

'That's not the point, Ms Godfrey. Even if you answer all of her questions, you will, unfortunately, be spending the night in jail. I should be able to bond you out first thing in the morning.'

'That's not soon enough. I think I'll take my chance with the ugly cop.'

'Sorry, Lieutenant. That was uncalled for,' Prager said to Lucinda, then turned back to his client. 'Ms Godfrey, you are not helping yourself here. Just plead the fifth and let's call it a night. Tomorrow is another day.'

'Save me your platitudes, lawyer. As I said, you won't be the one in that snake pit all night. Yes, Lieutenant, I did have a good reason for being in that house and it had nothing to do with the murders.'

'Ms Godfrey . . .' Morgan cautioned.

'Shut up, Edwin. Lieutenant, we talked about my relationship with Jeanine. When I told you, you seemed quite surprised. And I don't think your reaction had anything to do with shock over lesbian intimacy. Am I correct on that?'

Lucinda sat in silence waiting for more.

Prager couldn't bear to remain quiet. 'Ms Godfrey, I must warn you . . .'

'Shut up,' Pamela said again. 'I believe I'm right about that, Lieutenant. And I believe your reaction to my revelation was surprise because you were unaware of our relationship.'

Pamela paused, waiting for an acknowledgement from Lucinda. When she got none, she continued. 'To me, that meant you hadn't confiscated the photographs or videotapes.'

'Photographs? Videotapes?'

'Of me and Jeanine making love. Parker shot them. You didn't find them, did you?'

'Perhaps not,' Lucinda said. 'Or perhaps we hadn't processed that evidence yet.'

'Whatever. Anyway, I assumed you hadn't taken them and I went in to get them. I was just trying to protect myself from a scandal. The snapshots and video have nothing to do with the murder. Nothing.'

'Maybe they don't. Maybe they do. That will be the prosecutor's decision.'

'No! You can't turn those over to the state,' Pamela shouted as she jumped to her feet.

'Please instruct your client to return to her seat, Mr Prager,' Lucinda asked.

Pamela sat back down and said, 'If you turn that evidence over to those guys, when you arrest someone, the prosecutor will have to release it as discovery to the defense attorney. Then that lawyer will introduce it at trial to raise reasonable doubt about his client's guilt. Don't you see? It's not in your best interests to do that.'

Lucinda stood. 'Someone will be arriving shortly to escort your client to the jail, Mr Prager.' She turned and headed for the door.

'Wait,' Pamela shouted. 'Are you familiar with Rodney Conners?'

Lucinda closed her eyes and cocked her head. 'The CEO of It Is?'

'Former CEO. Parker Sterling's Dodgebird swallowed up all the It Is clients and Rodney's business went belly up.'

Lucinda nodded. 'I was aware of that.'

'But did you know that he's still talking about revenge? I've overheard him, more than once in the last month, say that he would bring Parker Sterling down and pluck the feathers off Dodgebird's back.'

An honest tip? Or a diversionary tactic? 'Thank you, Ms Godfrey. The officers will be with you soon.'

'What, do you mean I'm going to jail? I explained myself. I gave up a viable suspect. And you're still sending me to jail? You can't do this.'

'Ms Godfrey, we will have to make some changes to your charging document. If it's true you had a key, then you can't be charged with breaking into the Sterling home. But, in order to enter, you had to break the police department's seal. It was a closed crime scene, Ms Godfrey. When you ignored the yellow tape, you broke the law.'

'You can't hold me overnight for that.'

'Oh, yes I can,' Lucinda said. The sound of Pamela's rants trailed Lucinda down the hall, making a smile dance on her lips.

TWENTY-NINE

A glass of wine, a book and bed were all Lucinda had on her mind as she pulled in to her apartment complex. She reminded herself that she couldn't forget to make a detour between the doorway and the bedroom to feed the cat. That brought another smile to her face – *as if Chester would ever let me forget.*

She stepped out of the elevator and looked down the hall toward her apartment. A rounded bundle lay on the floor right by her door. She tensed and reached for her gun. Holding it straight by her side with the muzzle aimed at the floor, Lucinda took cautious steps, ready to raise her weapon at the slightest provocation.

The unknown object moved. Lucinda's gun swung up as she shifted her body to shooting stance. It was a person. A small person. Lucinda lowered her gun and took two more steps forward. 'Charley? What the heck are you doing here?'

Charley sat up, looking startled and confused. Then she smiled and stretched. 'Hi, Lucy. I didn't think you were ever gonna get home.'

'Does your dad know you're here?'

'Nah. Daddy's in Iraq – you know, that Doctors Without Borders thing he does.'

'Yes, OK. So who's watching after you and Ruby?'

'Kara.'

'Does Kara know you're here?'

'No. She was asleep when I left.'

'Did you leave her a note?'

'She wouldn't read it, Lucy, she's asleep.'

'Is she staying with you and Ruby at your condo?'

'Yeah.'

'Let's go in and give her a call,' Lucinda said as she unlocked the door.

'I want to come in, Lucy, but I don't think you should call Kara. She's asleep.'

'If we don't call her, how are you going to get in your place?'

'Well, I have a key but I don't want to go home. I need to talk to you – oh, there's your kitty cat. Here, Chester,' Charley coaxed.

Chester was not interested. He stuck his tail straight up in the air and scampered back down the hall.

'Aww, Lucy, I wanted to pet him.'

'He'll be back. When he does, I'll let you feed him – then you won't be able to get rid of him.'

'Good.' Charley smiled and walked into the living room. 'See, I could sleep right here on your couch. And – oh, look, you can see the river, too.'

'Not as grand as the view from your balcony.'

'But it's still so pretty. Look at the moon shining on the river. The water sparkles like the moonbeams tickle.'

Lucinda stood in front of the window beside Charley. 'I never thought of it that way but you're right. Now, what's going on, girlfriend? Is there something wrong at home?'

'Nope. I just need to talk to you about something important.'

'So, what is it?'

'First, can I spend the night?'

'Charley . . .'

'Please, Lucy. If I have to worry about going back home tonight, I'm going to feel rushed and I'll booger it all up. And I've been practicing and I want to say it right. Please.'

'OK. But I'll need to call Kara . . .'

'She's asleep, Lucy.'

'I think it'd be a lot better to wake her up now than for her to get up in the morning and discover your empty bed. That would really scare her.'

'OK.' Charley sighed.

Lucinda punched in the numbers. A groggy Kara picked up the phone. 'Kara, this is Lieutenant Pierce. Everything's OK. I'm not sure how Charley managed to get here but I found her on my doorstep. I'll bring her back tomorrow morning before I go to work.'

After disconnecting the call, Lucinda said, 'OK, Charley, what's so important?'

'You.'

'Me?'

'Yes, Lucy, you didn't go in to see Rambo like you promised. And you didn't return any of his calls today.'

A flash of ire jolted Lucinda's body. 'I am sorry, Charley. Dr Burns should not have dragged you into this.'

'He didn't, Lucy. I kept calling him and calling him, every day. I've been asking him lots of questions about the surgery and stuff. You didn't show up for the appointment I made for you. This morning, he promised me he'd talk to you but I called him this afternoon and he said he called you but you wouldn't return his calls. Is that true, Lucy?'

Lucinda squirmed. 'Yeah, Charley, but you don't need to worry about it. Why don't we go feed Chester?'

'Lucy, I'm not a baby. You can't trick me like that. I do need to worry about you. You are my best friend. And you need to go to see Rambo so's he can explain everything. He can make you better.'

'It's really a lot more complicated than that.'

'No, it's not. It's simple. You're scared.'

'I am not scared, Charley.'

The young girl put her small hands on her hips, thrust out her chin and waggled her head as she said, 'Are, too.'

Lucinda's childish side was poised on the edge of the conversation, ready to inject 'Am not'. Instead, she accepted the fact that what Charley said was true. 'How'd you get so smart?'

'Well, my daddy's smart. And my momma was smart.'

Lucinda looked at the little girl closely – no signs of tears. It was the first time she could remember Charley mentioning her murdered mother without crying. She hoped that meant the worst of the pain had passed.

Charley continued, 'We're still not sure about Ruby, yet. Daddy says she shows a lot of promise. But I said I wasn't sure. I told him I worried I might have to take care of her all my life. Daddy just laughed at me. But Ruby is four years old and still sucks her thumb – mostly at night in her bed. It gives me bad dreams sometimes 'cause it makes me remember her sitting on the basement floor, next to my momma's body.' The tears swelled in Charley's eyes and spilled down her cheeks.

Lucinda dropped to her knees and enfolded the little girl in her arms. She kissed her on the forehead and said, 'I love you, Charley.'

'I love you, too, Lucy,' she sniffled.

Lucinda pulled back and placed her hands on Charley's arms. 'So, tell me. What do you want me to do?'

'I want you to go see Rambo – right away.'

'Charley, I'm in the middle of a difficult investigation.'

'What if Rambo could come in early in the morning and see you before you went to work? Would you go then?'

'Yes, Charley, but it's a doctor's office. They don't open that early.'

'We'll see,' Charley said as she punched numbers into the phone.

'The office is closed now, Charley.'

'I know. I'm calling Rambo's house.'

'It's a little too late for that, Charley.'

'Hi, Rambo. It's Charley,' she said into the phone and then paused. Lucinda could hear the rumblings of a voice on the other end but couldn't understand the words.

'I'm sorry I woke you up. But it's important.' Charley nodded her head and then continued. 'Yes, it is Lucy. She'll come in and see you tomorrow if you can get to the office early.' She stopped to listen again, then said, 'It's gotta be earlier than that.' She turned and flashed a smile at Lucinda. 'Thank you, Rambo, we'll see you tomorrow morning.'

Charley returned the receiver to its cradle and said, 'There. It's all settled. Seven o'clock tomorrow morning.'

Lucinda sighed. 'OK, but we'll have to leave early so I have time to drop you off at home.'

'No. I'm going with you.'

'There's no need for that. I can take you home first.'

Charley hung down her head and turned her eyes upward. 'I'm sorry, Lucy, but I have to tell you the truth. I don't want to make you feel bad. I trust you about almost everything in the whole wide world. But, Lucy, I don't trust you about this – I can't believe you'll tell me the truth.'

Lucinda knew Charley was right but that didn't make it any easier to hear.

THIRTY

D r Burns stood inside the glass door waiting for their arrival, sleep still whispering at him to return to bed, puffing up the bags under his eyes and putting a slump in his shoulders. He unlocked the door with a smile, let them in and locked it behind them. 'We need to go into the examination room first. I need to take a fresh look at your face and make sure I'm on the right track. Do you want Charley to wait in my office?'

Lucinda looked down at Charley's face – the message in her expression was clear: Don't you dare. 'That's OK, Dr Burns. She can come in with us.'

Lucinda sat down at the end of an examination table and the doctor asked her to close her eyes. He pulled the arm of a light fixture away from the wall and pointed the bright spot on to her face. She felt his breath on her skin as his fingers traced her cheeks and her lips. He placed his index finger beside her nose and pushed it to the left. Then he moved his digit to the other side, giving her nose a small shove in the opposite direction. He didn't say a word throughout the examination, just grunted from time to time.

Lucinda contemplated the odd noises he made, wondering if it were a doctor thing but then deciding no woman doctor would grunt like that – it had to be a man thing. Burns flipped off the light and swung it back to the wall. He folded his arms and looked at her for a moment. 'Lieutenant, I look at you and imagine a set of full, plump, kissable lips – not that I'd ever attempt to try them out.' He grinned. 'Ethical concerns would stand in my way, unfortunately. But I'd love for you to use a beautiful pair of lips to paste a kiss of gratitude on my cheek.'

'I haven't agreed to another procedure, Doctor.'

'No, you haven't,' the doctor said with a sigh. 'Come on, let's go down to my office, I've pulled together something to help explain it all to you.'

Burns pulled out a laptop and placed it on the desk facing the chairs occupied by Lucinda and Charley. He stood beside the computer and brought up a slide show. Lucinda cringed at the first image – the screen filled with the damaged side of her face while she still had an empty eye socket. 'Here is a photograph of you the first time you visited me. For starters, you have to understand the extreme difficulty of dealing with facial wounds. The skin on your face covers a complex muscle network. Scarring restricts the function of those muscles. Now, I know you are unhappy with the scars that resulted from the last lip reconstruction procedure – I am disappointed in them, too. But, if you recall, I never said that one operation would get your mouth back to its original shape.'

He pressed the enter key and brought up the next slide, a split-screen image of Lucinda before and after the first set of procedures. 'Now, it's easy to see the improvement from here to here,' he said, clicking again.

'The differences between these two pictures are more difficult to discern. There is a shot of you before the last procedure and here is a picture taken of you after that procedure. Look closely. The improvement is not so obvious, but it's there.'

Charley nodded and said, 'Yes, I see it.'

Lucinda grimaced – she saw nothing but the half-gargoyle face she loved to hate.

'Here's the problem,' the doctor explained. 'Working on your face is a lot like reconstruction after burns. Burned skin contracts, causing scars that affect not just the immediate area but other parts of the face. Similarly, the shotgun pellets scorched and shredded your skin as well as the underlying muscles.

Burns brought up an illustration of the muscles across a skull. 'The damage to your face ran deep. It is not unusual that the initial procedure, in any particular area of the face, does not produce satisfactory results. What I plan to do next is use z-plasty sutures to redirect the scars from the earlier surgery – both mine and the quickie repair job they did immediately after your accident – and that will help your face look more natural. Then we'll plump up your lips. After that, I want to focus on the damaged side of your nose and make it conform to the shape and size of that on the undamaged side. Next, we'll move on to the skin on your cheek, removing scars, smoothing it out. When I finish with you, Lieutenant, the application of a little make-up will be all you need to look flawless once again.'

'Dr Burns, please, one step at a time,' Lucinda said, holding up her hands as if pushing him away. 'I really don't care about flawless. I am just tired of scaring kids and capturing stares wherever I go.'

The doctor smiled. 'Of course, Lieutenant. We'll go one step at a time. Let's just schedule the next procedure.'

'I can't,' Lucinda said and earned herself a baleful look from both Burns and Charley.

'I mean, I can't set a date right now. I'm in the middle of an intense investigation. I can't just drop it.'

Burns and Charley ganged up on her, countering every argument she made. In the end, she bowed to the pressure from both fronts, lifted her right hand and swore to schedule a surgical procedure as soon as the Sterling homicide case was solved or turned cold.

The thought of the latter possibility sent a dagger of ice into Lucinda's mid-section. Two people demanded justice – the idea that she might not be able to deliver made her feel ill.

THIRTY-ONE

Leaving Charley at her family's condo, Lucinda entered the office shortly before eight that morning. Despite the hour, Ted was already elbow deep in work at his desk. 'In early today?' she asked, hoping he hadn't labored through the night in the office.

'Yeah, I had some stuff I wanted to take care of before I go visit Ellen,' Ted said.

The news of a visit to his wife pleased Lucinda but she wasn't sure what to say. If she reacted the wrong way, it could botch things up. Before she could think of the right words, Ted said, 'I'm trying, Lucinda.'

'I know, Ted. I am very happy that you're making the effort.'

'How much is enough?' he asked.

'You don't have to ask me that, Ted. You know the answer – help her find her way home. After you take care of her, you can look to your own future,' she said.

'Our future?'

'Ted, I told you, we are not going there. Not now.'

'When, Lucinda? I called my feelings "fantasies" in the courtroom for Ellen's sake. But you know it's more than that. When can we try to rebuild our relationship?'

'Maybe never, Ted,' she snapped and regretted it immediately. 'I'm sorry. You're trying, I owe you more patience. I just don't want to go there until Ellen's mental health problems are resolved.'

'What if they never are?'

'Ted, one day at a time. OK? Now, have you got anything new for me in the Sterling case?'

'Yeah, I contacted the Texas Rangers and the state criminal authorities in all the states between here and there. They're all willing to help. I sent photos and a description of our suspect, Jason King and all his known aliases. They'll alert all law enforcement in their jurisdictions to be on the lookout, pick him up if they find him and call us right away. Are you sure he's our doer? And do you think he acted alone?'

'The print under the toilet seat convinces me of his complicity in the murders. I can't say I'm certain but I'm pretty sure he didn't act alone. One body treated with scorn, the other with respect – two victims Jason King didn't know or didn't know very well – the contradiction doesn't make sense without another person on the crime scene.'

'Pamela Godfrey?'

'Maybe, but so far, no one's turned up a connection between her and Jason King. But he has to know someone in the area besides Freddy and his grandmother. We need to ferret out information about his associates to see if anyone else is a likely partner in this crime. Back to Godfrey – I'd like to see if she'd admit to knowing Jason King before her attorney bails her out this morning but, after last night, I'm sure she won't talk to me. Could you go see her and play the Pierce-is-a-miserable-bitch card and see if she'll open up to you?'

'You ever wonder why that card is so effective with other women when I play it, Lucinda?' Ted grinned.

'Shut up, Ted,' Lucinda said, laughing.

As Lucinda walked up the sidewalk to the Sterling home she tried to visualize the duo of Jason King and Pamela Godfrey as accomplices. *Could they watch from a car on the street, waiting for Freddy's departure?* Lucinda stood on the porch

with her back to the front entrance and scanned the neighborhood. *A few cars parked by the curb. They could do it and
not be noticed.*

*Or maybe their arrival after Freddy left for school was a
coincidence?* That word made her squirm as it always did.
She didn't like the concept of coincidence and was reluctant
to acknowledge it as a possibility. *If it were a coincidence
and they had gotten here before Freddy walked out this front
door, would we now have three victims instead of two?*

She turned and faced the door. *Pamela had a key – entry
would be easy. But what if it wasn't Pamela by his side?* She
dismissed that question as a distraction. She wanted to focus
on the possibility of King and Godfrey right now.

She stepped inside the house and closed her eyes, reviewing
her scenario. *King and Godfrey sat in the car and waited until
Freddy left. Then they went inside. Did they approach the
house as soon as the car drove off with the boy? Or did they
wait for the adults' routine to re-establish itself? Ten minutes?
Fifteen minutes? Does it matter?*

*Would they stand here just inside the door and listen for
any sounds of someone on the first floor before they went
upstairs? Could they hear the sound of running water in the
master bath from here?* Lucinda made a mental note to check
that out before she left.

She paused halfway up the stairs and closed her eyes again,
listening to the house, wondering if her suspects barreled up
at top speed or ascended with caution. The memory of her
tumble down the steps in Texas intruded in her thoughts. She
shook her head to chase it away.

She continued up to the second floor, entering a library with
three walls lined with shelves, broken only by long windows
looking out on the front lawn. Four comfy chairs – each with its
own ottoman and all flanked by a table with a reading lamp –
spread out, filling the space. To her left was the door to the master
suite. On the right a hallway led to three doors. The first appeared
to be a guest room, tastefully done but without any touch of
personal identity. The next door was a bathroom – not as spacious
as the master bath but still much larger than the one in her apartment. The third led to Freddy's room. *Would they go down this
hall first? Check out these rooms? It would be the smart thing
to do. Wouldn't want to leave open doors at their backs.*

After walking through those rooms, she entered the master bedroom and went to the bath where both victims died. According to ballistics, all the bullets came from the same gun. *One shooter? Probably. King or Godfrey?* She had a hard time imagining Godfrey pointing the gun at a human being and pulling the trigger. King, on the other hand, had demonstrated his lack of scruples all across the country. *King had to be the shooter.*

Did Godfrey watch while King butchered Parker Sterling's body? Or was she busy beside the bed, caring for the body of the woman she claimed to love? Lucinda decided Godfrey might be cold enough to not give a damn about what King did to a dead body but thought the woman was probably too squeamish to watch it happen. *That puts her right here. In this spot.* Lucinda listened, imagining Pamela hearing the roar of the chainsaw and the crunch of bone, inhaling the iron-rich tang of fresh blood in the air.

Lucinda could see it, accept it as a possibility. Nonetheless, something about the scenario seemed off, as if a piece of the puzzle had been forced into an interlock that was wrong. She shook her head and returned to the bathroom where she turned on the shower and went downstairs to listen. She discovered that although she couldn't hear the actual sound of water running in the master bath, she could easily discern the quiet rush of it as it coursed through the pipes in the house.

Returning to the master suite, she turned off the water and began looking for photographs and videotapes. In her mind, she visualized a clunky rectangle of plastic designed to shove into the mouth of a VCR player and snapshot-sized photographs printed on glossy paper. She assumed that none of this evidence would be in a family area of the home – they wouldn't want Freddy to stumble across them.

She stepped into the walk-in closet. Although the stills could be slid into a pocket or tucked inside an envelope, she searched, at first, in places where something the size of a video cassette could hide. *But I could be looking for a DVD.* With that thought, she moved to smaller hiding places, sticking her hands in any pockets she found on shirts, pants or jackets. She retrieved near-empty packs of mints, ticket stubs and lint. *Jeez, how many pockets can two people own?* She felt overwhelmed by the size of their wardrobe.

This realization strained her focus, so she shoved it away and continued on, pocket to pocket. When her fingers brushed against small, hard objects in one of Parker's sports coats, she first thought they were just more pieces of life's debris archived away until the next time the garment was worn.

Pulling her hand out, she spread open her fingers and looked into her palm. *Memory chips?* For a moment, the relevance of this find eluded her – then it hit her. *Duh, Lucinda! Welcome to the digital world. Of course, the still images and the video would be stored on removable chips, easily inserted back into the device to record new input or into a computer for easy viewing. Gotcha, Godfrey!*

THIRTY-TWO

Before Lucinda answered her ringing cellphone, she looked down at the read-out on the screen. *Damn. I forgot to call Ricky.* 'Hey, little brother, sorry I didn't return your call. I really meant to but . . .'

'That's OK. I called back because it was important.'

'What's up, Ricky? Is Connie giving you more grief? Or is it our sweet sister?'

'I sure haven't heard anyone call Maggie "sweet" in a decade or two,' he said with a laugh.

'And it will probably be a couple more before you hear it again.'

'Listen, Lucinda, I've got more bad news.'

'What kind of bad news?'

'Family obligation kind of bad news.'

'Did someone else die?' Lucinda laughed.

'Yeah.'

'What? I was just joking.'

'Well, it's Aunt Connie . . .'

'Aunt Connie? She didn't seem to be that distressed over Uncle Hank's death.'

'That wasn't it. In fact, she was the same old bitter self she was when Hank was still alive – she just didn't have him to kick around any longer. She was coming down the front steps of the church, looking back over her shoulder, scolding the minister for something or another, and she slipped. When she fell, she broke her hip.'

'You're kidding?'

'Wish I was. Man, was she in pain. She bellowed so loud, everyone rushed out of the church – shoot, you probably could have heard her halfway across the county. Anyway, we got her to the hospital. Once they got enough drugs in her to make her comfortable she got all weepy about Uncle Hank not being there to take care of her. Then she got to feeling a bit too good and started in on me for not being there to help her down the steps. Same old Connie, as much vinegar as sauer-kraut. But she was acting like herself so I thought she'd be fine.

'She had surgery the next morning and the doctor said it went well – it was a successful procedure. And she looked good – I mean, for someone who's just come out of the oper-ating room. I wasn't worried about her the next morning, so I took care of my chores before I came into the hospital. But when I got there she was gone.'

'What happened?'

'Doctor said it was an embolism. Since it was the hip on her good leg that broke, they couldn't get her up and walking around right away – doc said that might have prevented her from throwing a clot. But they couldn't, she did and it's over.'

Lucinda felt a twinge of guilt for not making peace with her Aunt Connie the last time she saw her. *Another weight I'll carry on my back for the rest of my life – Connie wasn't the nicest person in the world but she didn't deserve to die.* 'I don't know what to say, Ricky.'

'Nothing much to say, Lucinda. I was hoping you might come on up for the funeral – it's the day after tomorrow.'

'I'll be there, Ricky,' she said and ended the call. *Aren't I the lucky one? Two funerals in two days. And I'll face hostility at both.*

Ted settled in an attorney conference room awaiting the arrival of Pamela Godfrey. She walked up to the opposite side of the table and settled into a chair. At Ted's nod, the guard stepped out into the hall.

Pamela looked haggard, as if she hadn't slept at all the

night before. 'Listen, Sergeant, I don't know what you want, but I want to be real clear. I am here for one reason and one reason only: I'd agree to talk to anyone to get out of that damned cell. I can't believe you all kept me in here overnight. It's outrageous. It's a travesty.'

'It's Lieutenant Pierce, I'm afraid.'

'What a bitch!'

'You won't get an argument from me. She's a real hardass to work with, too.'

Pamela wiggled in her seat, straightening her posture, and brought a hand up to pat at her hair. 'What can I do for you this morning, Sergeant?' she said with a smile.

Ted couldn't believe it had been *that* easy. 'I was wonderin' – do you know a guy named Jason King?'

Pamela's brow furrowed. 'You know, the name sounds familiar but . . .'

Ted slid out a photograph. 'Here, look at this. Does he look familiar?'

She peered down at the image. 'That's Jason King?'

'Yes, it is.'

She shook her head. 'Can't say I recall ever seeing him. But the name – it sounds so familiar.'

'Concentrate – think back. Where did you hear the name? See it written?'

Pamela lowered her head, shook it and looked up. 'It's not coming to me at all.'

'Was it recently?'

'I think so.'

'Who have you talked to in the last week or so? Who might have mentioned the name?'

She shook her head again and then gasped. 'It was Jeanine. She mentioned him. She said she only met him once but she despised him. He's her mother's boyfriend. He's the reason why she cut off her mother. And she was feeling guilty about it, too. But she didn't see what else she could do. She didn't want Freddy exposed to him or his weird ideas. She said her mother believed every word he said but he was just making it all up to take advantage of her.'

'Making what up?'

'Something about Parker being involved in some occult nonsense – it was pretty stupid. But she was concerned because apparently her mother and this Jason King guy had convinced Freddy that his father was evil.'

Leaving the Sterling home, Lucinda went straight to the lab to see if Beth Ann Coynes had performed any miracles. As she stepped through the doors, her cellphone rang. She looked at the number and answered with a smile. 'Hello, Beth Ann.'

'Lieutenant, I've got something for you.'

'And I for you; look down the hall.'

Beth Ann's head popped out of a doorway. She laughed and disconnected. 'I've got results for you right in here.'

Lucinda joined the lab tech in front of a computer monitor. 'Look at this,' Beth Ann said. 'Lots of similarities in the profiles of Freddy and the sample you gave me. I'd say they are related.'

'Do I hear a "but" in there?'

'Yes, you do, Lieutenant. Since we know that Jeanine is Freddy's mom, I can tell you with absolute certainty that this guy is not his biological father.'

'Can you tell anything else about the relationship?'

'I'll run a Y-STR profile but it would help if I had additional samples from other males in their family. Any chance of that?'

'I'll prioritize the report on William Blessing with the research department. We think he is the sample's father.'

'If I know a bit more about him, I might be able to find a colleague with access to the DNA and pull the right strings to speed up getting a profile or sample. Now, c'mon, you gotta have a name for that "sample" – after all, you turned in his razor.'

'Yes, but you don't want to know,' Lucinda said.

'Where did you get that razor?' Beth Ann pressed.

'You don't want to know.'

'Oh, so I guess that makes me an accomplice to your nefarious deeds.'

'I'm sorry. I forgot that, with Audrey out of the office, it all falls on your shoulders.'

Beth Ann laughed. 'Not hardly. If I get caught, I'll plead ignorance. I'll just tell Dr Ringo, "That Lieutenant Pierce tricked me." Trust me, she won't doubt it for a minute.'

'Yeah, well, so it goes,' Lucinda said and walked away.

'Hey, anytime, Lieutenant. I'll be back with you soon as I have anything.'

Lucinda raised her hand and waved it without looking back.

Sometimes Lucinda reveled in her image as the tough, difficult scourge of small-minded and stiff-necked people everywhere. But now, with the rawness of her recent family encounter still fresh in her mind, it rubbed old wounds raw. She felt as if everyone imposed their values, agendas and perspectives on her, assuming that their motivations were her own. She tried to shrug it off but this morning, the judgment of others hung round her neck like a dead and bloodied albatross.

She stopped by the research department and got the good news that the folks there had read her mind – a report on William Blessing was in the process of compilation and she'd find it in her email box soon. She picked up the supplies she needed to help Charley with her science project and returned to her desk. Ted dropped by and briefed her on the conversation he'd had with Pamela. 'She fell for the nasty-you bit with ease,' Ted said, laughing.

'That's good but, Jeez, did you get the feeling she was telling you the truth and not playing out a role herself?'

'Yeah, I did. In fact, I find it really hard to believe she had anything to do with the murders.'

'Aw, Ted. You're just a sucker for a pretty face.'

'C'mon, Lucinda, that's not fair.'

'Chill, Ted, I was just jerking your chain,' she said, knowing that she was more serious about what she said than Ted would ever know. She turned to her computer, opened her email window and was rewarded with the familiar ping that heralded incoming messages.

She opened the attachment to the email from the research department and started reading. William Blessing was a biochemist and geneticist with doctorates in both fields as well as an MBA in business administration. Even his critics praised him as a visionary and a genius but took issue with his stance on genetic engineering, calling him a Nazi. Unlike those dreamers of a master race, he did not place emphasis on ethnic origins but, instead, he advocated intelligence as the indicator of suitability for survival. He advocated the sterilization of all who tested below normal and promoted the increased breeding of those with high or genius level IQs.

Despite his philosophical shortcomings, he was universally praised as a pioneer in artificial insemination. He founded the still successful company IQ Genetics, a sperm bank that specialized in cognitively superior donors. In order to make a deposit, a candidate had to demonstrate the ability consistently to score at 140 or above in intelligence testing.

Lucinda already found the man distasteful – an arrogant narcissist, at the least, more likely a dangerous sociopath who would enjoy toying with those whom he deemed inferior. She scanned through a list of awards and other professional aspects of his life and then slowed as she reached the personal details.

He was in his forties before he married Viola Kidd. They had one child, John Blessing. William walked out on his wife and son, cutting off all contact with them, but he never filed for a divorce. Viola never pursued the dissolution of her marriage either nor did she demand the child support she deserved. However, she did revert to using her maiden name and had her son's name legally changed to John Kidd. Lucinda swallowed hard. The initials were too much of a coincidence. Jason King had to be John Kidd.

William Blessing suffered a debilitating stroke in 2003, lingering on – attached to a ventilator – for five months before he died. His widow committed suicide in 2004. His son's whereabouts were unknown.

Lucinda forwarded the email to Beth Ann, picked up her phone and called down to research. 'Pierce here. Thanks for the great report. I really appreciate it – please express my gratitude to everyone who helped pull it all together. Beth Ann Coynes down in forensics is going to attempt to find Blessing's DNA but it wouldn't hurt if you guys were searching for a profile in case she comes up empty-handed.'

Lucinda felt as if she were driving blind through a blizzard. No matter how she steered, she collided with obstacles that slowed her progress and she couldn't seem to recognize the truth until she saw it fading in her rear-view mirror.

THIRTY-THREE

Lucinda used her lunch hour to visit Charley Spencer. The young girl bounced up and down with excitement from the moment she opened the door. She didn't settle until Lucinda said, 'Come on, Charley. I know you're excited but if you can't calm down and pay attention, it would be a waste of time for me to show you what to do.'

Charley stiffened her body, arms at her sides. 'Yes, ma'am. I'm good.'

'Yes, you are, Charley,' Lucinda said, smiling as she noticed that Charley's movements had slowed but a quiver of antici-pation made her vibrate in place.

'First thing you need to do is take fingerprints of everyone in your home – Ruby will be the hardest because she won't understand why you need to take it slow and easy. But if you go too fast, you'll smudge the prints.' Lucinda inked each of Charley's fingers and rolled them on the fingerprint card. 'Now, let me show you an alternative that will work if you don't have the right equipment.'

Lucinda picked up a pencil and scribbled a dense rectangle on a piece of white paper. 'Give me your index finger,' she said and pressed Charley's digit into the lead-covered spot, rolling it from side to side. 'OK, hold it straight up.' Lucinda ripped off a piece of transparent tape and carefully placed it on the little girl's finger. She lifted it off and attached it firmly to a blank spot on the paper. 'See – your fingerprint.'

'Wow! But it's not as good as the ones with ink.'

'No, but it'll do in a pinch.'

Looking very solemn, Charley said, 'Like a fingerprint emergency?'

Lucinda stopped the laugh that struggled to escape and answered in a serious tone, 'Yes, you never know when that might happen.'

Charley nodded her agreement and Lucinda wondered just what Charley's imagination had set free to frolic in her head.

'Now, I need to demonstrate how you recover fingerprints.

Let's use the surface of your door right by the door knob. There should be scads of prints there. The trick will be finding ones that aren't smudged or overlapped.'

Lucinda crouched down, brushed on the powder and peered at it with a magnifying glass. She let Charley look through it as she pointed out the print she wanted to lift. She went through the procedure with care, explaining every step. She laid the tape on a recovery card and held it up for Charley to see.

'OK, supposin' I had an emergency and didn't have all this good stuff, is there an in-a-pinch way for this, too?' Charley asked.

'Sure. All you need is a little paintbrush – like you'd use for doing watercolors – a tin of cocoa, Scotch tape and a thick piece of paper like an index card – but you've got to use the side without the lines.'

'Then, when you're done, you can lick the mess away – mmmmm,' Charley said.

Lucinda tried not to choke at that thought. 'Don't lick the fingerprint powder, Charley, it tastes nasty.'

'How do you know? Did you taste it?'

'Well, no,' Lucinda admitted. 'But look at it. It looks kind of nasty, doesn't it?'

'Looks like powdered licorice. Think it tastes like licorice?'

'Charley, even if it does, I don't like licorice.'

'I do, can I taste it?'

'No!' Lucinda said but suspected that she wouldn't get to her car before Charley did just that. 'I gotta run, sweetie. Call me if you have any problems.'

'Where ya goin'?'

'I have to go see Ms Whitehead and her grandson Freddy.'

'Who's Freddy?'

'He's a boy who lost his mom. He's going to her funeral tomorrow.'

'Was she murdered, too?'

'Yes, honey.'

'Well, I'll go with you and talk to him. I've been there and done that.'

A bittersweet lump jammed in the back of Lucinda's throat. She choked on it as she responded. 'That is sweet of you, Charley. But I don't really want you going over there and getting caught up in the middle of my investigation. Everything is a real muddle right now. When we have more answers, then I'll make sure you and Freddy get a chance to talk.'

'Will that be soon?'

'I hope so, Charley. But right now, I'm having trouble finding the answers to all the questions.'

'Oh, you'll figure it out, Lucy.'

Charley's faith in her abilities touched Lucinda. *Dear Lord, please let me live up to her expectations – or at least, get close.*

Victoria Whitehead jerked the front door halfway open and stood in the gap. 'Mercy, Lieutenant! You can't give a moment's peace to a grieving mother, can you?'

'I'm sorry to intrude, Ms Whitehead. But I have some important new information about Jason King that I think you need to know.'

'My daughter's funeral is tomorrow, Lieutenant,' she said, stretching her arm across to the far frame of the door, blocking Lucinda's entrance.

Lucinda sighed but didn't say a word.

For thirty seconds, Victoria didn't budge. Then she broke down, dropping her arm in defeat. 'Very well, Lieutenant, if you insist.'

Victoria slipped into her familiar southern belle pose on the sofa beneath the front window as Lucinda slid into a chair facing her. Victoria spoke first. 'Out with it, Lieutenant. What is so important that it couldn't wait until after my daughter's funeral?'

'I just got back from Texas.'

Victoria blinked her eyes much faster than normal. 'Really? And did you speak with Jason?'

'No, ma'am, but I did spend time with Karen King. In fact, she gave me a complete tour of her home.'

'In her wheelchair?'

'No, she was walking,' Lucinda said.

'That is a miracle. What wonderful news. I wonder why Jason didn't call and tell me about that.'

'As a matter of fact, Ms Whitehead, Karen King is a robust, vital woman of your age with no outward signs of any illness at all.'

'Oh, yes. She would put a front on for you. She's a very brave woman. I hope you didn't distress her. You could cause her a serious setback if you did.'

'Ms Whitehead, I believe that you believe what Jason told you about Karen King but it simply isn't true. Karen is not ill or bedridden. In fact, she's not even Jason's mother. She's his lover and is quite proud of the fact that she can keep up with the sexual demands of a younger man.'

Victoria paled and covered her distress with bluster. 'Her boyfriend is none of my concern. My only interest is in her son.'

'That's just it, Ms Whitehead, she does not have a son. The man you call Jason King is Karen King's lover – only she knows him as Jeremy Kneipper.'

'That explains it then. You're confused. It's two people. That Jeremy person is her lover, Jason is her son.'

Lucinda wanted to jump up and shake her. Instead she shut her eyelids through one deep inhale and exhale. 'As I said, Karen King denies that she has a son.'

'That's what she told you. Mothers are protective, Lieutenant. You don't have any children, do you?'

'No, Ms Whitehead, I do not.'

'See. You just don't understand how it is with mothers. We will lie, cheat, do almost anything to protect our children. Maybe she just didn't trust you. Maybe she didn't like your looks – that would be easy to understand, wouldn't it?'

Lucinda wanted to wipe the smug look off of Victoria's face. It was obvious that she was very pleased with herself for hitting the mark with her allusion to Lucinda's facial deformity but the detective refused to give her the satisfaction of reacting to her nastiness. 'And when did you last speak with Jason?'

'I told you. I kissed him goodbye before he left here to go to Texas,' Victoria said and a soft blush rose from her neck-line to her face.

'Are you telling me you have not spoken to him since then?'

Two bright red spots bloomed on Victoria's cheeks. 'That is what I said, Lieutenant. Are you questioning my veracity?'

'You're not a very good liar, Ms Whitehead.'

'How dare you?'

'I know you've spoken to Jason. More than once, actually.'

'You know nothing of the sort.'

'Even if I hadn't known, I would know now. The blush on your face betrays your dishonesty, Ms Whitehead. Now, please tell me about your conversations with Jason in the last couple of days.'

'You are a horrid woman! My face is flushed because I am under so much stress. You come in here, interrupting my grief, and you expect me to act as if nothing is amiss. What's wrong with you?' Victoria shot to her feet and raised her chin high. 'I am distraught, Lieutenant. My daughter has been murdered. And you sit here badgering a poor old woman instead of doing your job. Don't you have a single shred of human decency? You should be ashamed.' Victoria raised her arm and, pointing her finger towards the front door, shouted, 'Leave my home, right now. And please don't return here again. And in the name of common decency, don't show your ugly face at my daughter's service.'

Lucinda unfolded her legs and, with great deliberation, rose from the chair. Taking two steps in Victoria's direction she looked down at the woman. 'You can rest assured that I will be attending the funeral tomorrow. With or without your help, I will find the truth. You are right, though. Shame does hang heavy in this room – but it doesn't rest on my shoulders.'

In four long strides, Lucinda was out on the porch. Victoria stood in the open doorway staring at her with enough ill will in her gaze to curdle a fresh-from-the-udder stream of cream.

THIRTY-FOUR

Lucinda stood against the back wall of the sanctuary observing the crowd in attendance at Jeanine Sterling's funeral. She strongly doubted that Jason King would show up here today. *He has to know we're on to him by now.* However, she suspected his accomplice did not feel as vulnerable. She scanned through the audience looking for any reaction that didn't appear appropriate.

When the service ended, she stood a short distance from the double doors, watching the mourners depart. She saw nothing out of the ordinary until she spotted a woman who hung back from the crowd. Her face was covered by an old-fashioned widow's veil. She seemed determined to cling to her anonymity. To Lucinda, that was a bright red flag.

The woman exited and Lucinda followed. As she emerged

into the sunshine, the woman bowed her head and veered over to the far side of the broad concrete stairs. She fast-walked to a car and Lucinda went to her own vehicle, ready to move as soon as she knew the course of the other woman.

When Lucinda saw her pull into the procession line, she drove over and eased into place, three cars behind her. Lucinda knew that, at any point, the woman could turn off in a different direction. If she did, Lucinda would have to make a decision and she knew whatever choice she made, it could be regrettably wrong.

Fortunately, the woman crawled with the others into the cemetery. Lucinda parked near her and kept her in her sights as she walked in the direction of the plot. Again, the woman hung back, keeping her distance from the others. Lucinda leaned against a large oak tree just ten yards away.

The hum of the minister's voice at the graveside reached them at this distance but his words were not discernible. Still, the woman repeatedly reached under her veil to dab her eyes with a tissue as if moved by his speech.

The crowd dispersed, migrating back to the cars. The funeral director escorted Victoria and Freddy back to the limousine. Freddy spotted Lucinda and flashed a woeful smile. Lucinda put a finger to her lips and he signaled his understanding with a thumbs-up gesture.

The mystery woman remained rooted in place, her head turned slightly in the direction of the departing funeral home vehicle. When it pulled away, she took a few tentative steps forward. She paused, looked around and then walked with purpose to stand beside the gaping hole of the grave. Lucinda approached her, hearing the sound of quiet sobs as she drew close.

'Excuse me,' Lucinda said.

The woman's head jerked in her direction and she took a step backward.

'I'm sorry,' Lucinda said. 'I didn't mean to startle you.'

'I thought everyone had left,' the woman said, taking another step back.

'Pretty much. I stayed because I wanted to talk to you.'

'I have nothing to say.'

'Ma'am, I just . . .'

'Please, I have no desire to speak to the media.'

Lucinda slid her identification out of her pocket, flipped it open and said, 'I'm not the press. I am a homicide detective.'

'Oh dear, I guess you know who I am, then?'

'Actually, I don't,' Lucinda said. 'But I would like to know.'

The woman turned her face to the ground and stood silently for a full minute. Then she raised her head and said, 'I am Susan Livingston.'

The name was meaningless to Lucinda. She pondered its significance as she waited for the woman to continue.

'Susan Pippin Livingston – Jeanine's older sister.'

Lucinda was disappointed that she hadn't taken that logical leap on her own. 'I'm delighted to meet you, Ms Livingston. All I knew about you was your first name and the little bit of information I was able to pry from your mother.'

'Oh, I'm so sure *that* was complimentary.'

'Let's put it this way, Ms Whitehead does not score high on my credibility scale.'

'Thank you for that,' Susan said. She scanned the grounds, pulled out a hatpin and lifted the veiled covering off of her head. 'I didn't want my mother to recognize me. I haven't talked to her in years, and I certainly didn't want to talk to her now. I couldn't have borne it today.'

'Could we sit and talk a bit, Ms Livingston?'

'Is there any place nearby we could grab a cup of coffee in a quiet corner? I'm definitely in need of a little caffeine. And, please, call me Susan.'

Lucinda smiled. 'Certainly, Susan, there's a funky little coffee shop just a couple of blocks away. You can follow me there.'

Lucinda led Susan to an older bungalow, with a broad front porch, converted to commercial use. Inside, a series of small tables with chairs huddled in the center of the room. The perimeter of the room was occupied by clusters of conversation areas – groupings of overstuffed sofas and chairs around coffee tables piled high with tattered magazines and battered paperbacks.

The women placed their orders and took their mugs to a far corner. Susan eased into a love-seat covered by a worn, ancient throw – tufts of cotton poked through the fabric of the uncovered arms. Lucinda settled into a winged, high-back upholstered chair positioned at a right angle to Susan.

Susan took a sip of coffee and said, 'How can I help you?'

'I'm hoping you can shed some light on the darkest corners of my investigation. Some things simply make no sense to me.'

'I certainly will do my best.'

Lucinda repeated Victoria Whitehead's story about Parker
Sterling selling his soul to gain immortality, her belief in
Parker's culpability in Jeanine's murder and her claims that
her boyfriend was Freddy's half-brother.'

'That sounds like my mother, I'm afraid. Truly off the wall,
as usual. She is a sucker for anything occult and willing to
embrace the most bizarre conspiracy theories – she's always
been that way. I don't believe, though, that she made it all
up. I'd bet the boyfriend fed her this line and she took every
word as the gospel truth.'

'Quite possible,' Lucinda said. She described the strange
genealogy charts recovered during the search of Victoria's
home. 'Does that make any sense to you?'

'I'd guess that William Blessing might be Freddy's sperm donor.'

'Excuse me,' Lucinda said as the sharp click of a perfect
fit echoed in the back of her mind.

'Jeanine couldn't get pregnant. She and Parker went to a
fertility clinic for testing. It seems it was all Parker's problem.
He had an older brother who was autistic. His parents blamed
childhood immunizations for their first son's condition and,
as a result, refused to get shots for Parker. In high school,
Parker came down with the mumps and the doctors believed
that is what made him sterile.

'Jeanine and Parker still wanted a baby so they decided to
attempt artificial insemination. But Jeanine didn't want just
any biological father for her child so she ferreted out a sperm
bank specializing in donors of better than average intellect
and flew to California for the procedure. I told her that was
a bit over the top. But who pays attention to their big sister,'
she said, ending with a laugh.

'IQ Genetics?' Lucinda asked.

'That could have been the name,' Susan said, 'but it was
so long ago, I simply don't remember one way or the other.'

Distracted by her own train of thought, Lucinda asked Susan
a few perfunctory questions about Jeanine, expressed sympathy
for her loss and then excused herself with the promise that
she would call her when she had any new developments.

Susan provided important information that answered a lot
of questions. But those answers spawned more questions.
Lucinda zoomed back to the office. She had work to do.

*   *   *

Even without DNA confirmation, Lucinda felt certain that William Blessing, founder of IQ Genetics, was a donor to his own sperm bank. In all likelihood, there was truth in the genealogy papers – no direct interaction with the women on those pages, but a biological bond with their children, just the same.

Lucinda ran down the list of Jason King's victims. She couldn't reach them all but with every successful contact, she received the same response. Each one of them had used the services of IQ Genetics.

She placed her next call to the company. She slogged through a number of people before she reached someone who actually had answers – but at that point, she hit a brick wall.

'I am sorry, Lieutenant. We cannot divulge any information about our clients – it's all confidential.'

'What would you say if I told you someone else has detailed information about one of your sperm donors and about the women who withdrew his deposits from your bank?' Lucinda cringed at her own language but couldn't think of a less crude way to say it.

'It is simply not possible that anyone received that information from us.'

'What if I told you that the person with this information is probably the biological son of the founder of your company.'

'That, Lieutenant, would put it in the far reaches of the possibility scale. We certainly wouldn't violate our founder's privacy. We do have an open-identity program. That allows a child who reaches the age of eighteen to submit a request to receive information about the donor's identity. We honor all those requests; however, that is the only information we provide. We reveal nothing about any other children from the same donor.'

'Listen. I am investigating a homicide. Outside of that context, I do not care about who fathered whom.'

'I empathize, Lieutenant. And I wish I were at liberty to help you. I would suggest that you contact any suspected progeny and convince them to file a request for information. That would be the only appropriate way to obtain the data you want.'

'How long does that take?'

'We respond to all requests within ninety days.'

'Oh, Jeez!' Lucinda exclaimed.

'I caution you not to attempt to short-circuit this process,

Lieutenant. I know you can get a court order rather easily. But we have ethical principles to uphold. And we have an attorney who will block your every move claiming medical privilege. You may win in the end but, trust me, he will stall you for far longer than three months and, in the interim, we may need to freeze our records and delay our responses to the requests from offspring.'

Lucinda felt like telling him what he could do with all that sperm in his care but stopped herself. She said, 'Thank you,' between clenched teeth and hung up the phone. She had no proof for her theory but she knew she was right. Still, even with that knowledge, Jason King's motivation remained veiled in mystery.

THIRTY-FIVE

C hewing over her theory, Lucinda thought she spotted a flaw. *Is it really possible for one sperm donor to have children decades apart?* She logged on to the Internet seeking answers. As she browsed, she jotted down notes.

Fifty to eighty per cent of sperm die in the freezing process.
The sperm that perish do so within the first forty-eight hours of freezing. Very little attrition after that.
Frozen sperm can be stored for as long as fifty years without additional sperm deterioration.

Now that Lucinda knew her theory was possible, she couldn't find the answer to the big question of 'why' without more information. She had to find someone who knew Jason King's mother. *No*, she corrected herself, *John Kidd's mother*. She searched the Internet for Viola Kidd but found nothing of any use. She pulled out her phone and sent a text message to research requesting the information. At this late hour, she knew that she probably wouldn't hear back from them until the next day when she was heading to Charlottesville for her Aunt Connie's funeral.

*   *   *

Victoria Whitehead stood at the bottom of the stairs and shouted up to the second floor, 'Frederick, dinner is ready.' She returned to the kitchen, making several trips between there and the dining room, placing fresh salads, water goblets and a steaming casserole on the table.

Her grandson, however, had still not come downstairs. She hollered up again: 'Frederick, did you hear me?' Getting no response, she climbed up to his bedroom. On his bed, lay a piece of paper. She unfolded it and read: 'If I go down, I'm taking you with me.'

Victoria threw her hand in front of her mouth and gasped. *No. No. It can't be true.* She raced through the four rooms on that floor, shouting her grandson's name. She hurried down the steps, stumbling once but grabbing the railing in time to prevent a fall. She ran from room to room on the first floor. 'Frederick. Frederick. Please answer me, Frederick.'

She searched the basement, looking behind the washer and dryer, under the stairs, between the wall and the furnace. No Frederick. She trembled on the edge of panic. Back on the main floor, she picked up the telephone receiver, moved her finger towards the nine button and froze. *Should I call nine one one or not? What if this is just a test?* She pressed a finger down to disconnect the call. Despite everything, she did not want to lose Jason.

She returned the receiver to the cradle and took two steps toward the dining room. When the phone rang, she staggered and nearly fell again. She picked up the call but said nothing.

'Victoria?' the voice said on the other end.

'Jason! Do you know where Frederick is?'

'Of course I do. He's with me.'

'Bring him home. Bring him home now,' she said, her attempts to sound firm foiled by the quaver in her voice.

'I'm keeping the boy until my demands are met. Go ahead – contact the cops. You'll need their help to get what I want,' he said, then slammed down the phone.

Victoria's breath came in short, fast gasps. She was afraid to call the police – terrified of where that might lead. She feared for her grandson's safety. And, yet, she still wondered if it was a test and if she would fail if she brought in the authorities.

Numb, she walked to the dining room and sat in her place. She toyed with her salad but never took a bite. She wandered away from the laden table to the liquor cabinet where she poured a large glass of sherry and slugged it down as fast as she could swallow and, leaving everything on the table, went up to her bedroom.

Lucinda rose the next morning with dread. She put on a new blouse with the black suit she'd worn the day before to Jeanine's funeral. She was halfway into her drive when her cell pinged, indicating the arrival of a text message. She picked it up and read the phone number for Constance Green, Viola Kidd's younger sister.

She stuck the Bluetooth in her ear and called – it was still very early in California, the better to catch her at home. Constance answered on the first ring. 'Hello.'

'Hello, Ms Green. I'm Lieutenant Lucinda Pierce, a homicide detective with the Greensboro Police Department in Virginia.'

'Homicide? You mean murder?'

'Yes, ma'am, we do investigate murders and that is why I am calling you. I need some information about your nephew, John Kidd.'

'Oh, my God! Someone killed him? Thank heavens Viola didn't live to see this day.'

'No, ma'am. To the best of my knowledge, John Kidd is still alive.'

'Surely, you don't suspect him of being involved in a murder? I must admit it wouldn't have surprised me if he killed his father – he was full of rage about that man. But he died years ago – of a heart attack or stroke or something. I can't imagine John ever hurting another soul.'

'Ms Green, he's simply come up in the investigation and we need to eliminate him as a possibility so that we can move on.'

'Well, then, what do you want to know? I'm not sure if I can answer your questions, I haven't seen John since my sister's funeral – that must have been five years ago now. What a horrible tragedy.'

'Yes, I understand she committed suicide.'

'Afraid so. I rue the day that my sister ever met that damned William Blessing.'

'But he died before her, Ms Green. Did she miss him that badly?'

'Heavens, no. Not for one minute. He might have left her but she was well rid of him and she knew it – I told her so. But, after he died, his place of employment sent his personal effects home. They hadn't lived together since John was born, but they never divorced. Anyway, she didn't even want to look inside the box. But John did, and he found a journal belonging to his father packed inside. And all that Blessing bastard's secrets were there.'

'Secrets?'

'Apparently, Blessing had a very active sex life after my sister and his son. Never sent Viola a penny for child support but had plenty of money to fool around. Why she didn't take him to court, I don't know. But they scraped by all those years. My husband and I had to help them out from time to time. Viola was faithful to her husband throughout it all, so her heart was broken when John pointed out the many liaisons in his father's journal. Viola felt distraught, humiliated and betrayed. The last time I spoke to her, I never imagined she was thinking about taking her own life. But there you go. A woman's heart is an impenetrable jungle.'

'But, Ms Green, are you certain he had a string of affairs? He ran a sperm bank. Isn't it possible that William Blessing kept a private record of the artificial inseminations using his sperm?'

'Don't much matter what I think. Viola imagined romance – with all those women. She talked to me about candlelight dinners and dancing under the moon. I told her not to let her imagination run away from her. I told her he wasn't worth it. I thought she was listening to me. I didn't learn I was wrong until it was too late.'

'So, you hold William Blessing responsible for your sister's death?'

'I most certainly do – indirectly, that is. To hear John talk, though, you would have thought that Blessing reached his hand out of the grave and forced those pills down Viola's throat.'

THIRTY-SIX

Victoria Whitehead awoke that morning with a headache and a sick sensation of dread in her stomach. She walked downstairs, fixed a cup of tea and returned to bed. She kept running over her decision not to call nine-one-one. She stared at the phone, willing it to ring. She wanted to hear Jason say, 'You passed the test. Freddy and I will be there for lunch.'

But noon came and went without a call. *Maybe he won't call. Maybe they'll just show up at the front door grinning and laughing.* She jumped out of bed and quickly got dressed to be ready for their arrival. By the time she made it downstairs, though, her optimistic thought turned on itself. *You are a fool – a silly old fool* beat a tattoo in her head.

She roamed around the house, uncertain and unsettled. She stopped at the dining room table a few times to clean up the mess she'd left the night before. No sooner had she started than she abandoned the project, drifting off into another room. It was three thirty that afternoon before she found the energy to go outside and retrieve the day's mail.

Opening the door, she spotted a box on the porch and smiled. She slipped two envelopes and a flier out of the mailbox, set them on top of the package and lifted. It was a lot heavier than she thought it would be.

She carried it to the dining room table and, pushing a place mat out of the way, set it down on the surface. She went into the kitchen for a pair of shears and cut away the tape. She'd only lifted one flap when the stench hit her nostrils and drove her back against the wall. She threw a hand over her mouth and nose in a vain attempt to block the smell.

Is that Freddy? Oh, dear God, don't let it be Freddy in that box. I've got to call the police. I've got to call now. No, I need to know. I need to look. Maybe it's just rotted food. Maybe it's a dead animal. 'Oh, but it could be Freddy!' she wailed out loud.

One foot after another, she forced herself to walk back to the table and open the box. Inside, a plastic bag held a head.

She jumped back. 'Oh, my God! Oh, my God! Oh, my God!' *Breathe deep, calm down*, she urged. Halfway through one hard inhalation, she gagged, doubled over and vomited on the floor.

Shaking inside and out, she leaned against the wall again. *It's not Freddy. It's not Freddy. It's not Freddy. But I have to be sure. I have to know.* She staggered back to the table and stared into the box. *Not Freddy. Oh, thank God.*

She turned to launch herself into the kitchen. One foot hit the mess she'd left on the floor. Her foot slid backward, bringing her to her knees, and the inertia slammed her down on all fours. A sharp jolt shot through one wrist and up her arm. She whimpered and crawled the rest of the way into the kitchen.

Grabbing the door frame, she pulled herself up to reach the phone. With shaking fingers, she pressed 9-1-1, slumping to the floor with her back to the wall and the receiver clutched in the one hand that didn't throb with intense pain.

As Lucinda pulled into the parking lot of the funeral home, Ricky burst out of the front door. He was by her side as she stepped out of her car, wrapping her in a tight embrace. 'Thanks for coming, Lucinda.'

'Anything for you, little brother,' she said with a smile as they stepped out of their hug and walked up to the front door.

'People are going to start thinking I'm bumping off family members just to see you.'

'Hmm. Hadn't thought about that. Maybe I should investigate?'

Ricky pulled the door open and they were face to face with their sister Maggie.

'How can you dare show up here?' she snarled.

'No matter our differences, Mags, she was my aunt, too.'

'And, because of you, she's dead,' Maggie spat.

'Maggie, lower your voice,' Ricky urged. 'This is not the place. Lucinda was nowhere near here when Aunt Connie died.'

'Shut up, Ricky,' Maggie said and turned to her sister. 'You might as well have pushed her and then smothered her in her hospital bed. She'd be alive if it weren't for you.'

'You're out of your mind, Mags. Please let me come inside.'

Maggie stepped back. 'Oh, you come on in. But let me tell you this, sister dearest, I will make sure that everyone knows this is your fault. If you hadn't stressed out Aunt Connie so much, she wouldn't have lost her temper and taken that fall. You couldn't be more responsible if you shot her point-blank with your gun.'

Lucinda brushed past Maggie and headed up the hall. She heard Ricky hissing an urgent whisper to their sister but had no hope his words would do any good.

No one in the room with Aunt Connie's casket gave the slightest indication that they believed she bore any responsibility for her aunt's death. Those who knew Lucinda greeted her warmly, telling her it was good to see her again although they regretted the circumstances.

On the limousine ride to the cemetery, Lucinda kept her gaze out the window, never once acknowledging her sister's presence in the car. A couple of times, Maggie made baiting comments. Ricky chastised her but Lucinda didn't even turn her head.

The mourners gathered at Ricky's house after the graveside service. For an hour, Lucinda succeeded in never being in the same room with her sister. Then, she was cornered. Maggie was in her face.

'I know why you're here,' Maggie said in a loud, booming voice. 'You want to make sure you get your piece of the pie. You want us to sell the farm so you get your money. You hated Aunt Connie while she was living but now you're here picking over her bones. Go ahead, tell Ricky – he should know you're going to force him to sell the farm. Go on, tell him.'

Lucinda turned her back on Maggie and walked across the room to her brother. Speaking in a low voice, she said, 'Ricky, as far as I'm concerned, this farm belongs to you. You built a house on this ground. You worked these acres all of your life – tended to the cows, the chickens, the pigs. You have earned this place. Have an attorney draw up the paperwork transferring all my interest in the property to you. I'll sign it the moment I get it.'

The room was silent. Everyone there had heard every word. Lucinda scanned the room and heads dropped in embarrassment at overhearing the family drama. She turned around and left the room. Behind her back, Maggie shouted, 'You are such a liar.'

Ricky hesitated only a moment before racing out of the farmhouse, calling Lucinda's name.

'Ricky, I can't stay any longer. I have to go.'

'I know. I know. I just wanted to say goodbye.'

Lucinda stopped and hugged her brother. Over her shoulder, she saw the funeral guests drifting out on to the front porch, observing their interaction.

'I feel a vibration in my chest – is that your cellphone in your pocket or did you just taze me?'

'Funny boy,' Lucinda said, backing out of the embrace and pulling out her phone.

'Pierce.'

Lucinda's faced turned ashen. 'Kidnapped?' She bent her head, listening intently. 'The head and one hand? Why not both?' She disconnected. 'I've got to go now, Ricky. You know the double homicide I'm working on? Well, someone just kidnapped the victims' thirteen-year-old son.' She drove off faster than she should, raising a huge cloud of red dust up from the packed clay drive.

When Ricky returned to the porch, Maggie said, 'What? Did someone else die and they sent out an urgent plea for vultures?'

'Please, Maggie. A young boy's been kidnapped.'

'Well, good Lord, keep her away from him – she's apt to shoot him as soon as save him.'

THIRTY-SEVEN

A few miles down the road, Lucinda realized that the FBI would have to be involved. She groaned, grabbed her cell and called Captain Holland. 'Captain, this is Lieutenant Pierce.'

'Pierce, I heard you were on your way in. Sorry to take you away from a family funeral.'

'Nothing to be sorry about, Captain. I wanted to talk to you about the FBI.'

'I was all ready to contact the local office when you called.'

'No, Captain. Please don't.'

'Pierce, the FBI has to be involved. This is an abduction – a child abduction.'

'I know that. But get me Special Agent Jake Lovett.'

'There's a chain of command here, Pierce.'

'Captain, please. The local guys all worked with my ex-husband . . .'

'They are all professionals. That shouldn't be a problem.'

'Yeah, Captain. How about if I told you that you had to work with your ex-wife's cronies in an already difficult situation?'

'OK, OK,' he said with a sigh. 'I'll do what I can.'

Walking into Victoria Whitehead's home, Lucinda grimaced and shook her head in reaction to the vile and obvious odor of human decomposition. She spotted Ted in the living room, holding one of Victoria's hands and talking to her quietly. The woman's other hand was wrapped in an ice pack. When he saw Lucinda, he excused himself and approached. 'You made good time.'

'Not bad,' she said. 'Where is it?'

'The head and the hand?'

'Yeah.'

'It's down at the morgue.'

'Whew, as bad as it smells in here, I didn't think the box had left yet.'

'Oh, yeah, it's the aroma that keeps on giving. I told the pathologist to get a sample for DNA testing up to Beth Ann Coynes as soon as possible. In fact, she probably has it by now.'

'What about the other hand?' Lucinda said. 'Why wasn't it in the box?'

'Man, you got me. Might not be a reason. But we did find a note in the box. I sent that down with the body parts but I jotted down the message before I did.' Ted pulled a notebook out of his pocket. 'It was addressed to "My dearest Victoria".'

'That's enough to make you gag.'

'Tell me about it,' he said, then read, '"Just wanted to make sure you knew I was serious. You and the cops need to meet my demands or else."'

'What are his demands?'

'Don't know yet. We've set up a tap on the phone. Ms Whitehead needs to be here in case a call comes in but I'd rather have her down at the emergency room.'

'What happened to her?'

'She slipped in her own vomit, went down and I think she sprained her wrist. We've got ice on it but I really think it needs to be X-rayed.'

'As long as she's not screaming, that will have to wait. Did you get her some pain meds?'

'We started with a few ibuprofen from her medicine cabinet but a little bit ago, we had a doctor come by. He gave her some stronger stuff with codeine in it. But he wasn't too happy that she wasn't getting an X-ray.'

'Yeah, well, too bad, isn't it?'

'What now, Lucinda?'

'Damn, I wish I knew. We've got to wait for a call and – wait a minute, Ted. Let me see the wording in that note again.'

Ted handed her the pad. 'What is it?'

Lucinda tapped on the page. 'This isn't his first contact. He wouldn't say he wanted to *make sure* she knew he was serious unless he already talked to her,' she said and walked into the living room. Sitting down beside Victoria, she said, 'Ms Whitehead, were you expecting this package?'

'Oh, good heavens, no!'

'But this isn't the first time you've heard from Jason, is it?'

'Of course it is.'

'Then, tell me, Ms Whitehead, how did you know that Jason left that package on your porch?'

Victoria's head bobbed as she stammered, 'Wha – what – what do you mean?'

'For one, the note in that box was not signed. Secondly, the wording of the note makes it obvious that this was not the first contact you had with the kidnapper. I strongly suspect you knew it was Jason because you talked to him before the package arrived.'

Victoria squeezed her eyes tight and shook all over.

'Right now, this isn't looking good for you. You're looking at possible accessory charges. You need to tell me everything you know.'

Victoria breathed in deeply, her shoulders rising to her ears. With her loud exhale, they slumped back down, even lower than they were before. 'He called last night and told me he took Frederick.'

'And you didn't call nine-one-one?'

'I was afraid. I thought it was a test. I thought if I didn't call the police, that he'd bring Frederick back. I thought they'd be laughing. I thought . . .'

'You just weren't thinking at all, were you, Ms Whitehead?' Lucinda snapped.

'Oh my, oh my, oh my,' Victoria wailed.

'You were so desperate to cling to a man that you didn't give a damn about your grandson, is that right?'

'Oh, no, no, no,' she whimpered, bending at the waist and burying her face in her hands.

Disgusted, Lucinda rose and walked away. 'Damned stupid woman.'

'Making people cry again, I see.'

Lucinda jerked her head around, following the familiar voice. 'Jake!' Her heart pounded, her throat tightened and she cautioned herself to hide her emotions.

'FBI at your service, ma'am,' he said, making a mock bow. 'It seems the local agents had as big an aversion to working with you as you did with them. So here I am.'

Lucinda's eye trailed down his body to the signature high-top Chucks on his feet. 'Nice shade of yellow, Special Agent Lovett.'

Jake looked down at his feet and wiggled one in her direction. 'They're gold, Lieutenant. Aztec gold.'

Lucinda laughed. 'Let's go into the other room and I'll get you up to speed.' *It feels so good to see him again, to hear his voice, to be near him, to know he has my back. Focus on that last one, Lucinda, girl. This is a professional relationship – don't forget it. He has a job to do. I have a job to do. Keep that in mind.*

They were deep into their conversation when Ted stepped into the room with a smile that quickly flatlined and became a frown. 'Special Agent Lovett,' he said with a nod, then turned away from the man he was certain was a rival for Lucinda's affections. 'Lucinda, Whitehead said that she didn't notice that Frederick wasn't at home until dinner time. Jason King called a short time later.'

'He told her that he had the boy, he expected her cooperation and that she should call the police because she'd need their help to get what he needed. But because he told her to call the police, she was certain it was a trick or a test and so she didn't call.'

'You buying her story?' Jake asked.

Ted glanced at the FBI agent, and then shifted his eyes to Lucinda before he spoke. 'I know it sounds stupid, Lucinda. But I think she's telling the truth about that call.'

'Thanks, Ted,' Lucinda said. She turned away from him and resumed talking to Jake.

For a moment, Ted stood and watched them. They gave no indication that they were aware he was still in the room.

A commotion arose at the front door just before eight o'clock. Jake and Lucinda walked into the foyer and smiled. Officer Robin Colter clutched two urns from Starbucks and the patrolman behind her carried a huge sack of sandwiches. 'Colter!' Lucinda grinned. 'Your instincts are excellent.'

'Thanks, Lieutenant. Hope you'll keep that in mind. I'm taking my sergeant's exam next month – when I ace it, I'll be looking for a new place on the roster.'

Lucinda laughed. 'You see an opening in my department, let me know, and I'll put in a good word.'

After setting up the food in the kitchen, Robin carried a steaming Styrofoam cup of coffee into the living room and offered it to Victoria Whitehead. When the woman demurred and asked for a cup of tea, Robin returned to the kitchen to prepare it.

For a while, everyone was content – stomachs full, caffeine replenished. But as the clock approached ten, restless energy bounced off the walls. Lucinda, Jake and Ted all found it impossible to sit still – each one walking off into another room, then turning around as if they forgot their purpose and walking back again.

Victoria turned snippy, taking out her nervousness on Robin who stuck to her side despite the abuse. A shout of 'Lieutenant!' rang out from the family room. Lucinda followed the sound, Jake and Ted at her heels. She took in the scene before her – three uniformed officers gathered around a television set watching the news. 'What?' Lucinda asked.

'Your sister,' one of them stammered. 'She's gone now. But . . .'

Lucinda snatched the remote out of the patrolman's hand and clicked to another local newscast and then to the third. Her sister Maggie stood in front of Ricky's house, an array of microphones curved around her.

'All that my sister ever thinks about is herself. When she –' Maggie said, turning to face the camera and enunciating with care, '– Lieutenant Lucinda Pierce – when she should have been at work, protecting that little boy – she knew he was in danger – but no, instead of doing her job like she should, she was here. Right here. She forgot about that little boy and rushed up here to try to steal this farm from our brother. She is the most greedy, self-centered person I have ever known.'

'Damn her!' Lucinda said, slamming the remote into the floor. Everyone flinched as they watched it bounce, but no one said a word.

'Anyone want a sister from hell? I'll sell her cheap. Damn, I'll pay you to take her off my hands,' Lucinda said and stalked out of the room. Furious with her sister, embarrassed in front of her colleagues and frustrated with her inability to help Freddy, Lucinda paced back and forth in the dining room, her fists clenched tight by her sides.

Ted stepped in front of her, putting a hand on each shoulder. She jerked away from his touch. 'Get out of my way, Ted.'

'Lucinda . . .'

'I'm warning you.'

Ted backed away, passing Jake as he left the room, and shrugging his shoulders in response to the questions on the agent's face. Jake came to a stop before intruding into Lucinda's space. 'Lieutenant, we have a job to do.'

'Oh, Mr Special Agent, are you critiquing my performance? Would you please tell me what I haven't done or haven't done correctly? Please, enlighten me.'

'Cut the crap. You need to let this go and calm down.'

'The hell I do. I need to fume. I need to pace. I need to burn off my anger so I can focus. Can you understand that, Special Agent man?'

Jake paused, looked at her and said, 'Actually, I can. But could you please stop taking it out on all the rest of us?'

Lucinda knew he was right but she glared at him anyway and resumed her fast walk, back and forth across the room. She jerked to a stop when the telephone rang, switching gears without a moment's hesitation. She barreled into the living room, slapping on a pair of headphones. By the end of the second ring, Jake was by her side, donning his pair. Lucinda nodded to Victoria.

With a trembling hand, the woman picked up the receiver. 'Hello?' she said in a cracking voice.

The voice of Freddy's kidnapper filled Jake and Lucinda's

ears as he spoke to his erstwhile girlfriend. 'Tell the cops to stop wasting their time trying to trace this call. I'll let them know exactly where I am in the morning. They won't have any trouble finding me.'

'Freddy?' Victoria asked.

'The boy's fine.'

'Can I talk to him?'

'No time. Here's what I need. Listen carefully and don't screw it up. I need a candy apple red '68 Camaro with a Hurst shifter and a big block eight delivered to my front door.'

Lucinda's jaw dropped. She looked at Jake who smiled and nodded his head. *Jake's impressed?*

'A what?' Victoria asked.

'You're recording this, right?'

'Uh, uh . . .' Victoria darted frantic eyes to Lucinda.

'Of course, you are. I also need a fast, seaworthy boat with a pilot and supplies waiting for me in slip seventeen at the Atlantic Yacht Basin in Norfolk. They've got live streaming video online. So don't even think of setting a trap up there.'

'Then I'll get Freddy?'

'I'll tell you how it will all go down in the morning. No surprises for anybody. Just start getting it ready.'

'But, Jason—'

'Tomorrow. Goodbye.' The click of the phone made Lucinda wince. She turned to the audio technician with anxious expectation etching deep lines in her brow. He shook his head. He wasn't able to trace the call.

THIRTY-EIGHT

Freddy hated the feeling that rested like a burning ball of slime in the middle of his body. He knew it was a combination of his fear and the disgust he felt over being so stupid. Understanding the reason behind it all didn't make it go away, though. In fact, the more he thought about it, the worse it became, but he couldn't put it out of his mind.

He tried to calm down but when he closed his eyes in search of peace, a video ran in his head – one that made him feel like a childish dumb-bell. He'd been stretched out on his bed when he heard Jason's voice. 'Hey, Freddy!'

His initial reaction was the right one. He bolted upright, as his heart lurched into a hard, fast, throat-clenching rhythm. His nerve endings jangled as adrenaline surged through his bloodstream. His muscles all tensed in instinctual preparation to react to any emergency. He held his breath, listening and assessing the danger he faced.

'I didn't mean to startle you, little man. I just need your help. I've got a surprise out in the car for your grandmother. It's not too heavy but it's bulky. Put down your book and give me a hand, OK?'

When Freddy thought about his reaction, self-hate and loathing oozed from his pores, making him feel soiled, greasy and repulsive. He despised himself for reacting just as Jason knew he would – he got excited like a little kid and jumped off the bed, saying, 'What is it?'

'Come see!' Jason said and Freddy followed him out of the bedroom. At the top of the stairs, Jason paused, placed an index finger on his lips and pantomimed sneaking down the stairs.

Freddy threw a hand across his mouth to hold in the giggles that threatened to tickle his lip. He crept down the stairs, with extravagant care, making sure no sound reached his grand-mother in the kitchen preparing dinner. *Stupid! Stupid! Stupid!*

Jason led him to the back of the car, prolonging the moment by waving around the key fob without pressing the button. *And I bought into it. I bounced up and down and whispered, 'Open it, open it!'*

'All right, little man, here you go!' Jason said. After that, everything moved too quickly, as if someone pressed the fast forward button on the remote control. He wasn't sure of what was happening until the lid of the trunk slammed over his head. He squeezed his eyes tight and jiggled his legs to stave off the simultaneous urges to let loose his bladder and burst into tears.

Now, he sat with his wrists bound together, his arms tied behind his back and his ankles fastened to the legs of a chair. *How could I be so dumb? I'm supposed to be smart. I was a baby – a stupid baby – and I didn't get just me in trouble.* He looked to his right, at the nice farm lady, Ms Martha. Jason busted into her house a couple of hours earlier, yelling and threatening, pushing and shoving. Freddy knew the lady was frightened when Jason tossed him at her feet but she took care of him and soothed him doing her best to hide her own fear.

Now, they sat side-by-side, with her limbs bound and her mouth duct-taped like his. She tried to smile at him with her eyes. But he knew she was still scared – a constant quiver ran through her body, sometimes getting so intense it made the chair legs clatter on the vinyl floor.

Past her was another chair, with Ms Martha's husband, Mr Frank, secured to its frame. Freddy never noticed any fear in Mr Frank's eyes. But he did see flashes of rage burn in them, that he covered up quickly with a vacant stare. That blank look was on Mr Frank's face now, filling Freddy with terror. *We're all gonna die!* A whimper escaped from behind Freddy's duct tape.

Ms Martha jerked her head in his direction. The intensity of her stare sent waves of warmth and comfort across the space between them. Freddy knew she was as helpless as he was, but somehow she seemed to have a power he could not define – a strength that would not bend. He flared his nostrils and pulled in a full chest of air, absorbing some of her energy. His shoulders relaxed and he gave her a nod. He couldn't see her mouth, but somehow Freddy knew she smiled.

That instant of hope shattered as Jason re-entered the room. He walked toward Freddy, not stopping until they were toe to toe. He bent over and brought his nose right up into Freddy's face. 'Well, little man, time to call your grammy.' Jason straightened up and walked to the phone mounted on the wall.

Freddy listened, every word ratcheting up his fear. His insides felt like a wet washcloth held in a large, strong hand that squeezed without mercy. He wondered if his stomach could get so tight it would explode – if he could die, right here in the chair, without Jason ever raising a hand to harm him.

He heard his abductor saying that he would tell them what would happen when he called back in the morning. *That's the hardest part* – Freddy fretted – *the not knowing what's coming next. But if he's calling in the morning, that means I will live through the night.* Then, he remembered what happened when one of them made Jason mad and his hope died with the memory.

Earlier that evening, Mr Frank raised his chair up off the floor and lunged. Jason stepped aside and laughed as Mr Frank fell, face first, into the wood stove. Jason chuckled as he picked up the man and the chair and positioned him back next to his wife. He walked in front of Miss Martha, with a grin. Suddenly, a flash of movement filled the space in front of her face, as Jason back-handed her so hard he knocked over the chair – the back of Miss Martha's head barely missing the radiator as she landed on her back. *It could have killed her.*

Now, disconnected from the phone, Jason laughed again, stopping in front of Freddy's chair. 'Well, little man, looks like I'm going to need your help again.'

Bile churned and shot up into Freddy's throat. He wanted to throw up but he knew with the duct tape on his mouth, he had no place to hurl. He swallowed hard over and over again as Jason unfastened his legs and arms from the chair, leaving his wrists bound. 'Up!' he shouted at Freddy.

The boy tried to rise but the prolonged time in the chair made his knees and back stiff. Jason grabbed a fistful of hair on the back of his head and jerked him upright. 'Now, Miss Martha, Mr Frank, you sit still down here. If I hear one little sound of movement, I'll kill the boy and then I'll come down here and find out what's going on. Are we clear on that?'

Freddy saw them nod before Jason jerked on his hair again and led him up the steps into the couple's bedroom and over to the computer in the corner. 'Now, little man, I'm going to untie your hands. But you try anything – no matter how silly – I'm going to haul you downstairs and make you watch while I kill those two and then I'll kill you. You got that?'

Freddy nodded. Jason untied the knots on Freddy's wrists and shoved the boy into the desk chair. 'I want you to be my research assistant. You've heard of extradition treaties?'

Freddy's brow furrowed and then he nodded.

'OK, little man, this is what you need to do. I want to know which countries don't have one with the good, old U S of A.'

Freddy put his hands on the keyboard. He struggled to make his numb fingers work. After two clumsy attempts, he managed to bring up locations on the Google search page. The first link he clicked led to a long list of countries with the extradition status detailed beside each one.

Jason clunked the back of Freddy's head with the butt of his palm. 'You can do better than that. I just want to see the ones without a treaty – not a list of countries, all mixed up.'

Freddy clicked back to the search results and connected with another link.

'Now, that's what I'm talking about, little man.'

Jason read through the list of countries that maintained diplomatic relations with the United States but had no extradition treaty. Then he saw the list of those nations that had neither treaty nor relations. He tapped on the screen. 'This is it,' he said and read out loud, 'Andorra, Angola, Bantu Homelands, Bhutan, Bosnia, Cambodia, Ciskei, Cuba, Iran, North Korea, Libya, Maldives, Serbia, Somalia, Taiwan, Transkei, Vanuatu and Vietnam. Never heard of at least half of them. I know North Korea is a hellhole – and it's too far away. So are Vietnam, the Maldives, Taiwan and Cambodia. Shit! Cuba? That's it? Nothing else? Cuba? Why not Venezuela? I'd rather go there. It's a big place – lots of pretty country to get lost in. What do you think is wrong with that Chavez, little man? You'd think he would have cancelled all the treaties with the big white devil, wouldn't you?'

Freddy shrugged his shoulders.

'Wish I could take off that duct tape and let you talk. You're smart enough; you could do me some good if you wanted to. But I know I can't trust what you'd say. And I don't trust those teeth of yours – kids bite and I bet you'd try. Well, little man, Cuba it is. Let's go join the party downstairs.' He entwined his fingers in a hank of Freddy's hair, forcing him to his feet and down to the first floor.

Tied back into his chair, Freddy mulled over the experience at the computer. *Cuba? I'm just a kid and I know that Cuba is a stupid idea. What does he think, they'll rush out in the surf to greet the boat and give him a ticker tape parade through Havana? He's dumber than I thought. I can use that. I know I can use that. I just have to figure out how.*

THIRTY-NINE

At the end of the call, Lucinda turned to Jake. The glazed appearance of his eyes and the soft smile on his lips made Lucinda roll her eyes. She snapped her fingers in front of his face. 'Hello, Jake. Please wipe the bliss off of your face and focus your attention in the here and now.'

'Wow! He's got excellent taste in automobiles.'

'Oh, good grief.'

'I wonder if I could convince him to let me ride with him down to Norfolk.'

'Hello, Jake. We don't really want him getting to that boat. And we've got a real problem here. Where the hell are we going to find a car like that at this time of night?'

'Piece of cake.'

'Oh, Jake, be serious.'

'Oh, I am. I know just who to call.'

'Really?' Ted interjected.

'Oh, sure, driving my dad's old '66 Impala Super Sport has put me in touch with a lot of interesting people.'

'A Super Sport? I am impressed. Convertible?' Ted asked.

'Of course! She's got a 396 under the hood with 325 horses . . .'

Lucinda interrupted, 'Yeah, yeah, yeah. And the ride is as smooth as glass. Much as I'm enjoying this male bonding moment, Jake, don't you need to make a call?'

Jake turned back to Ted. 'No appreciation for the finer things in life.'

'None whatsoever,' Ted agreed.

'Jake!'

'Hey, it's cool,' Jake said, sliding his cell out of his pocket. 'Hey, Grease Monkey, this is Jake. How's it shakin'?' Jake nodded his head a couple of times and said, 'Same ol' same ol'. I gotta problem that I thought you might be able to help me with – I need to find a car and have it delivered here before daybreak.' Jake ran through the car's specs and said that he didn't want to buy a car, just borrow it for a day or two. He nodded a few times while he listened and said, 'All right, man, I'll be waiting.'

'You'll be waiting? He has a car? Already?' Lucinda asked in amazement.

'No, not yet. But he will. He'll call back as soon as he finds out which one is available,' Jake said.

'Which one? You mean there's more than one around here?'

'He knows of several, right here in Virginia. A few more just over the line in North Carolina.'

'You're kidding?'

'It's kind of a bummer. You have a sweet machine like that and you like to think you're the only one but that's rarely

true – there were four other cars just like my dad's at the last
rally I attended.'

'You go to car rallies?'

'Yeah, they're a lot of fun. You oughta come with me sometime.'

Lucinda rolled her eyes, walked over to Officer Colter and
whispered in her ear. Robin spoke to Victoria, who protested
at first, but then allowed the officer to lead her upstairs to lie
down in her bed. 'I don't think I'll be able to sleep,' Victoria
said as she walked up the stairs.

'Don't you worry about that, Ms Whitehead. You just stretch
out for a bit and rest.'

Lucinda passed through the family room where all of the
officers leaned back in recliners and snored quietly in the blue
light of the television set. She paused to pick up the remote
and power off the TV. She slipped out the French door into
the back yard for a breath of fresh air. As she stared up at a
hazy moon, she heard the back door open and shut.

'Pretty damn humid out here tonight, isn't it?' Jake said.

'Ah, summer in Virginia – should call it mildew season.
Sometimes I worry if I stand still too long, it'll start creeping
over my toes.'

'Are you doing OK?'

Lucinda snorted. 'Yeah, sure.'

'It's a lot harder when you know the abducted kid.'

'Can't say I really know him. I've been trying to figure him
out but . . .' her voice trailed away, tinged with unspoken regret.

'But you have interacted with him and that makes it harder
to hold your center and maintain your balance.'

Lucinda made an ambiguous noise, halfway between a grunt
and a growl.

'And then there was that crap with your sister tonight,' Jake
added.

'Oh, please, don't remind me.'

'What's with that? Why is she so hostile toward you?'

'I don't know. She's been that way since Mom was killed.
I've tried to get through to her but it didn't seem to make a
difference so I finally gave up. She snaps at me when I see
her; she judges me and always finds me wanting. You saw
her tonight – she has no problem criticizing me anywhere, at
any time, to anyone.'

'Why is all this anger directed at you?'

Lucinda shrugged. 'Maybe she's this way with everybody.'

'You think?'

'I don't know, Jake. Let's drop it, OK?'

'Sure,' he said, stepping to her side and sliding an arm across her back, cupping his palm around her shoulder.

At his touch, a small electric charge coursed through Lucinda's body. For a few seconds she felt as if she never wanted the moment to end. She nearly turned to fall into his arms but a tight ball formed in her core and an ugly voiced hissed in her head: *Push him away. Push him away!*

She tried to squash her internal nay-sayer and nearly succeeded when they were interrupted by the opening bars of *Born to be Wild*, boogying from Jake's cell. She looked at him and laughed at his ringtone.

He grinned and shrugged as he answered the call. 'That you, Grease Monkey? Got good news for me?' Jake's browed furrowed, then he shot his arm up in the air and shook a fist at the sky. 'Thanks, buddy, I owe you, big time.' He disconnected, raised both arms and shouted, 'Yes!'

'What? What? Tell me! He found the car, right?'

'Yesssss! Yes, he found the car. It will be pulling up out front between five and five thirty tomorrow morning.'

Lucinda looked down at her watch. 'Correction, Jake – five to five thirty *this* morning.'

'Oh, man, we need to get some sleep.'

They walked inside, taking care not to disturb the sleeping patrol officers. When they reached the living room, they saw that they'd lost the audio guy. He sprawled in his chair, mouth wide open, a pair of headphones balanced precariously on one knee.

Lucinda kicked off her shoes and slid into a chaise next to a narrow floor-to-ceiling shelf of books. Jake tossed her an afghan from the back of the sofa and grabbed the other one for his own use as he stretched out to rest.

She didn't think she could sleep. Too many dire warnings raced through her head. She had no idea what the new day would bring but she knew it wouldn't be easy and it wouldn't be pretty. She stretched the covering over her long legs and closed her eyes.

She awoke with a start and looked at her watch. Four fifteen. *But what woke me?* She listened but heard no sound except for the relaxed light snore coming from the audio guy. She walked in her stockinged feet over to the sofa and looked down at Jake. *He looks even younger when he's asleep. Doesn't look old enough to carry a gun.* She sighed and padded into the kitchen to prepare a pot of coffee. Once she got the coffee-maker going, she pulled out the spare carafe – they were going to need more than one pot this morning to get the whole crew up and at 'em.

When the first batch was ready, she poured two mugs, and then paused. *How does Jake like his coffee?* She cast her mind back. *Black – unless there's half and half available.* She rummaged through the containers on the refrigerator door, emerged victorious and poured a big dollop into one of the mugs. She carried them both into the living room, set them down on the coffee table and crouched down by Jake's face. 'Jake,' she whispered.

He stirred but did not open his eyes.

She spoke a little louder. 'Jake!'

His eyes fluttered and a hand reached out to rest on the damaged side of her face.

A tiny gasp escaped her throat. She held her breath, waiting for the recoil of revulsion. It didn't come. Instead, he caressed her scars and moved his fingers into her hair. She trembled and fought back tears. 'Jake,' she whispered.

His eyes opened halfway. 'Lucinda.'

The sound of her name on his lips brought a flush to her skin.

He reached out with his other hand and placed it on the opposite side of her face.

She almost relaxed – almost moved to him. She was stopped by an insistent warning in her head. *Not the right place. Not the right time.* In a sharper, more urgent tone of voice, she said, 'Jake!'

His eyes flew all the way open. Puzzlement splashed across his face and then was gone. 'What time is it?'

'Four thirty. Here, I fixed you a cup of coffee,' she said, handing him the mug.

He took a sip, then pulled back the mug and looked inside. 'Mmm, you remembered the half and half.'

'Sure. I like it myself from time to time,' she said with a smile. 'Let's let the rest of them sleep as long as they can.'

They rose to their feet and went out on to the front porch, leaving the door open a crack to hear the phone in case it rang.

They sat in quiet harmony, rocking in the wicker chairs, sipping from their cups and enjoying the early morning quiet. Birdsong heralded the rising sun as light made its stealthy spread across the sky. 'I'd better go get Ms Whitehead up. Don't know when he'll call but it could be soon,' Lucinda said.

'I'll wait out here and watch for the car.'

'When it gets here, Jake, please don't embarrass us all by drooling on your shirt.'

Jake laughed. 'Just wait till you see her. She's a beauty.'

Smiling, Lucinda eased into the house and went upstairs. In Victoria's bedroom, she was surprised to see Officer Colter stretched out on top of the bedspread, in full uniform, with her hand resting on top of the other woman's. She walked over to that side of the bed and whispered, 'Officer Colter.'

Robin woke instantly. 'Sorry. Sorry, Lieutenant. I didn't mean to fall asleep. I . . .'

'It's OK. I'm glad you got some rest. Did she sleep OK?'

'Not at first. But she asked me just to lie down next to her until she drifted off. When I did, she slipped her hand in mine and, minutes later, she was out.'

'Thanks, Colter. That was a kind thing to do. Now, unfortunately, we need to wake her and get her downstairs. The sun is starting to rise and the bastard could call any minute.'

Lucinda walked into the guest bedroom and woke up the liaison officer from the state police. In Freddy's room, she found Ted curled up in a tight ball. She brushed the hair out of his face and whispered his name. He jumped. 'It's OK, Ted. Sun's up and there's coffee in the kitchen.'

He mumbled, 'Thanks' as he threw his legs out of the bed.

Lucinda went downstairs, waking the three uniformed officers in front of the TV and moving on to the audio tech. His first words were: 'I didn't miss anything, did I?'

'Not yet,' Lucinda said. 'But you'd better hurry to the kitchen before all the coffee is gone.' She was walking towards the porch when a whoop rang out She opened the door and spotted Jake doing a crazy jig down the sidewalk toward the screaming red car at the curb.

'Isn't she a beauty?' he squealed.

'Jake, you're drooling!'

He placed both hands over his heart and said, 'How could I not?'

Lucinda laughed. 'I'm going to get everyone together so we can run over what we might expect and see if we can work out a scenario for each possibility.'

'I'll be right there.'

Lucinda herded the still sleepy team into the family room, grabbed a fresh cup of coffee and returned just as Jake entered the room from the other doorway and gave her the thumbs-up sign.

'OK. The car is here,' she said.

The men in the room stirred as if ready to jump up and check it out.

'Wait. You can go see it in a minute. Let's just hash things out first.' She heard a couple of sighs as they all settled back down. She entertained theories, answered questions and expressed the confidence that they all could handle whatever situation arose – and hoped what she said was true.

When she finished, the men surged like one big beast outside to ogle the Camaro. She watched from the doorway as they took turns sliding behind the wheel, ran loving hands across the hood and just stood back and stared.

A harsh ring jarred Lucinda from her relaxation. 'Telephone,' she shouted and the men scrambled away from the car and up the walk. She raced across the living room, donned her headphones and flipped on the recorder as the audio tech skidded to a halt, muttering, 'Thanks.'

Lucinda gave him a sharp nod and a smile and then looked over to Victoria, repeating the gestures. Victoria cleared her throat, reached for the receiver and said, 'Hello?'

FORTY

'Listen up, Victoria, and listen good,' Jason said.

To everyone's surprise, Victoria bounded to her feet and shouted in a shrill voice, 'No, you listen, Jason, or whoever you are. I want to speak to my grandson and I want to speak to him now.'

Lucinda and Jake frantically shook their heads but Victoria would not look in their direction.

'Shut up. You will do what I say if you ever want to see him again!'

'You've killed him, haven't you?'

Lucinda waved her arms violently but still could not get Victoria's attention. Robin stepped up, put an arm around the woman's shoulder and whispered in her ear. Victoria shrugged her off, her eyes wide, her breath fast and furious.

'He's fine, woman. You want to see him, you listen to me.'

'No. I don't believe you. I don't believe anything you say. You let me speak to Frederick right now or I'm hanging up.'

'Have it your way,' he said and slammed down the receiver.

The echo of the disconnected call wiped the color from the faces of all the listeners in the room except for Victoria's – her face blossomed in a bright red. 'Don't you hang up on me! You have to talk to me. Get back on the phone!'

Robin eased the receiver out of Victoria's clenched fingers and threw an arm around her again. Victoria burst into gut-wrenching sobs as Robin eased her back down on to the sofa.

Lucinda and Jake looked at each other, removed their head-phones and walked out to the front porch. 'So, what now?'

'We sit and hope he calls back and hope he doesn't take it out on Freddy.'

Jason boiled with rage. He stretched out his arms and ran them across the nearest counter, sending canisters, salt and pepper shakers and cookbooks crashing to the floor. When the container of flour hit the vinyl, its lid popped off, sending a white cloud into the air, enraging Jason even further.

He walked to the wood stove, grabbed an iron skillet and flung it in the general direction of his bound hostages. They all ducked even though it flew through the air far from their heads, crashing into a window in the wall behind them, shat-tering glass and thudding to the ground outdoors.

Stunned by his fury, the wide-eyed trio could only watch as he pulled objects off counters and utensils out of drawers and threw them across the room. Frank cringed as a spatula bounced off his head. Martha's muffled cry escaped through the duct tape as she saw Jason pick up her prized blown-glass rooster and send it soaring through the air. Freddy tried to move his head out of the way but he wasn't quick enough. The fragile figurine smacked into his forehead and exploded into pieces.

A sliver sliced his eyebrow, sending a narrow, persistent streamlet of blood across his cheek and around the duct tape and down to his chin where it dripped on to his shirt.

Jason walked over to Freddy and chucked him in the side of his head. 'Why didn't you duck, moron? Look at the mess you're making. Damn it – I should have just killed you right away. You're more trouble than you're worth. OK, Miss Martha. I'm gonna untie you so you can tend to this boy. But you try anything and I'll kill him and your husband, too. You understand?'

Martha nodded her head. Jason unfastened her legs and arms from the chair and then untied her hands. He left the duct tape in place. Martha didn't dare reach up and pull it away. She went to a drawer, pulled out a clean dishcloth and ran it under the faucet. At the table, she grabbed a paper napkin.

She folded the napkin in fourths, pressed it against the small cut and held it there with the butt of her left palm. Her right hand used the wet cloth to wipe away the trail of blood. While she worked, she stared into Freddy's eyes. Her gaze calmed him, slowing both his breath and his pulse rate. She knew what she was doing mattered but it angered her that she could do no more for the frightened boy.

Waiting for the phone to ring again scraped Lucinda's nerves raw. She tried to stop her mind from racing down nasty little rabbit warrens of ugly possibilities. But as soon as she stopped one negative train of thought, another took its place. She waited ten minutes for her annoyance with Victoria to shift back to pity before speaking to the woman.

'Ms Whitehead, I understand why you did what you did, but I need you to be aware of the situation.'

'I don't know what came over me. I hope he doesn't hurt Frederick because of what I said.' Victoria hung her head and shook with sobs.

Lucinda waited for her to settle down before she continued. 'When he calls back, I want you to apologize to him and promise you'll do anything he says.'

Victoria nodded her head.

'You think you can do that?'

Victoria nodded again. 'Yes, if he calls. But what if he never calls again?'

Lucinda stuffed down her own worries on that point and said, 'Of course he will. We have what he really wants and he has to call us to get it.'

Lucinda returned to the front porch where Jake still paced. 'I talked to her,' she said.

'You think she'll handle the next call better?'

'She says she will, but I don't know; desperate loved ones of victims are unpredictable.'

The audio tech stuck his head out the front door. 'I only got the area code, the exchange and the first of the last four digits with that last call but I was able to narrow down the area. It's still pretty big but I thought it might be better than nothing.'

Inside, Lucinda called Ted over. 'Could you get hold of the Sheriff's Departments in Amelia, Cumberland and Powhatan Counties? Run down what we've got and tell them you know it's all vague but if the kidnapper doesn't call back, they may be our only hope to find the boy.'

'We already have a statewide Amber Alert so I won't be hitting them cold,' Ted said.

'Good. Thanks, Ted.'

'I want to head out there and drive around,' Jake said.

'C'mon, Jake, you know that would be futile.'

'Yeah, but at least it would be something to do. And, who knows, if I don't find anything, he might spot me tooling around in that beauty and instigate dialogue again.'

'You do realize the odds against that, don't you?' Lucinda asked.

Jake ran his fingers across the top of his head. 'Yes, yes, of course I do. But, damn it, doing nothing is making me stir crazy.'

'I know. Me, too. Let's go back outside.'

They tried to sit in the chairs and rock but couldn't stay still more than a couple of minutes at a time. They took turns jumping up and pacing the porch floor. Lucinda and Jake attempted casual conversation but it always died after a couple of sentences when one or the other drifted off to darker thoughts.

An hour after they returned to the porch, the phone rang. They both jerked like marionettes and dashed inside the house. Donning headphones, Lucinda said, 'Ms Whitehead, are you ready? Remember to stay calm and apologetic, OK?'

Victoria nodded and picked up the receiver. 'I'm sorry, Jason. I'm so sorry. I'll do whatever you say.'

'That's better.' He laughed. 'Now, you want to talk to your grandson so I'm gonna let you.'

A ripping sound tore through the receiver, followed by a yelp.

'What have you done to him?' Victoria jumped up, shrieking.

'Calm down, Ms Whitehead, calm down,' Lucinda hissed.

Victoria nodded and collapsed back down in her seat.

'Shut up. I just took the tape off his mouth so he could talk to you,' Jason snarled.

'Grandmother?' Freddy said.

'Frederick. Oh, Frederick. Are you OK?'

'I'm fine, Grandmother. I'm here at a farm with two nice people . . .'

'That's enough. You heard him, now listen to me. You need to go west on Highway Sixty and then turn off on Route Thirteen. If you look in your dresser drawer, Victoria, you'll see that a bunch of your silk scarves are missing. I took them and used them to mark all the turns from Thirteen to this farm – it's a nice little spread of bottom land on the Appomattox River, not too far from Tobaccoville. Just look for the scarves flapping in the breeze and you'll find the place, no problem.

'And tell those cops, no tricks. I saw the boat pull into the slip a little while ago. I'm keeping an eye on it; they try anything funny and I'll kill the boy and these fine farm folk, too. I'll know if they try to hide anyone or anything in that boat. Just pull my car up in front of the house and wait. No tricks there either. One of them messes with a car like that and it will be obvious. I see any alterations and they'll regret what they force me to do. I'll tell them what to do next after they get here.'

When the connection clicked closed, every law enforcement official shifted into motion. Lucinda turned to the audio tech. 'You stay here with the equipment. If he should ring again, call my cell.'

Then she was out the door and in her car. Jake piled into the red Camaro and pulled away from the curb with Lucinda right behind him. Four marked cars – three from the city and one state trooper vehicle – followed in their wake with lights flashing.

In each vehicle, someone picked up a phone and called in updates and requests for reinforcements. Every few miles, another vehicle joined their caravan as it raced toward the three hostages, hope in their hearts, fear in their throats and intensity jangling in their eyes.

FORTY-ONE

Jake slammed down on the brakes, squealing tires as he hooked a left at the first scarf. Turning off Route 13, the patrol cars killed their lights to make their approach less obvious from a distance. Until they reached the farm, they wouldn't know how far the abductor could and could not see.

All eyes were focused on barns, curves, dips in the road, seeking a spot of concealment where vehicles could hide and a roadblock would be effective. With cellphone and radio, they exchanged observations and made their plans. After several turns in the countryside, they reached the end of the road where the final scarf flapped from a mailbox beside a dirt drive. Jake stopped and the caravan halted behind him. They all knew what to do.

Several cars backed up to a turning point and travelled to a spot a mile away where the roadway passed between two high banks, making it easy to block off the road. Other vehicles positioned behind barns and clusters of trees to wait. Lucinda parked her car in the dirt in front of a gate with a cattle guard. She piled into the back seat of a patrol car and ducked down.

Jake pulled the red Camaro into the drive first, followed by four police vehicles, including the one carrying Lucinda. As they reached the curve in the road near the barn, they all slowed down to a near-stop. Lucinda rolled out of the back door and darted behind the outbuilding.

She checked the back of her waistband to make sure she hadn't lost her handgun in the maneuver. If all went well, she wouldn't need it; the high-powered rifle clutched in her right hand would do the job. The state guys hadn't been too happy with her role in the operation – they had no faith in her shooting ability – but the local folks defended her proficiency. One even called her 'Dead Eye Pierce', then blanched and apologized. Lucinda waved him off, assuring everyone that she hadn't taken offense. She grinned at the memory. No one had called her 'Dead Eye' since she lost one eye. It almost made her feel whole again.

She dashed to the other end of the barn. From there, she could see the driveway peter out in front of the farmhouse where Jake had parked the car. Not a sound came from inside the house. The quiet made her nervous. Jake stayed in the car, an easy target for the man inside the house. She wanted to scream at him to take cover, but she knew that was not an option.

The creak of the opening screen door sent shivers through her body. She drew a bead on the emerging body. The slam of the door's closing sent a small spasm through her legs. But the person on the porch was a woman – in all likelihood, one of the three hostages. Lucinda lowered her rifle.

The woman's hands were tied tight behind her back. She spoke but her voice was too low to carry past the porch. A trooper put one foot out of his car and stood with a hand to his ear. The woman began again, shouting, 'My name is Martha Drummond. This farm belongs to me and my husband Frank. I have instructions for you. You need to follow them or that boy or my husband will die.' She choked as a sob shredded a hole in the idyllic setting.

Martha sucked in a gulp of air. 'You all must get out of your cars, take two sideways steps away from your vehicles and place your hands on top of your heads – and that includes the man in the red car.'

As the car doors opened, Lucinda thought this might be the moment of diversion she sought. She scampered to the back of the house and flattened against the wall beside the back door, clutching the rifle to her chest with both hands.

Jake did not like standing there beside the car with his hands on top of his head – it made him feel vulnerable and powerless. It was made even worse knowing that everyone in the back-up cars stood in the same position. He could only hope that Lucinda found the right moment to get into position.

Martha told them she had to inspect their vehicles and she travelled to them one by one, looking in the back seats and in the trunks. She returned to the porch, turned and faced them. 'Thank you. I'm sorry.'

A shout from the house drew her eyes to the front door. She cringed and scampered inside, the wooden screen door slamming shut behind her. Again, they waited.

*   *   *

Lucinda eased open the back door just enough to listen. She heard voices coming from the front of the house. One, a female voice tinged with fear, must be Martha. The other, a male voice, snarled out orders. Without seeing what was happening, the terse words made little sense to her.

Praying the door wouldn't make a noise and betray her presence, Lucinda opened it a little bit further to slide inside. She stood in a kitchen that brought waves of nostalgia rushing through her thoughts, transporting her for a moment back to Hank and Connie's farmhouse. She shook her head and snapped back to the here and now.

Indentations on the vinyl floor indicated where the dining table once sat – it was now shoved against the wall. One window sported a jagged hole and small slivers of glass gleamed in the sunlight. Three chairs, side by side, occupied the middle of the room. From each one, rope hung from the backs and puddled on the floor by the front legs. Debris cluttered the floor – an egg beater here, a grater there – and everywhere shattered glass and porcelain. Lucinda didn't want to think about the terror this destruction had caused.

She didn't see a spot where she could look into the front room without revealing her presence. She considered bursting in with her rifle up and ready to fire but knew she couldn't risk it without knowing the position of the hostages. She strained to think of alternatives.

An odd noise came from the room, a shuffling sound that reminded her of a line of shackled prisoners entering a court-room but without the jangle of the leg restraints and chains. She risked a peek around the corner and froze at the sight of a pair of eyes looking in her direction. In a split second, she realized she had nothing to fear. The duct tape across his mouth made it obvious – it was the male hostage. He gave her a tiny, tight nod and fixed her with a pleading stare. He was tied to the kidnapper's back, making it impossible for Lucinda to see Jason King/John Kidd's head.

Damn. He thinks of everything. Lucinda refused to enter-tain that thought a moment longer. *He will make a mistake. A big mistake. And when he does, I will be ready.*

The front door opened, the screen door creaked and the tight group shuffled out on to the porch. As soon as it slammed behind them, Lucinda crept into the room and stopped. She waited for the four pairs of feet to make it down the porch steps, before getting into position and aiming her rifle at the most likely location of the killer's hidden head.

An ache burned in Jake's shoulders. The stress of the situation made it doubly difficult to keep his arms raised over his head. A sign of movement at the front door gave him hope that this part of the ordeal would soon be over. He hoped Lucinda was in place ready to take the shot that would bring it all to a quick end.

He groaned when he saw how they emerged from the house, the abductor's left arm wrapped around Freddy's throat. His right hand held a gun to the side of the boy's head. On his right side, Martha had her left arm tethered backwards. Jake couldn't tell from his position where it was attached. It could be to her captor – it could be to her husband. Frank was tied back to back with Jason King/John Kidd, making it impossible for Lucinda to get a clear sight of the kidnapper's head. *This pretty much sucks. Damn it.*

Kidd turned to Martha and whispered in her ear. She shouted out, 'You – next to the red car – step away from the vehicle but keep your hands on your head.'

Jake took two steps away. Kidd whispered again. Martha said, 'He says that's not far enough, go over by the barn.'

Jake brought his hands down without thinking. Kidd dug the muzzle into Freddy's head making the boy cry out. 'Hands on your head!' he screamed.

'But you wanted a driver. I'm your driver.'

'I changed my mind. Move!'

Jake backed away, fever burning in his eyes. He cast a glance toward the house but could see nothing in the gloom of the unlit rooms. He prayed the perfect opportunity would come for Lucinda who was ready and waiting to take the shot.

Lucinda knew that as long as Frank was attached to Kidd's back, there was no chance she could pick off Kidd without killing Frank, too. She waited, breathing deeply and purposefully – preparing for the moment when that might change.

Kidd stopped his bound entourage by the side of the Camaro and, grinning, looked down the line of officers standing in that humiliating pose. 'Miss Martha, untie your wrist from the rope attached to my waist and then go behind me and untie your husband. Frank, don't you move until I tell you to do so.'

Anger threatened to disrupt the peace and calm Lucinda knew she needed in order to do what had to be done. She forced herself to concentrate on her breathing to focus her mind and level her emotions.

Martha muttered and Kidd said, 'Good. Now, I want Frank to ease to one side and Martha, you get in his place but do it facing me and place one hand on each of my shoulders.' Once they'd exchanged places, Kidd said, 'Frank, back up a few steps. A few more.'

Lucinda beaded her gun sight on the top of Kidd's head but knew there was too little room for error – Martha was shorter but not by much. Kidd pulled open the driver's door and turned around. As he did, he hoisted Freddy up with a firm grip around his waist. The boy's new position blocked Kidd's head. Lucinda cursed him for being too smooth.

'Take your hands off my shoulders, Martha and slide behind the wheel. Start the car and shut the door. And don't forget, I still have a gun to the little boy's head.' With his back to the vehicle, he walked around it with Freddy held high. He shouted to Martha to open the passenger door. Over his shoulder, he said, 'Frank, your job is to make sure none of these fine officers move until I reach the end of the driveway. You got it?'

Frank nodded.

'Can't hear you, Frank.'

Frank mumbled through the duct tape. His words were not clear but Kidd accepted it as affirmation. Kidd crouched down, hiding behind Freddy as he set him on the ground. 'Now, little man, I'm going to remove my arm for a moment but the gun's still at your head, so don't try anything smart.' Kidd lifted up the lever on the side of the front seat, leaning it forward. He grabbed the boy by the waist again, using him for cover as he slid into the back seat.

'I'm going to let go of you, little man. You try to run for it and this lady is dead. I just want you to get into the front seat and shut the door.'

Freddy did as he was told. He reached for his seat belt and felt a finger brush his hand. He looked at Ms Martha and she gave her head a little shake.

'Move it, old lady,' Kidd shouted from the back seat.

Martha eased the car down the driveway, tires crunching over gravel. As soon as the Camaro curved around the barn and out of sight, Lucinda sprinted out the front door. Frank turned toward her, shaking his head. A patrolman slipped up behind him and cut the restraints on his arms. 'It's OK, sir. He can't see us from down there.'

Lucinda laid a hand on his arms and said, 'Frank, you go in the house and wait. We'll be back as soon as we can.'

Frank shook out his arms and tried to ease the tape off his face. He grew impatient and pulled it off fast, sending shrieks of pain up through his nerves and into his brain. He watched the patrol cars pull away but he didn't go inside. He stood sentry waiting for Martha's return. He prayed for good news but feared the worst.

FORTY-TWO

In the passenger side of the first patrol car in the pack, Lucinda grabbed the radio. 'Dismantle the roadblock. Get your vehicles out of sight. Now. He's travelling with two hostages.'

She dropped the device, picked up her cell and called Jake. 'I didn't take my eyes off of him for a moment. I never saw a chance. I don't think I missed a moment of opportunity but I don't know.'

'Trust me, Lucinda, you didn't have a chance. We're not dealing with your typically stupid felon.'

'But still, shit! I don't want to follow him all the way to Norfolk before we have another shot at him. Damn it, Jake, I should have tried.'

'No. Your instincts were right. We can't risk killing hostages to get to the bad guy. We'll be looking for opportunities along the way. Something will happen.'

'I sure hope you're right. And I hope we know it when we see it.' She clicked off and leaned forward in her seat.

Freddy wasn't sure what was going on. He knew Ms Martha had something in mind but didn't know what. He reached again for his seat belt but she hissed, 'No!'

Kidd kicked the back of his seat and said, 'You listen to her, little man, and don't try anything cute. Even if you get away, I'll put a bullet in the old lady's head and you'll have to live with that blood on your hands for the rest of your miserable life.'

'Where are we going?' Freddy asked.

'We're going to a boat and then to Cuba. Remember, you found that for me, little man.'

'I don't want to go to Cuba,' Freddy objected.

'Don't be a cry-baby. As soon as I get there, you can come back.'

Freddy knew enough about current events to know that wouldn't be happening but he didn't respond. He focused instead on Martha who kept glancing at him, jerking her eyes towards her door. Finally, Freddy saw that her left hand hovered over the door handle. He slipped his right hand over to his. Martha slowed the car.

'What are you doing? Get moving,' Kidd shouted.

'There's a nasty curve up ahead and a one-lane bridge. Take it too fast and I could run head on into a police car,' she said.

'Once you're past the bridge, pick up the pace.'

As soon as the car was moving as slowly as Martha dared, she shouted, 'Now!'

Freddy and Martha both pushed down on the door handles and plunged out of their seats, tumbling on to the road and rolling into the ditches along either side. Two shots rang out and the windows on the open doors shattered as the car drifted toward the side of the small bridge. The side of the Camaro scraped against the concrete and then swerved back into the center of the road. The driver's side door slammed shut and the car pulled away fast, the passenger door slapping back and forth in every curve.

Lucinda grabbed the radio and screamed, 'Get the roadblock back in place. Hurry. Now. Cut off the road. The hostages are out of the car. Repeat – the hostages are clear. Stop that car.'

The two vehicles transporting Lucinda and Jake zoomed forward. The two cars behind them fell out to locate and give assistance to the hostages. Lucinda switched to another channel on the radio and screamed for an ambulance.

Up ahead, one car was in place blocking most of the road. Kidd swerved, the tires on the left side tearing through the dirt. But he didn't turn the wheels sharply enough. The flapping passenger door collided with the front end of the marked vehicle, tearing it off in a deafening shriek of metal against metal.

The Camaro shuddered and barreled forward, running straight for the officers with drawn guns. They shot at the windshield, jumped to the side and continued firing into the side of the car. One bullet hit a tire, blowing it out, rubber flapping and metal rim digging furrows into the road surface, throwing sparks. Still Kidd surged forward.

Another roadblock was now in place at the intersection with Route 13. Kidd saw it moments before he reached the barricade. He swerved off the road in an attempt to cut the corner and escape behind the police line. The bare rim bit down into the dirt, jerking the car to a halt. Kidd's head flew forward in the sudden stop, crashing into the steering wheel and the horn, sending out a lonely, non-stop blare.

An ambulance turned the corner and slowed. 'Not here. Down the road,' a patrolman shouted and the emergency vehicle sped off.

Lucinda and Jake, guns drawn, reached the side of the Camaro first. They waited for a ring of uniforms to surround the car before moving closer. As they stepped towards him, Kidd raised his head. Jake and Lucinda froze. 'Put your fingers on the butt of the gun and toss it out the window,' Jake ordered.

Kidd paused, looking around the car, assessing the flight or fight probabilities and realizing the odds were not in his favor. He shrugged, reached down and raised one hand in an exaggerated move with the gun dangling from his fingertips. He moved his arm slowly to the window frame where some of the glass remained shattered into little chunks around the edges. Sticking his arm outside of the vehicle, he released his fingers and the weapon fell to the ground.

Jake reached in, grabbed him by the collar and jerked him out of the car. He threw the suspect face down into the ground, put a knee in his back, wrenched his arms behind him and slapped on the cuffs. Grabbing the chain between Kidd's wrists, Jake stood, yanking the cuffed man to his feet as he did.

'Hey, man, easy. I'm bleeding.'

Jake spun him around and saw a cut on his forehead turning his face into a bloody mess. He shouted to another officer who pulled a towel out of his trunk and rushed over to hold it on Kidd's wound.

When the ambulance returned up the road, Lucinda waved it down. 'How is everybody?'

'Looks like the lady fractured her ulna – we splinted her arm. The boy appears to have nothing more than abrasions and contusions – we cleaned up his cuts – and the older guy is delirious with joy that his wife is alive but concerned about her injury. The doc will give them a closer examination when we get them to the emergency room. You want us to take that guy, too?'

'Hell, no. But will the others be OK if you take a little time to bandage the cut on his head?'

'Sure, no problem,' the EMT said, grabbing a bag and sprinting over to Kidd. When the medical technician had finished patching up Kidd, Jake shoved the kidnapper into the back of a state car and sent them off to a nearby Trooper station.

Lucinda found a sorrowful Jake, hands on his hips, staring down at the damage to the Camaro. 'Damn,' he said. 'She once was a beauty.'

'Borrowed, not bought, right?'

'Yeah, 'fraid so. I hope I can find someone who can repair the damage and restore it back to the original. I could have done with a little less unpredictability today.'

'Yeah, but you gotta admire one unexpected turn of events. I am still amazed at Martha and Freddy. I didn't think either one of them had it in 'em. But thank God they did. It saved us a long, strained trip to the boat slip.'

'What?' Jake grinned. 'You didn't want a paid trip to the coast?'

Lucinda snorted in response.

'How about a ride on the Skyline Drive to the Blue Ridge Parkway and down into the Great Smoky Mountains – all with the top down feeling the mountain breeze – as soon as we wrap this up.'

'No can do, Jake, I have to go in for another surgery as soon as we close this case. I'll be out of commission for a few weeks.'

'That's even better. We'll go in mid October when the autumn colors are at their peak at the higher elevation.'

Lucinda felt a thrill coursing through her nervous system, threatening to flood out cogent thought. She didn't know what to say – she wanted to set a date right there, right then. But she was afraid. It would change the dynamic between her and

Jake and she didn't know if she was ready to take that risk. Ducking her head and heading to her car, she said, 'Let's talk about that later, Jake. Right now, we've got a suspect who needs our total attention.'

FORTY-THREE

A t the nearby state police headquarters, uniformed troopers escorted John Kidd into the interrogation room. Lucinda and Jake watched on the video monitor as they fastened his shackles to the leg of a sturdy gray metal table bolted to the floor and his left handcuff to the bolt and hook in the concrete wall.

Little remained of the smooth-talking con man with an easy smile and sparkling eyes and an ability to charm older women from coast to coast. The events of the day had scraped the veneer away to reveal the predator that lurked beneath the surface, ready to pounce on any opportunity. He was cornered and he knew it. Keeping up his false front demanded too much energy now.

Jake nodded at Lucinda. She returned the gesture and gave him a thumbs up. Jake walked out of the control booth and down two doors to the room containing John Kidd. As Jake entered the room, the three troopers departed, leaving him alone with the suspect. Kidd slouched in the chair with his free arm on the table surface and his forehead resting on his arm. When Jake began to read the man his rights, Kidd raised his head slightly and stared at the detective through hooded eyes. When Jake finished, Lucinda walked into the room.

Turning to her, Jake said, 'I read him his rights.'

'Why did you bother with that, Jake? John's a man and a man doesn't hide behind anyone – not even an attorney. Does he, John?

Jake leaned back against the wall and folded his arms across his chest. John raised his head and sat straighter in the chair. His focus was now on Lucinda alone. The surly expression vanished, as if a giant hand swept down across his face and wiped it away. He beamed a big smile, pulling his false front

back in place. 'Hello, ma'am. I am so glad to see you. I
thought I was stuck with macho man here,' he said, poking a
thumb in Jake's direction. 'Women are much more intuitive
and since you all don't tote around that testosterone-fueled
attitude, you can cut through the BS so much easier.'

Lucinda laughed at him. 'Spare me, Mr Kidd. I'm not old
enough for you and you're not pretty enough for me.'

Kidd's nostrils flared and his free hand formed a fist. The
veneer cracked but he smoothed it back in place. 'I'm not
coming on to you, ma'am. I'm afraid my reputation is clouding
your perception of me. I think if you'll set that aside for a
minute, we can both find a resolution to this situation that
will work for all of us.'

'A resolution? You kidnap a boy, hold him and a farming
couple hostage and you think there's some sort of nice little
compromise possible?'

'Listen, it's really simple, ma'am. You know, I'm sure, how
quirky things can get when we are dealing with affairs of the
heart?' He looked at Lucinda, waiting for an answer. When
he didn't get one, he continued. 'See, this is all a big misunderstanding around a lover's quarrel.'

'A misunderstanding?'

'Yeah, in fact, ma'am, all this is partly your fault.'

'My fault?'

'Yeah, you see, you told Victoria about Karen King and
all. And she was really angry about that. I mean, I don't blame
you or anything. I understand how women have to stick
together in the face of male trickery; but, you know, that's
why we fought. She said she was throwing me out. I couldn't
stand it. My heart was shredded. I knew if I had Freddy, she'd
come talk to me. That's all I wanted.'

'You just wanted to talk? That's why you left body parts
on her porch and sent her a ransom demand?'

'I don't know anything about body parts but I just made
the ransom request to get her attention.'

'You sure did that, Mr Kidd. But, you see, the kidnapping
thing is a federal rap. I'm not all that concerned about that –
I leave that to the Feeb here. I'm just an ordinary local cop.
And I've got this double homicide here that I was hoping we
could talk about.'

'Homicide? I don't know anything about murder.'

Jake interrupted. 'Listen, Lieutenant, I've got a real solid abduction case here and I want to deal with the problem at hand. Why don't you just go do some investigation and let me deal with my suspect?'

'See, ma'am, there's the perfect example of that macho behavior I was talking about. He's a man. He's gotta be in charge. Personally, I prefer demonstrating my testosterone in bed – if you know what I mean,' John said with a wink.

'Are you under the mistaken impression that you can play me like one of your old lady victims, Mr Kidd?' Lucinda asked. 'Let me set you straight. For one, a real man does not prey on helpless, lonely widows. And since I've taken on real men and won – you don't have a chance. Secondly, I have never been desperate enough to have a man in my bed to ever consider you as a possible candidate.' As she spoke, the change in his expression was so abrupt that Lucinda could have sworn she saw the veneer peel way.

He sneered at her, 'As if any man would ever crawl into your ugly bed.'

'Excuse me, is that another example of that macho shit you were telling me about?'

'Somebody sure messed your face. I'll bet you didn't feel so tough then, bitch.'

Lucinda looked down at him and blinked her eyelids with slow deliberation. She turned her head to the side and said, 'Later, Jake.'

'But, Lieutenant, the charge for the arrest is kidnapping . . .'

'Yeah, and with my help, you've got that wrapped up very nicely. So go on, give me a minute with my homicide suspect.'

Lucinda kept her eyes on Kidd. She didn't look back but knew Jake was gone when she heard the click of the closing door. She smiled at the realization that the script she and Jake had prepared was playing out just as they planned.

She placed two hands on the table top and eased into the chair. She pointed to her face. 'You think this looks bad, Mr Kidd?'

'Pretty awful, you ask me. Somebody must have been pretty ticked off at you. And I'm beginning to understand why.'

She leaned forward close enough to his face that she could feel the warmth of his breath. 'You think this is bad, you should see the other guy.'

Kidd laughed out loud. 'You think you're tough, don't you, bitch?'

'My title is Lieutenant. You can use that.'

'Don't think so, bitch.'

'My, my, my, Mr Kidd,' Lucinda said, leaning back in her chair. 'With a mouth like that, I don't know how you managed to con all of those women.'

'I don't know what you're talking about.'

'Don't be modest, Mr Kidd. We've tracked your trail of broken hearts and empty bank accounts all over the country. We know all your names. We know all your games. We own your sorry ass.'

'You don't know shit.'

'We know pretty much everything. We traced you all the way back to your genius Daddy, William Blessing. And we know he's the excuse you're using for committing your crimes.'

'You're crazy, bitch.'

Lucinda's hand clutched his collar and jerked him forward before the last syllable escaped his mouth. Out of the corner of her eye, she saw a twitch in his arm. 'Don't even think about it, Mr Kidd. Assaulting an officer will get you a very long sentence even if we can't prove the murders you committed.'

'My word against yours.'

Lucinda laughed, letting go of his collar, and gave him a sharp shove back into his chair. 'I have witnesses, Mr Kidd.'

Lucinda watched his eyes as they circled round the room. 'There's no one-way glass in here – it's all solid walls,' John noted. 'Oh, yeah, I get it. You have cops who will lie for you – swear to any story you concoct.'

'Oh, no, Mr Kidd. Welcome to the big time. This is a state-of-the-art interrogation room with a high-tech monitoring center where they can watch and record all six rooms at one time. Lucinda turned and pointed. 'See that vent high up on the wall? Look closely and you'll see a tiny pinpoint red light behind the louvers. That's a camera. And there are six micro-phones installed flush with the surface, around the room, to pick up everything you say in surround sound. And if I'm not tough enough for you, those three big, beefy troopers who brought you in, they're standing just outside the door, itching for a chance to slam you into the floor.'

'You don't scare me. They don't scare me. You might be

able to make the kidnapping stick but you don't have a thing to connect me to any murders. You've got my record. You know what I am – a con man, a scam artist – but not one violent crime. And you go talk to those women. For a while, I made every one of them feel like a queen and they loved me – each and every one. And unless they're lying, they'll tell you I never raised a hand to one of them. I'm not a violent man. I've no history of it – the judge will laugh you out of the courtroom. You want your killer, Lieutenant, I'll give her to you. But we've got to make a deal. I'm not spending the rest of my life in jail to protect anyone.'

'So, you're willing to pin your murders on a woman? Tsk, tsk, Mr Kidd. I guess chivalry truly is dead.'

'I'm not a violent man.'

'All of us are capable of violence; we just have to have the right motivation. We know why you targeted the people in the Sterling house but we don't know why this time you resorted to violence. It wasn't even the last one, so it doesn't make sense to me. You had one more to go. So why did you go so far this time around?'

Kidd studied her but did not speak.

'C'mon, Kidd. We know you were the shooter. Nothing else makes sense. But someone helped you? Who was she? Who was your accomplice? You're going down, but you don't need to take the fall alone. Cooperate and you might be able to waltz away from the death penalty.'

'I want an attorney.'

'What a disappointment. I thought you were smarter than that, Mr Kidd.'

'Screw you, bitch.'

'I don't think so, Mr Kidd. I'm too young for your senior citizen fetish.'

Kidd slammed his free arm down hard on the surface of the table.

Lucinda stood and walked to the door. When she opened it, she turned back and said, 'I hope you didn't hurt yourself, little man.'

FORTY-FOUR

'Any word from the hospital?' Lucinda asked as she stepped from the interrogation room.

'Everyone is just fine. Martha has a new cast and she and Frank are on their way to their son's house in the next county – we couldn't take them back to the farm because the forensics techs are still gathering evidence out there. We thought you'd like to take Freddy back home, so a trooper is bringing him over here. Should arrive any minute. But, if you'd rather, we can get the trooper to transport him.'

'No, not at all. That's perfect. Jake and I need to head back and it would be nice to have some time to talk to Freddy on the drive into the city.'

A civilian employee stepped into the back hall and informed Lucinda that Kidd was ready for transfer to her county's jail. 'And his attorney has been contacted. He will meet him there.'

Lucinda dreaded dealing with attorneys in general and assumed the one representing John Kidd would be particularly difficult. She just hoped that it wasn't one of the lawyers she'd already annoyed.

The back door opened and a bandaged, weary but upbeat Freddy walked through the door. 'Lieutenant Pierce! That sure was scary but it got really exciting at the end. I can't wait to tell everybody at school about what I did for my summer vacation. Nobody'll be able to call me a wimp ever again.'

Jake ruffled the young boy's hair. 'We're all proud of you, Freddy. What you did took a lot of guts.'

'Are you the FBI guy?'

'Sure am. And you'll be riding back home with me and the Lieutenant.'

'Do you have a cool car like the one you brought to the farmhouse?'

'I do, Freddy, but unfortunately, it's in DC. We're riding in the Lieutenant's boring-mobile.'

'Hey,' Lucinda said, 'it gets us where we need to go.'

'See, Freddy, women just don't get it.'

Freddy laughed and asked, 'Do you have to junk that red Camaro?'

Jake winced. 'I sure hope not.'

'Let's go, guys,' Lucinda said, putting an arm on Freddy's back and giving him a gentle push towards the door.

Before they hit the highway, Lucinda stopped at Dairy Queen and told Freddy to order whatever he wanted. He asked for a Butterfinger Blizzard. She thought about insisting on a meal, but then decided that after what the kid had been through, he deserved anything he wanted.

While he devoured the frozen concoction, Freddy babbled away about his recent experience. His hard-won freedom put a glossy shine on his days of captivity, turning it all into a grand adventure. Then he became serious. 'What makes people get that way?'

'That's something we study at the FBI all the time, Freddy,' Jake said, 'but we still don't have a clear-cut answer. It has something to do with abuse in their early childhood, brain injuries, drug and alcohol use at a young age – and then, there seems like there must be something in their genetic make-up because you can take a bunch of people with nearly identical lives and one person grows up a psychopath, another leads a life devoted to helping others, and most of them just end up like pretty ordinary folks.'

'How come my grandma didn't know he was a bad person?'

'I'm pretty sure she's come to regret that, Freddy,' Lucinda said. 'But she's not the first person to be tricked by a psychopath and she won't be the last.'

As they traveled the last few miles, Freddy grew quiet. Both Lucinda and Jake tried to bring him out again but he resisted all their attempts with monosyllabic responses.

Victoria Whitehead raced down the front steps as they pulled up front. She threw her arms around Freddy as soon as he stepped out of the car. She turned to Lucinda. 'Can you please come in for a bit? I have a few questions.'

Lucinda nodded and she and Jake followed Freddy and his grandmother into the house. Victoria prepared a snack for Freddy and, at his pleading, allowed him to take it downstairs where he wanted to go to play with his Wii.

The two investigators ran down the series of events and responded to all of Victoria's queries, assuring her that Freddy had received a thorough medical examination at the hospital. Lucinda was walking toward the stairs to say goodbye to Freddy when her cell rang. 'Pierce,' she said and then listened. 'You're kidding!' She paused again. 'Miracles do happen. Thanks for the call.'

'What is it?' Jake asked.

'He's ready to give up his accomplice in the double homicide. Fear of a possible death sentence does wonders for the level of cooperation.'

After their car pulled away from the curb, Victoria yelled down to Freddy, 'Get your Wii, your games and all the cable you need to hook it up and come upstairs.'

'You want me to bring my Wii upstairs?'

'Just do it, Frederick. And hurry.'

Freddy did as he was told and came up the steps. 'Grandmother?'

From the second floor, she shouted down, 'Set that stuff down in the foyer and get up here. You need to pack your clothes.'

'Pack my clothes? Where are we going?' Freddy asked as he mounted the stairs.

'Don't you worry about that. Just get busy. We may never come back here so pack everything you ever want to see again.'

'Grandmother, this doesn't make any sense. Jason or John or whatever is in jail. They're not going to let him out. We're safe.'

'No, we are not safe. There is more in this world to worry about than Jason's violence. We need to leave and we need to leave right away.'

In his bedroom, Freddy found an empty suitcase open on his bed. The thought of never returning frightened him and made it difficult for him to decide what to take and what to leave behind. He filled the bag, zipped it shut and rolled it out into the hall. 'Grandmother, I finished.'

'Good. Come in here and get another piece of luggage for your Wii – get the smallest one that will hold it all and grab an afghan from the family room and wrap it around the pieces so it won't get banged up.'

Freddy grabbed an overnight bag and rolled the two pieces of luggage down the stairs. After packing away his Wii, he sat down on a chair trying to figure out what was happening and why. He finally decided that his grandmother was just freaking out and in a few days she'd realize that and then they'd come home.

Victoria emerged from her bedroom pulling two big suitcases behind her. Freddy leaped up the steps to take one of the bags downstairs while she took the other one.

'Ready, Frederick?' she asked.

Ready for what? 'Yes, ma'am.'

Victoria led him through the kitchen and into the garage. She backed the car out and stopped. 'Say goodbye, Frederick. I don't know why any of us ever moved to this godforsaken town. I, for one, will never return – not even if I'm stone-cold dead. You remember that, Frederick. As much as I loved your mother, and as much as I'd like to rest beside her for all eternity, I can never do it here. My soul would never find a moment's peace.'

FORTY-FIVE

District Attorney Michael Reed and Federal Prosecutor Alicia Monroe greeted Lucinda and Jake when they arrived at the justice center. 'John Kidd is in the interrogation room with his attorney, Stephen Theismann,' Reed said.

'Not Theismann,' Lucinda groaned.

'Afraid so, Pierce. But it won't be a problem. Kidd's ready to deal, so we won't need the two of you in the room.'

'Excuse me?' Lucinda snapped.

'Pierce, settle down and hear me out. Here's how we're going to play it. You and Special Agent Lovett will be on the other side of the glass, able to hear every word. Prosecutor Monroe and I will be in the interrogation room wearing earpieces so that you can communicate with us – feed us any relevant details, suggest questions, whatever.'

Lucinda threw up her hands, 'Fine. Fine. But if he balks . . .'

'We hit a brick wall, Pierce, we'll bring both of you in.'

'OK,' Lucinda said, shaking her head in disagreement.

'Pierce, don't come barging in there without an invitation – you got it?'

'Whatever,' Lucinda said, walking down the hall and into the observation room.

Reed and Monroe entered interrogation, sat down across from Kidd and Theismann and put in their earplugs. Reed introduced Monroe to the attorney and his client, then said, 'Mr Theismann, for the record, what is your client offering and what does he want?'

'Mr Kidd is offering up the identity of the shooter and his willingness to testify against this perpetrator in a court of law. He is also prepared to plead guilty to desecration of a corpse and complicity after the fact. In exchange, he wants a sentence commensurate with those lower level felonies.'

'As if.' Lucinda chuckled.

'Providing that your client is completely truthful with us here today and testifies to the same, we are in agreement.'

'He's got to be kidding! I will not let them do that,' Lucinda said, reaching for the button to speak to the prosecutors.

Jake grabbed her wrist and pulled it back. 'Wait. They're only talking about dropping the murder charges. And what if there is another shooter? The kidnapping is a federal rap guaranteeing a stiff sentence and – unlike the state – in federal prison, the sentence given is pretty darned close to the time actually served. He's not off the hook, Lucinda. And if he makes one false statement, we'll prove it and the deal is off.'

'The murders of Parker and Jeanine Sterling are not irrelevant, Jake.'

'No, they're not. But we need to be practical. This could give us the best of both worlds – an accomplice and Kidd behind bars for a long time.'

'I still don't like it.'

'Let it play out.'

Lucinda nodded and returned her attention to the other room.

'Mr Kidd, are you claiming you are not the shooter?' Reed asked.

'Not just claiming. It's a fact. It was not my gun and I did not pull the trigger.'

'Who do you allege fired the weapon in the Sterling home that morning?'

Kidd looked at his attorney. Theismann nodded. 'Pamela Godfrey,' Kidd said.

'Holy shit,' Lucinda said, picking up her cell and speed-dialing

Ted's number. 'Go pick up Pamela Godfrey immediately and bring her in for questioning.'

'She's the accomplice?'

'That's what he says.'

'On my way.'

Lucinda turned back to Reed mid sentence. '. . . the nature of your relationship with Ms Godfrey?'

'She's a lesbian – we don't have a "relationship". I'm not her type.' Kidd laughed.

'Mr Theismann, will you please remind your client of the seriousness of this interview and request that he respond accordingly,' Reed said.

'Mr Reed, my client is well aware of the gravity of his position. He is apprising you of the situation, nothing more.'

'Well, Mr Kidd, can we start at the beginning?' Reed asked. 'Take me back to your arrival in town and why you came here in the first place.'

'You sure you're not a shrink? Taking me back to the horrors of my childhood?' Kidd asked.

'You weren't raised here, Kidd. You can skip the heart-wrenching biographical sketch.'

'Not really, Mr Reed. Not if you want the story to make sense.'

'OK, fine. Go ahead.'

'My father, the philandering William Blessing, fathered quite a few children in his lifetime. My mother knew nothing about it until after his stroke killed him. When he died, they cleared out his office and turned his personal belongings and papers over to my mother and that's when she learned the truth. He had extracted himself from our lives but since they were still legally married, my mother assumed that he was as faithful to her as she was to him. When she read his journal, she found out otherwise and took her life – she killed herself over that miserable son of a bitch.'

Reed looked back over his shoulder toward the glass and raised his eyebrows. Lucinda pressed the button. 'Yes, his mother did commit suicide.'

'I take it you saw the journal after your mother's death?' Reed asked.

'Yes, I did. I found a list of the women who slept with my father, complete with dates. And it was their fault that my mother and I had to struggle to exist – we lived on beans, rice and water for a long, long time. My father never gave us a penny after he walked out the door. So I set out to get what was owed to me by those slutty women. You found my papers, you saw all the women and the children they had with my father – children that replaced me.'

'Your father ran a sperm bank, Mr Kidd. Did it ever occur to you that all you found was a list of women who were artificially inseminated with your father's sperm?'

'Of course I thought about it. But that would have been unethical – he ran the place, he couldn't participate.'

That astonishing response left the prosecutor momentarily speechless. In his ear, Lucinda said. 'That was just one set of documents. What about the one that went back generations?'

Reed asked about the centuries-long genealogy chart and John Kidd laughed again. 'I just made that one up.'

'And why would you do that?'

'Well, that wasn't my original plan. I came looking for Jeanine Sterling – not Victoria Whitehead. I looked up Freddy's birth certificate and saw that Parker was listed as his father and I knew that wasn't true. I figured the easiest way to get the money Jeanine owed me for sleeping with my father was blackmail. I thought if I threatened to tell her husband about her affair and the paternity of her son, she'd pay me anything I wanted to keep quiet.

'Unfortunately, she just told me to go to hell. So I had to come up with another plan and that's when I discovered Victoria. She was easy pickings – most of those older women are; they're usually widowed or divorced with no one giving them a second glance. They're so appreciative of the smallest kindness and so grateful if you seduce them. It's kind of pathetic, really.

'I thought I could use her to get what I wanted. I realized she was a sucker for all that off-the-wall, mumbo-jumbo, supernatural stuff. So I created a story that Parker Sterling had sold his soul to the devil in exchange for immortality. Those phony documents I drew up made her a believer. I figured if she hated and feared her son-in-law, I could use that to my advantage.'

'So where does Pamela Godfrey come into the story?' Reed asked.

'The thing with Victoria wasn't working as I planned. Instead of convincing her daughter of the evilness of Parker, Jeanine grew furious at her mother and stopped talking to her. So I staked out the Sterling house, looking for something else to use. I knew I had it the day I saw a woman walk out the front door, then stop to embrace and lay a passionate kiss on Jeanine's mouth. That woman was Pamela Godfrey.'

'How did you figure out who she was?'

'I kept watching the house. I saw her come and go many times. Then one day, she stormed out, slamming the door behind her. I followed her to the parking lot of the complex where she lived. I approached her and told her I knew about her and Jeanine and thought she might be pissed off at someone in the Sterling house.

'She said she loved Jeanine but Jeanine had called off the relationship – said she didn't want to see Pamela any more. Boy, was Godfrey pissed. So I made her a proposition: we'd both blackmail Jeanine over the lesbian affair. No way could that woman survive in her social circle with her secret out. That's why we went to the house that morning. We wanted to catch both of them at home, thinking that if Jeanine balked, her husband would pay anything to keep that assault on his manhood private.'

'So you want us to believe that the two of you went into the house for no reason other than extortion?' Reed asked.

'Yeah, man, I swear, that was *my* only reason. I didn't even know Pamela was carrying a gun.'

'Then what happened?'

'We went upstairs and found them both in the bathroom. I told them why we were there and the next thing I know shots are firing and two people are dead on the floor. On top of that, Pamela was getting all weepy after killing them. I had to help her move Jeanine's body to the bed. She cried over her the whole time she was fixing her up. I kept telling her to make sure her tears didn't fall and leave traces of her DNA behind.'

'That explains the scene we found in the bedroom, but why was Parker's body mutilated?'

'Well, you see, I'd already fed my story to Victoria and she bought into it. So I figured if I made it look like Parker killed his wife and left some poor slob in the tub with his identifying features removed, she'd help me with an alibi and with cash when I needed it. After all, she would now control Freddy's estate, so she could get her hands on lots of money.'

'How did you know that? About her control of Freddy's inheritance?'

'Asked her about that a long time ago, just trying to figure out alternative ways to get to Jeanine's money.'

'That makes it sound as if you had a good motive for the shooting, Mr Kidd,' Reed said.

'Please, on the surface, sure, but I had this blackmail scheme going. I wanted to play that out and that damned Godfrey woman screwed it up.'

'I'm not buying this story, Reed,' Lucinda whispered into the microphone.

Reed just shook his head. He turned to Alicia Monroe and they exchanged nods.

'Wait!' Lucinda urged. 'Ask him about Parker's other hand.'

'Mr Kidd, we recovered Parker's head and one of his hands. Where is the other hand?'

John Kidd shrugged. 'Got me. Pamela wanted to keep it. Thought it was kind of weird but I let her have it – I guess she still has it.'

'Thank you,' Reed said. 'Mr Theismann, we accept your offer of a plea to the lesser charges.'

In the other room, Lucinda said, 'Jake how can they do this? It's outrageous!'

'Shh, Lucinda. Listen, we still have the kidnapping rap – we've got him dead to rights there.'

Jake and Lucinda turned their attention back to the interrogation room in time to hear Kidd's attorney ask, 'And the federal charges, Ms Monroe?'

'As long as your client continues to cooperate, tell the whole truth and testify at Ms Godfrey's trial, the abduction charge and all related charges will be dropped. The federal government will not prosecute your client.'

'No,' Lucinda screamed into the ears of both prosecutors. 'You can't do this!'

The prosecutors cringed at the loud noise, exchanged a glance, pulled the plugs out of their ears and flipped the switch, cutting off the audio feed into the observation room.

'I'm going in there,' Lucinda said. 'They can't do this.'

Jake grabbed her arms and turned her to face him. 'Listen, Lucinda, they can and they did. Confronting them in there right now will do no good. We need to prove he's lying. Even if most of the story is true, all we need is one inconsistency to give the prosecutors the option of negating the agreement.'

Lucinda jerked away from him.

'C'mon, Lucinda. You know I'm right.'

'I know it. I just don't like it.'

'Let's go see if Godfrey's here yet. You can take your frustration out on her.'

FORTY-SIX

Lucinda and Jake found Ted at his desk busy with paperwork. He looked up when they entered. 'Pamela Godfrey is down the hall. I've got an officer in the room with her and her attorney and another posted outside the door.'

'Great,' Lucinda said. 'Anything we should know?'

'When we got to her apartment, a packed suitcase sat on the floor by the front door. We smelled a faint whiff of decomposing flesh and knew that gave us the right to look for the source. We followed the odor to the bathroom. We found a human hand in a bag in the back of the toilet.'

'How did she respond to that?'

'She said, "Oh, my God! I called the landlord about that smell. I thought it was coming from the sewer lines." I asked her how the hand got in the back of her toilet and she clammed up, demanding her attorney before she answered any questions.'

'Well, this ought to be fun. If half of what Kidd said is true, her lawyer won't let her open her mouth. Let's go, Jake,' Lucinda said.

Lucinda introduced Jake to Edwin Prager and Pamela Godfrey. 'We'll start off easy, Ms Godfrey. Just where were you headed when the officers knocked on your door?'

'I was going down to the Outer Banks to get away for a few days.'

'A few days?'

'Yes, when you lose someone you love, you often need some time by yourself to grieve and heal.'

'Do you recall our recent conversation when you told me you didn't know Jason King?'

'Yes. And I don't – but I did recognize his name. I told you that.'

'Yes, you did. How about John Kidd? Does that name have any significance for you?'

'No. None at all. Should I know him?'

'He knows you, Ms Godfrey.'

Pamela furrowed her brow and shook her head. 'Are you sure?'

'Yes. In fact, he said you were with him in the Sterling house the morning Jeanine and Parker were murdered.'

'Well, that is a flat out lie.'

Jake jumped into the questioning. 'He told us you pulled the trigger. Why would he say that, Ms Godfrey?'

'I have no idea. But I know he is lying.'

Prager put a hand on Pamela's arm. 'My client has denied these allegations. Let's move on to another area of questioning or let us leave now.'

'Oh, I see,' Lucinda said. 'A man Ms Godfrey claims she doesn't know puts her at the scene of a double homicide. We're to take her word that John Kidd is lying, even though the male victim's hand was found in the back of her toilet?'

'You had no search warrant, Lieutenant. That so-called evidence will be thrown out of court.'

'I doubt it, but even if it is, you have a sloppy client, Mr Prager. I'm sure a complete search of her home and her office will lead us to the murder weapon.'

'Murder weapon? I don't have a murder weapon. I don't even know what it is.'

'Pamela, please, not another word,' Prager said.

'You didn't know Jeanine was shot in the head, Pamela? You spent an awful long time fixing her up in bed after she was dead not to notice that.'

'Shot? You mean a gun? I don't have a gun. I don't like guns. I loved Jeanine, Lieutenant. I had no reason to kill her.'

'Oh, yes, you did, Ms Godfrey,' Jake said. 'She broke off your affair. It's one of the oldest motives in the book.'

'It was a temporary break-up – just a timeout, nothing more. We were getting back together in the fall.'

Jake asked, 'So, if you weren't at her house the morning she was murdered, what did keep you away from the office until nine thirty?'

'Pamela, don't answer that,' her attorney urged.

'Oh, please, it's a simple explanation.' Pamela blew a forceful blast of air through her lips. 'It's an embarrassing situation that I hope we can keep in this room. The CEO of a major firm spent the night with me the evening before. In the morning, he was hung over, puking and generally making my morning miserable. I asked him not to return.'

'His name?' Jake asked.

'I told him I didn't want him in my bed again but I didn't say I didn't want him as a client. If I give you his name, I'm sure he'll cancel the contract. You can't expect me to do that.'

'And we can't expect you to be honest, now can we? Did you help cut up Parker's body, Ms Godfrey?' Lucinda asked.

'Pamela, I really mean it. Shut up now,' Prager said.

'But, Edwin, I didn't do anything. I'm innocent.'

'Unfortunately, Pamela, that doesn't always matter.'

'It does here, Mr Prager,' Lucinda snapped. 'All I need from your client is proof that John Kidd lied about some detail of the murders – anything. She gives me that, I can't say she'll walk free, but it will definitely improve her situation.'

Pamela shrieked, 'I don't know who John Kidd is! I don't know what happened in that room. I am heartbroken. I want to kill whoever killed my Jeanine! Can't you understand that? Don't you grasp simple human emotions?'

'Lieutenant Pierce, Special Agent Lovett, I am terminating this interview now,' Prager insisted.

'Fine,' Lucinda said. 'I'll go get the arrest warrant prepared and get a search under way.'

'You have no grounds for an arrest.'

'Oh, really? I have a victim's hand in the possession of your client – and even if you get that evidence thrown out in court, it's good enough for now.'

The door to the room creaked open. 'Lieutenant?'

'Not now.'

'Lieutenant, he said it was an emergency.'

'Too bad. Take a message.'

'But, Lieutenant, it's just a kid.'

'What? Who?' Lucinda asked, her mind jumping immediately to Charley.

'Freddy Sterling and he sounded really scared.'

FORTY-SEVEN

'Freddy, this is Lieutenant Pierce. What's wrong?'

'I don't know. I'm not sure. But I'm scared.'

'Are you at home?'

'No. I'm at a Shell gas station.'

'Where?'

'I don't know. It's near the airport. And it's near the Marriott.'

'What are you doing there?'

'I was scared. I don't know what's going on and I'm scared.'

'OK, Freddy, hold on a minute. I'm going to get a police officer near there to stay with you until I arrive. Just a minute, OK?'

'Yes, ma'am.'

Putting Freddy on hold, Lucinda called the dispatcher with instructions. 'No, I don't have an address – but there can't be that many Shell stations by a Marriott, next to the airport.'

'OK, Freddy, I'm back. Keep your eyes out for a marked police car, OK? Do not go to anyone else.'

'Yes, ma'am.'

'Now, tell me, how did you get there?'

'I walked from the hotel.'

Be careful of your words, Lucinda, this kid has an exceptional mind but his thinking is very literal and linear. 'When did you get to the hotel? Why are you at a hotel? Who is there with you?'

'After you left the house today, my grandmother made me pack and she said we may never come back again. But she wouldn't tell me where we were going. Then we came to the Marriott and she still wouldn't tell me. All she would say was that I needed to get to sleep 'cause we had an early flight the next morning. I don't know why,' Freddy said, sounding close to tears.

'OK, Freddy, everything's going to be OK. Someone will be there soon and then I'll hang up and come right over, OK?'

'Yes, ma'am.'

'Does your grandmother know where you are now?'

'No, she's asleep. When she started to snore, I looked in her purse and saw the papers she printed from the computer in the lobby. It says we're going to the Minneapolis-St Paul International Airport.'

'And your grandmother didn't tell you why you were leaving town so fast?'

'No. I told her we were safe 'cause Jason was in jail but she said we had more to worry about than Jason. Is that really his name?'

'No, Freddy. His name is John Kidd.'

'So he even lied about that?'

'Afraid so. He was not . . .'

'Oh, I see a police car,' Freddy said.

'You see the markings? Are you sure it's a police car?'

'Yes. He's pulling in right now.'

'Get the officer to come to the phone.'

Lucinda waited, her nerves afire. She couldn't imagine anyone could move quickly enough to snatch an official vehicle and get to Freddy that fast, but her imagination had disappointed her many times before. Finally, a male voice came down the line. 'Lieutenant Pierce? This is Patrol Officer McKenna.'

In her mind's eye, she saw him, she knew him and she relaxed. 'Thank heaven. Please stay with the boy. I'll be there as soon as I can.'

Lucinda dashed to the interrogation room and popped open the door. 'Jake!'

Jake opened his mouth to ask what she wanted but when he saw the urgency on her face, he jumped up and came out into the hall without a word. She briefed him on the situation.

Jake asked, 'Do you have any idea what all of this means?'

'I've got a lot of crazy ideas colliding in my head but I don't know what to think.'

'What about Godfrey?'

'Just leave her in there. If her attorney gets tired of waiting, he'll come out of the room and throw a fit. Let someone else deal with it. They won't let her go anywhere without talking to me first. We can continue the interview later.'

'You don't like that woman, do you?'

'She and her lover-attorney can rot in there for all I care.'

On the drive over, Jake asked, 'Do we need any back-up?'

'I don't think so. Freddy's out of the hotel room and in

safe hands. I think we can handle Victoria Whitehead, whatever's going on in her head. I want to keep all of this low key
and avoid alerting the media. If I'm wrong, we can call for
reinforcements later.'

They stopped at the Shell station to touch base with Freddy
and Officer McKenna before going to the hotel. 'Freddy,'
Lucinda asked, 'do you have a key to the room?'

'No. Grandmother wouldn't give me one,' he said with a
pout. 'I'm responsible – I really am – but she said I was too
young to be trusted with one.'

'I'm sorry, Freddy. In my book, you are very responsible
and very brave. We're going up to talk to your grandmother
right now. You stay here with Officer McKenna, OK?'

'Yes, ma'am.'

Lucinda looked into his mournful eyes and ached. She knew
firsthand the depth of the wound caused by a sudden and
violent loss of parents. And now, she was contributing to the
destruction of his last family connection. She knew the DA
would want to charge Victoria with something – obstruction
of justice, harboring a fugitive or who knows what. She sighed
and hopped into the car.

It took a little persuasion at the front desk, but at last they
had the room number. They rode up the elevator in silence.
Lucinda knocked on the door and got no response. Jake
pounded on the door with a fist. A man's head poked out of
the room next door. 'Cut that out or I'm calling security!' The
man scowled and then retreated back into his shell.

In front of them, Victoria swung the door open. 'Freddy,
where did you run off to? You . . . Where's Freddy? What have
you done with Freddy?'

'Freddy is fine, Ms Whitehead,' Jake said. 'But we need to
talk to you.'

'I don't want to talk to you,' she said, pushing the door shut.

Before it closed, Jake shoved a shoulder into the space
and pushed. Victoria ran into the bathroom. They heard the
lock click shut. They looked at each other and rolled their
eyes.

'Ms Whitehead,' Lucinda spoke through the door, 'we are
not going away until you come out and talk to us.'

'I'm not coming out.'

'C'mon, you can't stay in there for ever. And you sure can't crawl out the bathroom window – you're on the sixth floor, the fall would kill you.'

'Maybe that would be better,' Victoria whined.

Jake said, 'Ma'am, I could be wrong but I have a feeling you really care for your grandson.'

'I certainly do.' Victoria's voice cracked. 'I love that little boy.'

'Yes, ma'am, I thought so. But right now, he's really scared.'

'He should be. It's a dangerous world filled with terrible people.'

'I can't argue that, ma'am. But your grandson needs you. What frightens him the most now is that he doesn't under-stand what's going on with you. You are his rock, Ms Whitehead, and he is confused.'

Lucinda added, 'And you have nothing to fear – John Kidd, the man you knew as Jason King, is in jail. And his accom-plice is in an interrogation room at the justice center right now.'

'You have his accomplice?' Victoria asked.

'Yes, ma'am,' Jake said.

For a moment, Victoria was silent. Jake and Lucinda waited. When she spoke again, she asked, 'How did you find that person?'

'Kidd told us who was in the house with him the morning your daughter and her husband were murdered and we picked her up,' Lucinda said.

'He told you?' Victoria asked.

'Yes, ma'am,' Jake said.

The lock clicked and the door eased open. 'I'm sorry,' she said. 'I was scared.'

'That's understandable,' Jake said. 'Why don't you gather your things together and we'll all go down to the station and you can give us your statement.'

'You understand we need to know everything you know?' Lucinda added.

'Certainly,' Victoria said. 'Can I see Frederick?'

'We'll step out in the hall while you get dressed. Come out when you're ready and we'll take you to your grandson.'

Outside the door, Jake asked, 'Are you comfortable with her answers? Do you think her reason for running was fear of Godfrey?'

'No, I'm not. Something about her is off but I'm not sure

why – maybe she's just embarrassed. I don't know. But it struck me as odd that she didn't ask us the name of the woman we had in custody.'

'I hadn't thought about that – it is peculiar. I wasn't comfortable with her when she came out of the bathroom. She never looked either one of us in the eye. She kept her head down, staring at the floor in front of her feet.'

'I wonder what she's not telling us,' Lucinda said.

'I imagine we'll find out when we get her in the room. She doesn't appear as if she'd be tough to crack.'

'She may be tougher than she seems.'

FORTY-EIGHT

Back at the justice center, Lucinda and Jake paused outside the door leading to Victoria Whitehead. 'Should we stop in and speak to Godfrey and her lawyer before we talk to Whitehead? The attorney's been raising a fuss,' Jake said.

'Let him. Maybe Whitehead can give us some information about Godfrey we can use. Let's talk to her first. How do you want to play it?' Lucinda asked. 'Whitehead's not too fond of me; I could be bad cop – trite, but I think with her it would work.'

'All right, we'll try that. I'll start things off and you jump in and be surly when you think the time is right.'

'OK, but Jake, make sure you call her grandson "Frederick". She'll love you right away for that.'

'You're kidding?'

'Nope,' Lucinda said and pushed open the door.

'Good evening, ma'am,' Jason said. 'I understand you know Lieutenant Pierce well. I'm Special Agent Jake Lovett with the FBI.'

'Where is my grandson?'

'Don't you worry about Frederick, ma'am. We found a glass of milk and a granola bar for him and he's settled in the break room watching the Discovery Channel.'

'Why isn't he in here with me?'

'We need to talk, ma'am, and we didn't want to upset

Frederick. Could you tell us where you met John Kidd – or Jason King as you knew him?'

'I met him at the library. Everyone I ever met before at the library has been so nice. I had no idea.'

'When did he move in with you?'

Victoria blushed. 'I'm embarrassed to say, just two weeks after I met him. He told me that his lease was up and the house he lived in had been sold and he wasn't sure where he was going to stay. And, well, by that time I thought I loved him.'

'Oh, cut this romantic crap,' Lucinda snapped. 'What the hell were you doing sleeping with the man who killed your daughter?'

'I slept with him before that,' Victoria cried. 'What do you think I am? A monster? I loved my daughter. I still love my daughter.'

'But you slept with him the day your daughter was murdered, didn't you?'

'No, I did not. I did not see him after that morning. I . . . Oh . . . oh . . .'

'Lieutenant Pierce, you are upsetting the lady here,' Jake said. 'Why don't you step out of the room, get a drink of water and cool down for a minute. I know it's been a long day, but Jeez.'

Lucinda saw the hint of a smile cross Victoria's face before she spun on her heels and walked out. She went into the observation room to watch and wait for the right moment to return.

'I'm so sorry,' Jake comforted Victoria. 'Lieutenant Pierce is a little excitable.'

Victoria said, 'Thank you, Agent Lovett. But I guess if I was damaged goods, it wouldn't take much to set me off either.'

Jake clenched his jaws at that remark but moved on without commenting on it. 'Could you tell me about early that morning, before John Kidd left your house?'

'John? Oh dear, yes, it's so hard to think of him as "John". Well, we had breakfast, as usual. I imagine I fixed some sausages, a couple of fried eggs and toast – that's what he usually wanted. He left about seven that morning to run errands.'

'Wasn't it a little early for that?'

Victoria fidgeted with her fingers before answering. She renewed eye contact and said, 'Yes, I asked him about that. I can't remember what he said or where he was going. I'm sorry, I just can't remember.'

'That's OK. When did you talk to him next?'

Victoria's face flushed, her eyes darted, and settled on the table in front of her. 'Um, he called me from the airport. He said his mother had taken a turn for the worse and he had to rush to her side.'

Lucinda took that as her cue. It was obvious that Victoria was lying. It was time to kick the chair out from under her. *Not literally*, she reminded herself. She walked into the room and rested both palms on the table.

'Do you know Pamela Godfrey, Ms Whitehead?'

'Who?'

'Pamela Godfrey,' she said, slapping a photograph in front of her.

'No, who is she?'

'That's who Kidd said was with him in your daughter's house.'

'I've never heard of or seen her before. He said she helped him?'

'Ms Whitehead, take a good look at that woman. According to your boyfriend, she's the one who pulled the trigger. She's the one who killed your daughter.'

'No. She did not! Jason did!'

Lucinda eased into the chair. 'Jason? John Kidd? He shot your daughter?'

Bowing her head, Victoria mumbled, 'Yes.'

'How do you know that, Ms Whitehead?'

The only sound filling the room was the strained noise of Victoria's rapid breathing.

'Ma'am,' Jake said, 'do you have something you need to tell us about?'

Victoria hung her head, her shoulders shook but she did not respond.

'Ma'am, how do you know he shot your daughter?'

'Were you there, Ms Whitehead?' Lucinda added.

Victoria gasped and jerked her head up. 'Oh, no, I wasn't there – not when he shot her.'

'Afterwards, then?' Jake asked.

Victoria collapsed over the table, her head on her arms, sobbing. Jake and Lucinda sat back in their chairs letting her outburst run its course. When she raised her head, Jake placed a box of tissues in front of her. She wiped her nose and patted her eyes.

'Ma'am, I know this isn't easy, but why don't we start with the moment you got out of bed that morning.'

'When he told me, I believed him. Oh, dear Lord, I believed him.'

'When he told you what, ma'am?'

'He told me that Parker was ready to kill again. He said that he was about to kill my daughter and my grandson and fake his death so he could assume a new identity. Jason – uh, John – said he had to kill Parker before it was too late.'

'And you didn't try to stop him from killing your son-in-law?' Lucinda asked.

'I believed him. I thought it was the only way to save my daughter's life, my grandson's life. I thought Parker was evil. I thought he was centuries old and the devil owned his soul. I don't know what to think now but it must all be lies. Oh, God help me, it must all be lies.'

'Then what happened, ma'am?' Jake urged.

'He promised me he wouldn't hurt Jeanine before he left the house. And then the phone rang. He said it was an accident. He didn't mean to shoot her. She surprised him. Do you think that's true? Do you think it was an accident?'

Lucinda and Jake looked at each other. Jake turned back to Victoria and said, 'No, ma'am. I'm sorry but that doesn't seem likely.'

'Oh, my God, I can't believe I was so gullible!'

'Ma'am, let's just get it all out in the open now, OK?' Jake said. 'What happened then?'

'He told me I had to come over and help him clean up the mess. I told him I couldn't do that. Dead bodies, blood. I just couldn't. And he said, "Your daughter is lying naked on the floor with blood all over her face. Is that how you want your grandson to find his mother?"'

'So you went over?' Jake said.

'Yes, I did. I was so upset, I didn't think I could do anything. It was so awful to see my baby all bloody . . . but he yelled at me, he told me to think of my grandson. I had to take care of things for Frederick.

'And so I did. He helped me carry Jeanine to the bed and then he got the chainsaw. I lost it then. I screamed at him. I asked him why he was doing that. He just turned off the chainsaw, put down the toilet seat and pushed me on my shoulders until I sat down on it. He said, "Victoria, are you forgetting who he is? He's evil. And he's immortal. If we leave him here with a whole body, he will rise up again and destroy more families. This has to be done, Victoria." And, God help me, I believed him. I tried to block out the sound as I washed blood off of my daughter's face and cleaned her fingernails. I looked away when I had to go into the bath to get her hairbrush and make-up. But still I got a glimpse and it was hideous, so bloody, so awful.' Victoria collapsed forwarded, dropping her forehead on to her arms again.

'What happened then, Ms Whitehead?' Lucinda prodded.

Victoria raised her haggard face. 'I didn't want to leave. I didn't want to abandon my daughter. I didn't want Frederick to find the bodies.'

'But, you did leave, didn't you?' Jake said, encouraging her to continue.

'Yes,' she sighed. 'He said he had a plan. We'd get someone else there before Frederick got home from school. It just couldn't be us because no one would believe the whole truth – no one would understand how many lives we saved by killing and mutilating that monster. He said I had to be brave for Frederick's sake.

'So, I did what he told me. I drove my car, following him all the way downtown. When he pulled to the curb, so did I. He put a few coins in the meter by my car and we drove off in his. As we travelled a couple of blocks, I put on a pair of gloves and he gave me a note. It had my daughter's address on it and it said, "Call 9-1-1". We entered a parking garage and went around a few times and then he stopped and pointed to the windshield where he wanted me to leave the note. And I did it.'

'Did you know who's car it was, Ms Whitehead?' Lucinda asked.

Victoria's brow furrowed. 'No. Should I have?'

'It doesn't matter, Ma'am,' Lucinda said as she rose and walked to the door. She waved in a uniformed officer who cuffed Victoria's hands behind her back and escorted her away.

Watching Victoria Whitehead disappear down the hall, Lucinda turned to Jake, 'I'm glad this is over and we know what happened but I wish it hadn't ended this way. I've got to get someone here to take care of Freddy. I should call his aunt. I don't think he's ever met her but she's family and she loved his mother.'

'Shouldn't we go see Godfrey first?'

'Godfrey can wait,' Lucinda said as she punched the number into her cell.

A sleepy Susan Livingston muttered, 'Hello?'

'Ms Livingston, this is Detective Pierce, the lead investigator in your sister's homicide investigation. I'm sorry to bother you so late at night.'

Susan was instantly alert. 'Yes, I remember you, Lieutenant. What do you need?'

Lucinda explained the situation with the woman's mother and her nephew. Susan asked a few questions and said, 'I'll go online and book a flight now. I'll be there to take care of Freddy just as soon as I can.'

Relieved, Lucinda prepared herself to be excessively deferential when she spoke to Godfrey and her attorney. It galled her but she knew Captain Holland would have her head if she made the situation worse. After apologizing repeatedly, Jake and Lucinda escorted Pamela and her attorney out of the interrogation room. In the hallway, Pamela came to an abrupt stop. 'Lieutenant, I am certain the department does not want me to file a law suit.'

Lucinda jaw throbbed. 'Ms Godfrey, I don't think that the revelatory nature of a civil law suit would be in your best interests either.'

Pamela laughed. 'Please, you are forgetting my profession. I can spin anything to my advantage with a limitless budget.'

'We've apologized, Godfrey, what more do you want?'

'I want the original chips and any copies of the photos and video of Jeanine and I that you confiscated as evidence.'

'I'll talk to the D.A.'

Pamela stepped up to Lucinda's face. 'You do that, Lieutenant, and you make sure he knows that my father's friends will take a great interest in his decision come re-election time next year.'

'Is that a threat, Godfrey?'

'Hell, Pierce, don't be shy – it's blackmail, pure and simple. You know how the game is played. It's a boy's world out there, we only get what we need if we are not afraid to swing the low blows. And I'll be damned if I'll have a horny bunch of A.D.A.'s passing images of me and my lover from one sweaty palm to the next for who knows how many years. You get those image cards, make sure any copies are destroyed and I won't cause any problems. Deal?' Pamela took a step back and stuck out her hand.

Lucinda ignored her extended arm and planted her hands on her hips. 'One more question, Godfrey. Do you have any idea how Parker's hand got in the back of your toilet?'

'I'd guess the bastard stole Jeanine's key to my place the morning he killed her.'

'She had a key to your apartment?'

'Of course. Parker did too, for that matter.' Pamela turned, strutted down the hall and out of the building.

'I guess that's the key he used to get into her apartment to leave the hand. I wonder if he'll ever tell us what he did with it?' Jake asked.

Lucinda shrugged. 'She so creeps me out.'

'Why, she had nothing to do with the crime. She's just a victim, too.'

'Maybe. But I still don't like her.'

'The lesbian thing bother you?'

'Oh, good grief, no. She's not homosexual. She's not heterosexual. Heck, she's not even bisexual. It's not about sex with her. It's all about manipulation – manipulation and power. She's a predator – a self-controlled predator. And a very dangerous woman, in my opinion. I feel bad for anyone who crosses her path. Well, enough about her, let's go wake up some prosecutors in the middle of the night.'

'You betcha,' Jake said.

They both took great pleasure in delivering the news of Kidd's now defunct deal. To their credit, both of the attorneys, after a few moments of disbelief, congratulated them on their success.

When they finished with the calls, Jake asked Lucinda, 'What are we going to do with Freddy tonight?'

'We probably should call social services. But I have a better idea. I want him in a place where people will really understand what he's going through. I'm calling Charley's dad to see if we can drop him off there.'

Evan Spencer needed no persuasion, even now in the middle of the night. His empathetic response was instant. He urged Lucinda to bring the boy over. To Lucinda's relief, he didn't take the opportunity as a chance to hit on her again as he usually did. Her opinion of him inched up a tad.

After dropping off Freddy, Lucinda said, 'The test results came back. William Blessing is his father and John Kidd is his half-brother. At some point, he is going to have to be told the whole truth. But when?'

'His Aunt Susan will be in the best position to decide that. I imagine it would be best for him to get settled into his new home first.'

'I ache for him, Jake.'

'Yeah, I know. It's got to be hard on you to revisit your past every time a child loses a parent to a homicide you're investigating. Here's the hotel. C'mon up and raid the minibar with me.'

'Jake, I . . .'

'Lucinda, just come up, have a drink or two – you deserve it, we deserve it. You need some time to unwind and ramble over the case with someone who's been there – and here I am.'

Pleased but more than a little anxious, Lucinda parked her car and followed him into the elevator. Sitting on opposite beds, facing each other, they sipped on their first drinks while sharing random reflections and thoughts about the case. Midway through the second drink, the alcohol hit them both hard after their demanding day. Eyes slipped shut, bodies slumped. They fell asleep just feet apart and didn't awaken until daylight slipped around the drapes on the window.

EPILOGUE

Lucinda drove up to DC more nervous than she could ever remember. Jake reminded her repeatedly about their October excursion down the Skyline Drive to the Blue Ridge Parkway and into the Great Smoky Mountains. She tried to wiggle out of it but she didn't object too strenuously – she really did want to see him.

He promised separate rooms on their overnight stays and swore he'd do nothing forward without a direct invitation. The clincher for Lucinda came when he said, 'I'm not always sure what you think about me, but I know you love my car. You can't pass up a ride through mountains in her, can you?'

But what would *he* think of *her* now? Everyone seemed pleased with the results of the last surgery. Dr Rambo Burns even said her lips were the most kissable he'd ever seen. *Yeah, right, he's just pleased with his own handiwork. That's all I am to him, a pair of lips. Before that, I was just an eye socket and if I continue with his plan, I'll just be a reconstructed nose. Do all surgeons think it is always all about them?*

Still, although she knew Charley was biased, she was fairly credible. The young girl literally swore on a Bible that Lucinda's mouth was absolutely gorgeous. Lucinda laughed at the memory of her little hand on the black leather and the solemn look on her face. The clutch of anxiety in her core eased its grip a little.

She had thought her lips looked pretty good, too – almost like the originals – and, at times, she even thought they looked better than they did before the shotgun shredded half of her face. But now, she was no longer certain. *What if I'm fooling myself? What if Jake looks at my face and says, 'Never mind.'*

When she pulled up to Jake's office building, she waited in the car for a good ten minutes, trying to calm her nerves. She gave up and went inside. Jake took away all doubts the moment she walked inside. He smiled when he saw her, put one hand on either side of her face and gave her a big kiss.

Lucinda felt faint. She was shocked at how good it felt to have his lips pressed into hers. Nonetheless, when he released her she said, 'Jake, really!'

Behind Jake, the receptionist tittered into the hand she held over her mouth.

Jake turned and gave her a wink. He faced Lucinda and hung his head. 'Sorry, I couldn't help myself. Those new luscious lips drove me out of my mind.'

Lucinda grinned, shook her head and said, 'Are you ready to hit the road?'

'Yeah, we ought to get going if we want to hike a trail before sundown. I've weaseled our way into a group tour at Swannanoa Mansion at nine tomorrow morning.'

Following Route 66, they traveled from DC to Front Royal and entered the Skyline Drive. En route, they stopped at every overlook to take in the views and snap photos of the vistas and each other. They made a longer stop a little past mile marker 40 and hiked the circuitous 1.6-mile Stony Man Trail that led to an awesome view of the valley below. Excited by that sight, they set off on Little Stony Man, a shorter round trail with steeper sections but several incredible overlooks.

They ended their day about halfway down the 105-mile drive, at Big Meadows Lodge, situated in an unusual high-altitude meadow where early settlers once grazed cattle. They spent the night in separate rooms, just as Jake had promised.

Sleep did not come easily for Lucinda, though. She'd had a glorious day, filled with exercise and empty of stress. It should have meant she'd drift off easily and soundly, but when she closed her eyes, all she could see was a vast wall of concrete blocks encircling her, threatening disaster if she broke through them and opened herself to those outside of her self-imposed prison.

Lucinda didn't understand herself – she yearned for connection and yet she did all she could to keep everyone at a distance. *Not everyone. Not Charley. If I could break through to reach out to her, why can't I dismantle another hunk of the wall? Why can't I let go of my fear?*

She fell asleep at long last but awoke with a start several times that night. In the morning, she felt a bit ragged. *Can it possibly be worth it to rush out of here so early to get to the Swanee River or whatever he called that place?*

Jake's night hadn't been much better than Lucinda's. He couldn't get to sleep because he couldn't get Lucinda out of his mind. So close, yet so far away. He wondered if he needed to break his promise and make the first move but decided against it. Instinctively, he knew that though it might work with some women, it was the sure path to disaster with Lucinda.

The first few miles that morning passed in silence. Between the fresh mountain air and the incredible golds, reds and yellows in the trees, they both dropped their funk at the first overlook. By the time they reached Swannanoa, both were exhilarated once again.

Lucinda gasped when they pulled up to the enormous mansion built of Georgian marble. With its square towers shooting above the roofline, it looked more like a palace than an American home. She was even more impressed inside when she stood at the foot of the sweeping marble staircase. She was horrified to learn that the steps were once painted dark brown when it was used as a country club right after the great Depression.

Broader than four men laid end to end at its base, the elegant stairs tapered up to a landing where a beautiful and incredibly large Tiffany stained-glass window depicting a woman in a garden filled the wall. The tour guide said the face in the glass was that of Sally May Dooley, the wife of the man who, over eight years, paid more than three hundred artisans to construct the home. The stairway branched in two as it curved upward to the bedrooms on the second floor.

As the commentary shifted from the older history of the mansion to details of the post-Second World War occupation by Walter Russell and his University of Science and Philosophy, Lucinda stopped paying attention to the guide's words. *Just another Virginia crackpot*, she thought, and focused on the beauty of the historical home.

After the tour, they left the Skyline Drive at Rockfish Gap and continued south on the Blue Ridge Parkway. They had buckwheat cakes for lunch at a restaurant cabin along the way and paused at most of the forty-eight overlooks they encountered on the drive to milepost 86 and the Peaks of Otter Lodge. Jake pulled into the parking area and continued across the lot to the far side, stopping in front of a bar locked into a post that blocked the entrance to a narrow dirt lane.

'This place is special,' Jake said. 'I wish I could take you down there. I don't know if it has a real name or not but we called it Dexter's Descent – after the guy a few years ahead of me at school who discovered it.

'During my college years, I had an older friend named Van who drove a '67 Morgan. If we ducked down in the seats, his car could slip under the bar and we could drive this road all the way down the mountain. It's a little treacherous in spots but the views are unbelievable. The first time I went down it, I thought I died and went to heaven.

'As we approached a small rise, a wonderful, sweet smell tickled my nose. When we crested it and came down the other side, a vast valley opened at our feet, filled with apple trees all in bloom for as far as we could see. The scent in the air was powerful and overwhelming. We stopped the car and turned off the engine and listened to the buzzing symphony of a billion bees. I've never experienced anything quite like it.'

Jake turned to Lucinda and gazed at her face with longing in his eyes. 'More than anything, I'd like to find a low-slung car and drive it back here in the spring with you by my side. I want to share that with you. It was one of the most intense moments of my life.'

Lucinda put her hand on his cheek and pulled him towards her. After a long kiss, they embraced each other until their arms grew weary. Smiling, they dropped their arms and walked, hand-in-hand, into the lodge to check in. That night, they both shared the same room. Neither one of them got much sleep even though they barely rose from bed in time to make last call for breakfast the next morning.